AWARDS FOR *S.T.A.G.S.*

Shortlisted for the YA BOOK PRIZE 2018
Winner of the Warwickshire Secondary Book Award 2019,
the Great Reads 'Most Read' 2018 Senior Award and the
Sussex Coast Schools Amazing Book Award 2019

'*S.T.A.G.S.* is a pacey and well-plotted young adult story that champions outsiders and questions out-dated viewpoints in a constantly evolving world.'

CultureFly

'M. A. Bennett is brilliant at keeping the reader in suspense.'

Book Murmuration

'M. A. Bennett reinvigorates the boarding-school thriller ... This is a darkly compelling examination of the allure of privilege, and the unscrupulous means by which it preserves itself.'

Guardian

'*S.T.A.G.S.* is a thrilling and thoroughly enjoyable YA novel with dark undertones. A fun mystery thriller that sheds light on issues surrounding class and society. Highly recommend.'

Book Bag

'A gorgeous and compelling romp'

Times

D.O.G.S.

BOOKS BY M. A. BENNETT

S.T.A.G.S.
D.O.G.S.

The Island

D.O.G.S.

M. A. BENNETT

HOT
KEY
BOOKS

First published in Great Britain in 2019 by
HOT KEY BOOKS
80–81 Wimpole St, London W1G 9RE
www.hotkeybooks.com

A CIP catalogue record for this book is available from the British Library.

ISBN: 978-1-4714-0799-4
also available as an ebook

1

This book is typeset using Atomik ePublisher
Printed and bound in Great Britain by Clays Ltd, Elcograf S.p.A.

Hot Key Books is an imprint of Bonnier Books UK
www.bonnierbooks.co.uk

To Inca,
who was the very best of dogs

Let him but look,
And read,
He may be saved by thy book.

To Ben Jonson's Ghost
William Cavendish

ACT ONE

Scene i

So.

When someone's dead they're supposed to stay dead, right?

Well, that's what I thought. I certainly didn't think I was
going to be seeing Henry de Warlencourt again. But it turned
out I was wrong.

Everyone in the hospital keeps telling me that there's this
thing called the 'Anniversary Effect'. It's when you start
getting visions or flashbacks a year after a traumatic event.
In my case, Justitium weekend a year ago at Longcross, and
Henry's suicide. OK, death. Apparently the anniversary 'opens
up the neurological floodgates'. Now, I know all about the
Anniversary Effect. I watch *Stranger Things*. But *this* isn't
that. I know what I saw.

There's lots of other stuff before we get to the exceptionally
weird bit though. So I'm going to pick up the story exactly
where I left off – Justitium of my last year at STAGS – because

3

it annoys the shit out of me when stories are supposed to be sequels and then it's like: THREE YEARS LATER. I mean, what the hell is *that*?

I'm going to tell you what happened in the second half of that autumn term – God, was it really only six weeks ago?? – right after the chapel service, right after we broke up for Justitium, right after I'd figured out that the Abbot was the Grand Master of the Order of the Stag, a freaky, people-hunting cult hell-bent on maintaining some archaic social order.

So.

Here goes:

As soon as I'd told Shafeen and Nel what I had to say, the three of us went straight to see the Abbot. We strode through the ancient quads of the school, all hyped up and ready for confrontation. We'd decided to challenge the Abbot with his crimes – a pretty crazy idea on reflection, since we now knew he was Murderer-in-Chief. *Were* we crazy? Probably, but still we hurried through those sunlit courts.

STAGS looked beautiful and deadly in the autumn light. There was nothing modern to be seen, and only the distant howl of an ambulance siren and a flash of blue streaking along the Alnwick road reminded us that there was even a Savage world out there at all. I shivered despite the sun. Ambulances and blue lights brought back that last night at Longcross: Henry falling backwards into space, the roar of the waterfall drowning the sound of his body breaking on the rocks below, his ruined form in a body bag being filed away neatly into the back of an ambulance. It was time for all this to end. But when we entered the Abbot's study, the Abbot wasn't there. Friar Ridley was sitting behind the desk. Talk about the wind being taken out of our sails . . .

Friar Ridley was OK. He taught English and drama, and as they were two of my subjects I knew him a little bit, even though the term was only six weeks old. He was tall and had curling dark hair and green eyes. He looked a lot like that guy from *Batman v Superman*. Not Batman. Superman. Henry Cavill.

I wondered how the three of us looked to him – solemn Indian guy, perfect Barbie princess and me in the middle, all dark bob and bangs like some manga Joan of Arc. He nodded at the others but he knew me well enough to greet me by name. 'Greer,' he said. 'What can I do for you?'

We all sat down, uninvited, in the chairs across from him. We sat in the exact same configuration as when we'd told the Abbot all about the Medievals last year. What chumps we'd been, to give the Abbot warning so he could cover up for his evil little minions, the Medievals, and ship them off to Oxbridge before we could act. I raised my chin. *We* were the Medievals now, we were at the top of the school, and we were going to get to the bottom of this, right *now*.

'I . . . We want to talk to the Abbot.'

I was ready to be asked why. I was ready to say because he's the head of an evil, child-killing cult. But Friar Ridley didn't ask me why. In fact, he said something quite different.

'Ah,' he said, looking down at his long fingers on the blotter. 'I'm afraid that won't be possible.'

'Why not?' asked Shafeen, all belligerent.

'Because he's on his way to Alnwick Cottage Hospital. He was taken ill after Justitium Mass.'

'What's wrong with him?' Nel didn't mess about.

'I know no more than that, I'm afraid. He collapsed.'

'So who's in charge?' I asked.

He flattened his gown over his broad chest. Friar Ridley, I could see, worked out. There was no getting away from it. He was fit. I don't just mean ripped, but handsome with it.

'Well, for the moment,' he said, 'I am.'

We all studied him. He was probably in his thirties, but despite his height he barely looked old enough to be a teacher, let alone an Abbot. Behind that desk, he *kind* of looked like he was on a 'Bring Your Son to Work' day, waiting for Daddy to get back.

Friar Ridley was one of the slew of new teachers who had been hired throughout the year since we'd had our face-off with the Abbot. As we'd demanded, they were supposedly non-posh, non-STAGS alumni. But knowing what we now knew about the Abbot, I was wary of all his new appointments. Friar Ridley sounded pretty well spoken to me. Maybe he was one of *them*. 'Friar Ridley,' I said, looking at him through narrowed eyes, 'where did you come from?'

He narrowed his eyes to match. 'How d'you mean?'

'I mean, where were you before STAGS?'

'My last school was Ampleforth in Yorkshire, where I was head of house, then head of English, then –' he smiled –'head.'

Somewhere during that speech, I don't know why, I started to trust him. 'What about before that?'

'I could swear I'd already had my interview.' But he smiled

6

again. The smile was sort of lopsided. It was cute. 'Christ Church College, Oxford.'

That sounded alarm bells. Christ Church, I knew, was posh. And the reason I knew that was that it was the very college I'd applied to myself. More of that later. For now all I was thinking was that Ridley could be part of the whole STAGS set-up, radicalised at uni into the nostalgia posse, ready to murder us commoners just for fun. Warily, I asked, 'And before that?' I was trying to get to where he'd been to school, find out if he was part of the silver-spoon squad.

'Manchester Grammar School.'

'You're from *Manchester?*'

'Yes. Do I pass your test?'

That's why I'd begun to trust him. He'd said *last*, not *laaast*. *Pass* not *paaass*. He was a northerner.

'Do you know Arkwright Road?'

'Know it? My aunty lived on that street. Near Asim's newsagent's on the corner.'

That did it. I'd bought sweets in Asim's shop my whole childhood. I was totally Team Ridley.

I looked at the other two. Shafeen and then Nel both gave me a small nod.

'We've got something to tell you. Something about the Abbot.'

He leaned forward, hands clasped on the tooled leather of the desk. You can be sure I had a good old look at those hands, every single finger, before I spoke. But we were good – no signet rings stamped with antlers, no big, flashy head-of-a-cult rubies.

'The Abbot –' I began. 'You're going to find this quite difficult to believe . . .' – understatement of the year – 'but he's the head of a –'

Then, just like in the movies, the phone rang.

Typical of STAGS, if they had a phone it was going to be the oldest one they could find. This one was black with a rotary dial and a curly cord – it looked like it was straight out of some Ealing comedy of the 1940s. But there was nothing comedic about Friar Ridley's face as he listened to the muffled sounds of speech on the other end.

He said, 'I see. Thank you.'

He put the phone down very gently on its cradle. Then he looked at each of us in turn. Suddenly I knew what he was going to say before he said it.

'I'm afraid what you had to tell me may no longer be relevant,' he said. 'The Abbot is dead.'

Scene ii

Apparently the Abbot had had a heart attack and was dead on arrival at Alnwick Cottage Hospital.

In my head, of course, I'd now murdered someone else. Had the Abbot known, as he'd looked out across the congregation of STAGS pupils during Justitium Mass, that one of them had guessed his secret? Had he seen it in my eyes, eyes red with the reflection of his ruby ring, that I'd rumbled him and it was all over? Had the shock killed him?

That very evening there was a Requiem Mass for the Abbot, and Shafeen, Nel and I found ourselves once more in the chapel, this time by candlelight. The chapel choir, who were this professional-standard choir cherry-picked from the decent singers at STAGS, sang this song/hymn/whatever as everyone filed in. It seemed to be about misery cos they kept singing '*Miserere*' over and over again. It was fricking beautiful. Even though I didn't give a crap about the Abbot, I felt the corners of my mouth twitching downwards. Suddenly the choir seemed to be singing about Henry.

Luckily, just as it seemed that tears were inevitable, Nel nudged me in the ribs. 'They knocked this thing together pretty

9

quick,' she muttered out of the corner of her mouth.

Shafeen, on the other side of me, shrugged. 'Well, if you have a school run by a Holy Order then it doesn't take long to put together a Requiem Mass.'

'Unholy Order more like,' I said uneasily.

It all seemed a bit too neat. There was Friar Ridley, in the Abbot's robes, standing at the lectern, telling us that Justitium weekend had been postponed for a few weeks and that we were all to stay in school, as a mark of respect for the Abbot. This was greeted with a chorus of groans from the kids who actually liked their parents and were looking forward to going home, but Ridley shut them down with a look. He no longer looked like he was someone's kid. He had some authority about him, standing exactly where the Abbot had stood earlier that day, the rogue sunbeam catching not a ruby ring this time, but Friar Ridley's green eyes. His voice rang out. He had game. He was the acting Abbot now.

'The Abbot is Dead,' Shafeen said drily. 'Long Live the Abbot.' It was pretty much what he'd said when Henry had . . . died, and Cookson had taken over.

'Don't you like him?' I said, surprised. 'I do.'

He gave me a considered look. 'Yes,' he said. 'I could see that. Maybe that's why I don't.'

I decided to ignore Shafeen's snippiness. I actually thought it was cute. Although we were together – *really* together – in private, in public he wouldn't ever show how into me he was. To be fair, this was something we'd sort of agreed so as not to make Chanel feel like a third wheel, but that didn't mean I didn't like a bit of affirmation now and again. Don't tell the

BuzzFeed feminists, but I quite liked that he was a bit jealous. As one of the friars started droning through a Bible reading, I said, low-voiced, 'Now what?'

'Now nothing,' said Shafeen. 'It's the end of the line.'

'Are you sure?' I said. I nodded to a few rows in front, where the de Warlencourt twins sat, almost exactly where they'd sat earlier in the day.

'What have they done? They're not automatically guilty by association.'

'They smiled at me funny this morning.'

'Ooh, they *smiled*? Quick, call the Feds.'

'They invited Ty to Longcross.' I nodded to the new girl, her neat black cornrows next to those sleek blond heads.

'But they won't be going now. Justitium's cancelled. So she's safe.' He turned to the next hymn, snapping the pages of the hymnbook pointedly between his fingers.

After the service we had a bit of time before Commons (dinner to you). We gathered round the Paulinus well in the darkening light. This was a habit that, oddly, we'd adopted from our predecessors. I'm not sure why, we just kind of started doing it in a weird Medieval continuity, leaning on the stone wall looking into the depths of the well, or out into the night. I gazed into the shaft now and could swear I saw the Medievals' cigarette butts still stuck in the wire mesh halfway down. Had one of them been thrown from Henry's lips? 'So that's it?' I spoke down the well, my voice echoing back to me. 'We just drop it?'

'Greer,' said Shafeen, putting his arm round me in a rare Public Display of Affection, 'we have one year left at STAGS.'

He threw his other arm out in this big theatrical gesture, which took in all the silhouetted buildings. 'This is our school, and we're stuck with it. If we were going to leave, we should have done it a year ago after the Henry thing. It's too late to go anywhere else now, and besides, it has an academic record second to none. We have to take the good bits of the school and use them to our advantage. We have to trust that now Henry has gone and the Abbot has gone, all that other stuff is over.'

'Do you really believe that?' asked Nel.

'I have to,' he said simply. 'Because the alternative is that you and me and Greer spend our last year here obsessing over this, playing Sherlock Holmes and trying to reveal the machinations of a centuries-old cult – and if we do that we are going to mess up our exams.'

I straightened up and gazed moodily ahead at the massive hulking shadow of Honorius, the house that Henry was in when he was at STAGS. 'Maybe this is one of those times when your best friend dies and then you get all A-stars.'

Nel said, 'It was a year ago, and I don't think Henry would qualify as anybody's best friend.'

Shafeen gave me a funny look. 'Or would he? Anyway, I can't rely on that. I don't know about you, but I want to get my Probitiones. I need three As, Greer. I've got to concentrate on that.'

Probitiones were the final exams at STAGS. They were pretty much identical to A levels, but of course, being STAGS, no one called them A levels (except for me); it had to be something ancient and Latin. You took three or four Probitiones in the second year of sixth form, i.e. this year for us. Shafeen was right. Shit was getting real. He wanted to read medicine at university and he needed the grades. Nel, in contrast to (or perhaps because of) her dad's hi-tech world, had found a love of history and classics. I knew I wanted to be a director, but I'd agreed with my dad that I'd get a degree first, so I was going for drama. We all needed to work hard.

Determinedly, I moved my eyes away from the blond heads in front of me and looked instead at the stag window above the new Abbot's head. STAGS was my school and it was the only one I had.

Shafeen was right.

It was time to get my head back in the game.

Scene iii

It's funny to think, looking back now, that none of what happened *would* have happened if only I'd liked Shakespeare.

I've seen a fair bit of Shakespeare – admittedly on film. I've seen a trio of Hamlets – Kenneth Branagh (weird), Mel Gibson (weirder) and Laurence Olivier (weirdest). I've done the obligatory GCSE play (*Macbeth* in my case). But I could never get on with it. I don't know if it was the language, or the unfunniest comic characters in the universe (step forward, Porter in *Macbeth*. And you, Nurse in *Romeo and Juliet*.)

The whole point of this Shakespeare rant is that I had to direct a play for my drama Probitio. See what I always said about STAGS being different? In what other school would you be allowed to direct a play in a replica Jacobean theatre as part of your exam? Luckily for me, most of the drama folks were hell-bent on acting. No one was about to challenge me for the director gig, even though it was the director who was given the choice of what play we did. The problem was that the play couldn't be modern. The chosen text had to be old school, to fit the Renaissance theatre.

The Sunday morning after the Abbot's Requiem Mass I had

a meeting to discuss the play I'd chosen. The problem was, I still had less than no clue. I had researched and read, but still not found anything that floated my boat.

As I walked through the grounds to my drama meeting, working out what I was going to say, it was a late-October day, cold, with the sun shining and the leaves turning all shades of flame. STAGS really was an amazing place. Shafeen was right: if we were going to leave, we should have done it a year ago. Maybe with Henry gone, and the Abbot gone, this most vicious of cycles could be ended, and we, the new Medievals, could make it a good place. Buildings couldn't be bad in themselves, could they? Bricks and mortar couldn't be made from murder.

I walked from my room at Lightfoot, all Tudor splendour and diamond windows, across Bede's Piece iced with frosty grass, avoiding the hideous sporty types rushing about with lacrosse sticks, to the long, low medieval buildings of the library. I swished through the lovely quad to the English Schools, where I was due at 10 a.m. to discuss the practical element of my drama Probitio. I wasn't sure who'd be taking the meeting now, probably some BTEC friar who'd been parachuted in to replace Friar Ridley now that he was Abbot Ridley. But when I knocked on the ancient studded oak door of the English Schools and went in, it was Abbot Ridley himself who was perching on one of the desks, tapping his foot with a metre ruler. He looked completely different again to his chapel self, the strong leader who'd taken the reins of the school without missing a beat. He looked younger again. More approachable. Funner. He laughed at me.

'Why that face?'

I was surprised into honesty. 'You always turn up in places I don't expect.' I felt I could speak to him like a peer, not like the Abbot he now was.

He indicated a chair and I sat in it.

'I've been your English and drama teacher for six weeks now. I don't know you *very* well yet, Greer, but you don't strike me as someone who is slow on the uptake.'

'Yeah, I know, but . . .'

'But what?

'I thought, with you being the new Abbot and all, you'd have, well . . . bigger fish to fry.'

'Ah. I am merely an Interregnum Abbot, made so because I have experience of headship, as we discussed. So it's true, I do have some extra . . .' he searched for a word, 'administrative duties. But I assure you, none of those take precedence over the paramount importance of seeing my class through their English and drama Probitiones. So –' he banged the ruler smartly on the floor, making me jump a little – 'until graduation, you may consider yourself, if you don't mind me borrowing your phrase, the biggest fish in my fryer at this time. "Call me Ishmael."'

I caught the reference. '*Moby -Dick*,' I said.

He looked pleased. 'You've read it?'

I could've easily bullshitted, but then *he* could've easily caught me out by asking me my favourite part. 'Seen the movie,' I admitted. 'Gregory Peck.'

'Ah yes. Well, speaking of dramatic representations, let's talk about your drama Probitio. Have you decided which play you'll be directing for the performance element?'

He was talking like a teacher again, but I still thought it was worth chancing my arm. 'I don't suppose it could be a *film*, could it?'

'It couldn't. The syllabus specifies a play written before 1660.'

I mentally rolled my eyes. Typical STAGS.

'How about Shakespeare? That would be the obvious choice.'

'Exactly.'

'I beg your pardon?'

'It's the obvious choice. And – don't take off for Mars, but – I *hate* Shakespeare.'

He smiled his half-smile. 'Then I recommend you take yourself off to the library and do some research. He wasn't the only Renaissance dramatist. Look at Nashe, Dekker, Jonson, Marlowe. There might be something more to your taste.'

He got up from the desk, his robes falling to his feet, rippling like a superhero cloak. I did find myself wondering what he would look like out of his Abbot robes. Not *naked*, before you go thinking that. That would be creepy. Just in normal clothes.

I got up too, as the interview was clearly over. 'OK. I'll have a look.'

'And Greer –'

'Yes?'

'I wouldn't waste much time choosing. Term's marching on. The practical element represents two-thirds of your overall drama mark. You'll have to perform your play at Christmas. That's a little over six weeks.'

* * *

I spent a long, butt-numbingly boring afternoon in the Scriptorium, the most ancient bit of the library. Most of the time I spent watching patterns of stained-glass-refracted light crawling across endless tomes of Shakespeare, Dekker, Beaumont and Fletcher, Marlowe and Webster. The only good thing to be said about the afternoon was that I didn't once think about the Medievals or the Order of the Stag. Friar Ridley had really scared the bejeezus out of me about how little time I had, and there's nothing like losing your bejeezus to really make you focus. Finally I checked out *The Complete Works of Shakespeare*, a huge brick of a thing, and went to Commons. I plonked myself down between Shafeen and Nel on one of the long refectory benches.

'Any luck?' asked Shafeen through a mouthful of cottage pie.

'No,' I said. 'They're all so stupefyingly *boring*. I mean, I could do yet another horrible school production of *Macbeth*, or *Hamlet*, I guess, but . . .'

'But what?' asked Nel, who was peeling a tangerine in one long, satisfying curl, aided by her perfect acrylic nails.

'They've all been done to *death*. I mean, can you imagine someone saying, "To be or not to be", or "Is this a dagger that I see before me?" as if you're hearing it for the first time?'

'Then do something new,' said Shafeen, ever practical.

'This is STAGS. Has to be a play, has to be from before 1660.'

'Ah.'

Shafeen (history and triple science) had no further advice, and even Nel (who was actually doing drama too, along with history and classics) had no clue.

This *sucked*.

Scene iv

Nel and I walked back to Lightfoot in the dark and we said goodnight at the top of the stairs.

As Medievals we each had our own suite of rooms – no more sharing – and mine was a lovely big one with a study in the eaves of the house. Usually I would hang in the evenings with Nel or Shafeen or both in the Medieval Common Room, or in one of our rooms, or even, if it wasn't too cold, by the Paulinus well. But tonight I needed to get this play decision made, so I sat at my desk in a pool of lamplight, poring over the Shakespeare I'd brought from the library.

I got that familiar prickling feeling that I often got when I was alone, that Henry-behind-the-curtains feeling, as if I was being observed. However hard I tried to banish him, Henry hung around in my memory, impossible to forget. I didn't know if I felt guilt or a lingering sorrow, or whether I just plain missed him – all feelings far too complicated to share with anyone else. Particularly Shafeen. I couldn't tell Shafeen. Things were going so well, and I really, *really* liked him, way too much to present him with the fact that he was sort of sharing me with a ghost.

Henry hadn't been forgotten online either. Even though tech was still officially forbidden at STAGS (*Festina Lente*, right?), I would charge up my phone and check occasionally. His cult was growing. Those Oxbridge dining clubs still ate by waterfalls at moonlight in their black ties; fan pages grew in number on Instagram and Twitter. The presence of Henry's face and name in all my timelines made me stay away from my phone and embrace the Medieval life even more. But he still intruded, hanging about in the shadows. And tonight this made it hard to concentrate, and the tiny text, the stupid names and the improbable plots swam before my eyes. I threw the Shakespeare across the desk and sat back in my chair, shoulders aching, pushing my hands into my hair. It was then that I heard the sound.

It's funny how sounds can take you right back, like a time machine that can whisk you away to your past. That whispering, paperknife sound of something being pushed under a door transported me back a year, to The Invitation. A simple piece of card, which had set in motion the train of events that had led to the weekend of twisted huntin' shootin' fishin' and, ultimately, to Henry's death. For a moment, the dread turned me to stone and I physically couldn't turn round, but then I told myself not to be stupid. I should get up and go to the door, and there would be nothing there.

I got up and went to the door.

There *was* something there.

Not a single envelope this time, but a bunch of yellowing pages, covered in black scrawl, shoved under my door.

I picked up the pages and read, with difficulty, what was

on the front. It was old-fashioned script like you see written with a quill in films like *Anonymous*. It said:

The Isle of Dogs
A Tragedy
Acted in the Year 1597
By Pembroke's Men
With the Allowance of the Master of Revels
The Author Ben Jonson

I turned the page and read: *Act One, scene i*.

It was a *play*.

I whipped open the door and looked frantically up and down the oak-panelled passageway. Of course there was no one to be seen. I closed the door behind me and, for some reason, locked it. I stood for a moment with my back against the hard oak, heart pounding. I was suddenly sure, surer than anything I'd known in my life, that the play was from Henry. I walked slowly back to my desk, clutching the pages, and by the time I'd got there I'd given myself a good talking-to. There was no mystery here. The play wasn't from a ghost. There was only one person who could have given it to me, and that was Abbot Ridley. He was my drama teacher, my mentor for the drama Probitio, and the one who had been hounding me about choosing a play.

He'd obviously rooted out this copy from somewhere, thought it might be a bit pervy to actually come *into* my room, but, mindful of the shortness of time, decided to push it under my door tonight and give me a head start. And, since he'd gone to all that trouble, I thought I might as well read it.

It didn't take me very long – as it turned out, it was only one act, not an entire play. But it was fantastic. It drew me in immediately, because it was narrated by this sardonic poet character called Poetaster, who I was pretty sure was the playwright Ben Jonson himself, so you were seeing the whole thing through his eyes. The play was about a queen, called Queen Cynthia, who lived alone in this magnificent Longcross-esque palace on the Thames called the Palace of Placentia. She was rich, brainy and beautiful. She was also entitled and sometimes cruel, but endlessly charming. She had everything she wanted, and was bored out of her skull. She reminded me of Henry.

The play opened when the queen had, for the first time in her life, found something that she couldn't have. She had fallen in love with a penniless noble, the Earl of Greenwich, and decided that, after many years of ruling alone, she wanted to marry. But her chief courtiers, a father and a son called Lupo and Volpone, insisted that she couldn't marry him – if she was going to take a husband, it had to be this foreign king called the King of El Dorado. Queen Cynthia raged furiously against them like a caged animal trapped by duty. The whole thing was explosive – the two father–son courtiers simultaneously working for her and against her, and the earl sweet-talking her into making him her king. It set up this terrific power struggle at court, as well as this queen struggling with her duty versus her heart, and her love of her independent power versus her giving it up to a man if she married. The language was all Elizabethan (obvs) but somehow accessible. It was much, much darker than Shakespeare. The character of the queen was dynamite – such a strong, flawed heroine. I knew I had to direct *this* play. If anything was going to make me forget the events of the last year and concentrate on my work, it was *The Isle of Dogs*.

Without knowing why, I slept with the pages under my pillow. They crackled and whispered to me every time I turned.

Scene v

Despite being knackered from my late-night reading, I was up before the alarm and ready to go.

I had drama first thing, so I swerved the Refectory, just grabbing a banana, and went to class super-early, clutching *The Isle of Dogs* so hard that the buttons of my black Tudor coat bit into my chest. It was like I'd written the damned thing.

Our drama class was timetabled to be in the theatre that day, so I made my way across Bede's Piece, the low mist still clinging to the grass, the school buildings rising over the playing fields like a mirage. The De Warlencourt Playhouse (seriously, there was no getting away from that family) was built in the 1960s, way back when Shafeen's dad was at STAGS, but since it was an exact replica of a Jacobean theatre, even down to the thatched roof, it totally fitted with the rest of the school. If you've ever seen the film *Shakespeare in Love*, it looked just like the Globe Theatre in that, except for when you went inside: it wasn't open to the air but was enclosed, and entirely lit (with classic STAGS attention to traditional detail) by candlelight. It was pretty weird walking in there, through the timbered doors underneath the de Warlencourts' commemorative plaque, out of the bleak winter sunshine, into the candlelit dark.

For a moment I couldn't see a thing, but after a bit I could make out Abbot Ridley in the middle of the stage, lighting the candles around the proscenium with a taper. The flames flowered under his hand like he was some wizard from *Fantastic Beasts* or something.

I was suddenly shy, something I usually am not. I walked down the auditorium, between the wooden benches. 'Thanks for the play,' I said, by way of a hello.

He spun round in his superhero manner, robes flying. 'Oh, you found one?' he said. The theatre played tricks with his voice, projecting it out over my head. 'What did you go for? *Wives of Windsor* or *Gentlemen of Verona*?'

I held out the pages. 'Neither.'

He came closer, squinting a bit in the low light. 'What's that?'

'You tell me.'

'I don't understand.'

'Didn't you give this to me? Didn't you push it under my door?'

'Under your door?' He frowned. 'In Lightfoot? No. No, of course not. I assure you, I wouldn't even know where your room is.'

He seemed shocked by the suggestion and I saw then how mistaken I'd been – he was quite freaked by the implication that he'd been wandering around the girls' house after dark. He blew out the taper in his hand, as if to extinguish the very thought. He was obviously convinced that I was one of those bunny-boiling schoolgirls who get a crush on the hot teacher, like in *Wild Things*.

I wanted to reassure him that I wasn't about to go all #MeToo on him, but there was no earthly way of saying that without sounding mental. So I just said, 'It's a play called *The Isle of Dogs*.'

Then a weird thing happened. He started to *laugh*. 'Very good, Greer,' he said. 'You got me. But seriously, what have you chosen? I'd like to get everyone's production schedules done today so we can book rehearsal time in here. Between you and me, the music department can be very greedy with this space.'

I wasn't sure why he wouldn't believe me. 'I've chosen this. *The Isle of Dogs* – by Ben Jonson, it says.'

I climbed onto the stage and held the pages out to him. The Abbot looked at them for a moment and then took them in the manner of someone wary of a practical joke. He read the title page and went suddenly still. He actually sat down on the edge of the stage so that he could read in the candlelight. I sat beside him, but not too close. He lay each page down as he'd finished it on the stage behind him, as tenderly as if they were made of butterflies' wings. I waited nervously, as if I *had* actually written it myself. Had he got to *that* line yet? Had he got to the bit where this happened, or that happened?

I distracted myself by looking round at the De Warlencourt Playhouse. It must've cost the family a bomb, and I wondered then why theatre was so important to them that they'd put up the money. It was basically an oak structure built inside the circular brick shell. We were sitting on a thrust stage with a musicians' gallery behind us and an ornately painted ceiling above, with this kind of heavenly sky painted on it, clouds and stars and a sun and a moon – day and night at the same time. There were two horseshoe galleries, so the audience would be quite close to the actors, and I felt for the first time a shiver of nerves. The candles were not just ordinary ones like you'd buy in a supermarket, but made of beeswax, which gave off a funny olde-worlde smell. They were mounted in sconces, and in six high candelabra that could be winched up and down. (The theatre was basically a massive firetrap.) Sitting there, next to the Abbot in his dark monastic habit, watching him leaf through a handwritten manuscript, with the Christmassy candle smell in my nose, I could've been transported back in time.

When the Abbot looked up, the air of being constantly wry and amused had gone and he looked deadly serious. 'Where did you get this?'

'Like I said. Someone put it under my door last night. After Commons. What's up?'

He gathered the pages together again as he carefully formed his reply. 'This play doesn't exist.' It was almost a whisper and his voice sounded around the theatre spookily.

'How do you mean? It's right there.' I pointed foolishly, now thinking it was *me* who was on the business end of a practical joke.

'I mean, it *did* exist. But there was no surviving copy.'

'Explain.'

'The play was written in 1597, at the end of Elizabeth I's reign. It was performed, then quickly suppressed.'

'What does "supressed" mean? They closed the play?'

'Closed the play, closed the theatre it was performed in, closed all the other theatres too, and burned all the copies.'

I whistled, and the sound was amplified in the auditorium. 'Jeeesus. That sounds like overkill. *Why*?'

'Blasphemy. Sedition. Treason. Demonic practices. Black magic. The full house of Elizabethan sins.'

Wow. 'But it's pretty tame so far. I mean, I think it's really good, but it's not *offensive*.'

'No. Act One does seem pretty blameless. Perhaps the dangerous bits are in the later acts, and that's why only this fragment survives.'

Huh. 'So what happened to Ben Jonson?'

'The queen had him thrown in jail.'

'So that was the end of Ben.'

'Not at all. He was released, and fell out of favour – but the queen was quite an old lady by that time. When she died, Jonson became rather a favourite of Elizabeth's successor, James. He ended up as court poet.'

'Posh boy then?' I decided, my lip curling.

'Hardly. He was the son of a bricklayer, and had become a bricklayer himself. He was once described as having a trowel in one pocket and a book in the other.' He looked at me sideways, a smile in his voice. 'He wasn't a fan of Shakespeare either – thought he was overrated.'

'I'm starting to like him.'

'You should,' he said. 'You've got a lot in common. He got a scholarship to a very prestigious school in Westminster, and then went on to Cambridge. But he had to leave to make a living, and went into the theatre. At his death he was considered to be the greatest playwright of his time. Much better than Shakespeare.'

'Wow. Good for Ben.'

'Yes. But sadly he died penniless. He was buried standing up in Westminster Abbey, because he could only afford a grave that was two feet square, not six feet long. Then he became less popular after the Restoration, and Shakespeare started to take over. And now, of course, barely anyone on the street would know who Ben Jonson was.'

'OK, but still, if he was such a genius in his day, shouldn't this be in a museum?' I looked at the pages in my grubby hand, and moved my fingers so I was holding the manuscript carefully by the edges.

'If it was given to you here, I presume it was in the Scriptorium. I imagine it must be from the school's manuscript collection, and therefore it belongs to STAGS. But I'm new here. Have you spoken to Friar Waterlow?'

Friar Waterlow was the librarian who worked in the oldest bit of the library, the literally medieval Scriptorium. 'Not yet. But . . .' My mind was whirling. 'How could the manuscript have got this far north, even? If Ben Jonson lived in London.'

Abbot Ridley thought for a moment. 'Good point. I do know that later in life Jonson went on a pilgrimage from London to Edinburgh and that he had a very dear friend in the North by the name of Esmé Stuart. He may have risked all to bring a copy north to give to her so that it would at least survive for posterity. He knew he could trust Esmé Stuart.'

I recoiled. The name Esme to me would always mean Esme Dawson, Medieval, Mean Girl and would-be murderess. 'Who was Esmé Stuart?'

'A powerful noblewoman. Jonson's patron and protector. He lived in her house in London and visited her home at Lennox Castle in Scotland. She sometimes summered at Alnwick Castle, just down the road from here. Perhaps Jonson sought lodging here at STAGS on his way to visit her.'

'Huh.' I wasn't really interested in Esmé Stuart. I was still thinking of Queen Cynthia, the slimy father–son courtier team who were simultaneously working for her and against her, and the earl she loved but couldn't have. I had to ask the question. 'Could I direct *this*? I mean, if it belongs to the school, that's OK, right?'

'Of *course* you could direct it. You *should* direct it.'

'Even though there's only one act?'

'Well, that's a pity. But you still should present it as an extract.' He studied me for a moment. 'Greer, where are you up to in your university admissions? Remind me.'

'Oxford,' I said. 'I've got an offer. I just need to get the grades.' I grimaced.

He looked pleased. 'Then this is what I suggest: you perform it here. It's a wonderful discovery. Think of it, Greer. If you put this play on here, not only would it be an amazing coup – the first time those words have been spoken in four hundred years! – but if you are the first to direct the rediscovered *Isle of Dogs*, and you do as well as expected in your other Probitiones, then I don't see how Oxford could possibly turn you down to read English and drama.'

He had me there. The idea of making history began to take hold in my mind. Then the chapel clock struck nine and some of the other drama students started to filter in from breakfast and began to sit, dotting around the auditorium. Nel waved at me and motioned to a seat beside her. I nodded and slid off the stage, holding the pages like they were gold leaf. Which they kind of were.

Abbot Ridley spent the rest of drama briefing the others about the play. 'An exciting lost manuscript' at STAGS, which had recently been uncovered 'by our own Greer MacDonald'.

Nel turned to me, china-blue eyes very wide. Of course, the last she'd heard, I was floundering about trying to find a play to direct for the class, and the next thing, here was I, clutching a lost manuscript like Nic Cage in *National Treasure*.

The rest of the lesson was lots of chat about the rehearsal schedule, the performance date (last Friday of term, just before we broke up for Christmas). I wasn't exactly concentrating, because I was briefing Nel, low-voiced, about how Act One of the play had been pushed under my door the night before. Her eyes got wider and wider, and even in the gloom of the theatre you could see the whites of her eyes all the way around her irises.

Despite her obvious surprise, I had to ask the question. 'I don't suppose it was you, was it?'

'Me?'

'Yeah. I'd just left you – you could have gone to your room and picked up the manuscript to give me.'

She shook her head. 'No. If I'd had that up my sleeve, I'd have told you at Commons.' She smiled. 'Saved you from all that Shakespeare.'

Scene vi

When the class was over I didn't go to the Paulinus well to meet Shafeen like I usually would. I went to the Scriptorium instead, to find Friar Waterlow.

Nel came with me, because she was almost as excited by the mystery of *The Isle of Dogs* as I was. We went into the rare-books bit, which looked so old that I wouldn't be surprised if St Aidan himself used to hang out here. It had lots of stained glass, dark-wood shelves crammed with ancient texts and these kind of crossribs holding up a wooden ceiling, like you see in *Harry Potter and the Chamber of Secrets*. We looked among the shelving for the librarian and it was then that I started to get a weird sense of foreboding. It was some moments before I realised why. Everything about this particular bit of the library, appropriately the medieval bit, reminded me like a punch to the gut of the library at Longcross where I'd found the hunting books. But more than anything, more than the dark wood, or the stained glass, or the ornamental ceiling, it was the smell. The smell flipped me back like a time-machine, straight to Longcross library, and that very particular fusty, dusty aroma of ancient manuscripts. Modern libraries don't smell like that – there's something about the paper and the ink and the binding that's very particular. That smell, the smell of History, had a dark association for me. I was suddenly hiding among those ancient tomes in Longcross with that mastodon Perfect prowling around below, the barrels of his shotgun gleaming. I swear the memory scared me so much that if Nel hadn't been there I would have run right out of the place into the sunlight. But just then we caught sight of the shambling figure of the librarian, his friar's habit absolutely fitting his surroundings.

Friar Waterlow was about a hundred years old and had definitely been there in the days of the old Abbot. Probably due to his lifetime of expertise with rare books and manuscripts he'd escaped the cull – when all the old friars had been retired and replaced – so I was plenty wary of him. But I supposed if I was only asking about books, he couldn't do me any harm, and there was no doubt that books were his life. 'Friar Waterlow?'

The old friar turned and straightened up. 'Ladies? What can I do for you?' He spoke with this olde-worlde courtesy, but he was a pretty formidable-looking dude. He was small, and stooped, but he had these milky blue eyes that looked at you very directly, like he was straight out of *The Name of the Rose*.

'We were just wondering,' I began casually, 'do you have any of the works of Ben Jonson?'

'Oh yes, my dear,' he said. He pointed waveringly back to the more modern bit of the library – by that I mean Tudor – where the printed books were kept. 'Have a look in the second carrel on the left, in Renaissance drama. We certainly have the better-known ones, *The Alchemist*, for example, and *Volpone*.'

I'd spent the entire afternoon there yesterday. 'No, I didn't mean copies. I meant the *real* ones.'

'Are you talking about original manuscripts? Not here, I fear. The best I can do is a facsimile of his folio edition, collected plays, poems, masques, et cetera.'

'This folio – does it . . .' I licked my lips. 'Does it have *The Isle of Dogs* in it?'

'Dear me, no,' he chuckled. 'You're out of luck there, I'm afraid. That play no longer exists – every copy was destroyed when it was suppressed in 1597. Although . . .' He stroked his chin with a papery hand – I didn't realise people actually did that when they were thinking. And I don't think Nel or I breathed till he spoke again. 'It's funny you should mention that play. The only recorded mention of the script, written in Jonson's own hand, was held at Alnwick Castle in the private collection, oddly enough.'

So it seemed Abbot Ridley had been right. Ben Jonson *had* been in the 'hood. That seemed like a massive coincidence to me. Alnwick Castle (used as the film version of Hogwarts, irony of ironies) was just down the road. The Old Abbot had died en route to the cottage hospital in its very shadow.

I knew it was time to show the Friar the play. I'd put the pages carefully in a folder in my standard-issue deer-leather STAGS satchel. My fingers twitched towards the clasp, but I didn't get the manuscript out.

'So, his other plays, the ones that *do* exist,' I asked, 'where would their originals be?'

'The British Library,' he said. 'The Bodleian Library in Oxford. Possibly the library of St John's College, Cambridge, to which he was briefly admitted as an undergraduate.'

Again, just as Abbot Ridley had said.

'They later honoured him there when he became court poet. The other likely place would be Christ Church College, Oxford, where he taught for a short period.'

Another coinkydink. Like I said, that was the very college I was applying to. This was just weird.

'And how much would an original Ben Jonson play be worth?' said Nel.

I had to smile. Nel was always interested in money and how much things cost – I wondered if she inherited this commercial side from her dad.

'Well, given that in his lifetime he was considered the foremost poet of England,' said Friar Waterlow, 'far superior to Shakespeare, such a thing would be . . . priceless.'

I stopped smiling.

'Van Gogh's *Sunflowers* priceless?'

He smiled a wet, formless smile. He didn't have the greatest teeth, so the effect wasn't very pleasant. 'I should imagine so. And then some.' He looked at us beadily with his creepy-monk eyes. 'May I ask where these questions tend?'

'Well,' said Nel, 'you won't believe –'

'The time!' I trilled, grabbing her arm. 'You won't believe the time – we have to get to history. Thanks a lot, though, Friar Waterlow, you've been really helpful.'

He waved his hand in a little flourish and turned back to the stacks.

I dragged Nel away before she could blurt anything out. But I needn't have worried. In the last year we'd learned to read each other and she left quietly with me. When we were well outside, safely crossing the moat between Honorius and Paulinus, she spoke. 'You don't trust him?'

'Are you kidding? I don't trust *anyone* after last year.'

'Hmm,' she said. 'I can't picture Friar Waterlow running around Longcross in the 1960s hunting schoolkids.'

'That's what we thought about the old Abbot,' I reminded her.

Nel twisted a rope of her blonde hair around her manicured hand, like she always did when she was thinking. 'I s'pose so. But he might have had some clues. Not showing him the manuscript doesn't help you find out who gave it to you.'

'Does it matter?'

'It might. If the play doesn't belong to STAGS, then it belongs in a museum, and surely you won't be able to just keep it and put it on here at the end of term. You'll have to tell Abbot Ridley it's not from the Scriptorium.'

I looked at her sideways. 'I might forget to tell him. I might just let him, you know, *assume*.'

'Greer MacDonald!'

'What?'

'That's *lying*.'

'It's not *lying*. It's just . . . not telling the truth.' We were crossing the manicured lawn of the Honorius quad and I stopped dead centre and turned to her. 'OK,' I said. 'Suppose I tell him. He calls in the Government and they come along in their helicopters or some shit.'

'*Helicopters?*'

'Well, *I* don't know what they do. They take away the play

and we don't get to put it on, we don't get to make *history*, Chanel.'

She was silent, and I could see that I was getting through to her. I toyed with the idea of saying how fantastic the play would be for my Probitio, but realising that that didn't make me sound all that great, I went another way. 'Also, try *this* for size,' I said. 'What's a play meant to be?'

'How d'you mean?'

'Well, if a play had a wishlist, what would be top of it?'

'Well, I s'pose, to be performed.'

'Ex-*act*-ly. And I bet you old Ben Jonson, if he came back to life right now . . .'

'. . . like that's going to happen . . .'

'. . . if he came back to life right now,' I persisted, 'would be totally chuffed that his play was *finally* getting performed, and that this time no one's going to get thrown in jail.'

Nel let her hair go and it unwound itself. 'Still be good to know where it came from though.'

'Yes,' I mused, as we started to walk again. 'I do have one more notion about that, actually.'

Scene vii

I caught up with Shafeen after Commons – I'd missed him all day because he was in pretty serious work mode, but I tracked him down to his room in Honorius.

He opened the door with his glasses on, so I knew he'd been revising. He had his triple-science mocks just after Christmas. When he let me in he pushed his glasses up into his hair. His eyes sort of had this special light in them when they looked at me. He looked lovely. 'Hello, stranger.'

'Am I disturbing you?'

'Yes, but it's very welcome. I can't read one more molecular formula.' He collapsed backwards on his bed, dead straight like a tree that had just been felled. Without opening his eyes, he put out a hand and pulled me down beside him.

I told him all about the play, and the day, and Abbot Ridley and Friar Waterlow. He propped himself up on his elbow, turned towards me and gave me his full attention, frowning slightly, dark brows drawn down over dark eyes. When I'd finished he said, 'Can I see it?'

I opened my satchel and put the play in his hands. As he leafed through it, I said, 'Shaf?'

'Mmmm?'

'Was it you?'

'Was what me?'

'Was it you who put the play under my door?'

'Don't be dumb,' he said, but affectionately. 'Why would I do that?'

'Well,' I said, 'you were so keen to get my mind off the Order of the Stag and on to my exams.'

'Where would I get a genuine Renaissance play?'

I shrugged. '*I* dunno.'

'You're barking up the wrong tree. You need to look at the guy who is going to benefit from all this. Mr Teacher-of-the-Year.'

'You think that Abbot Ridley gave it to me?'

'Oh, he *definitely* gave it to you. He's a clever fellow, our friendly neighbourhood Abbot, I'll give him that.' There it was again, that unmistakable edge. Shafeen really didn't like Abbot Ridley, and I wasn't sure that it was just jealousy after all. I put that aside for the moment.

'I don't think it *was* him,' I said. 'You should've seen his face when he read the title page. It was like he'd just looked into the Lost Ark. He couldn't have *been* more gobsmacked. It looked like genuine surprise to me.'

'Well, whoever gave it to you, I'm glad you were given it,' Shafeen said. He rolled onto his back and addressed the ceiling. 'You're the one who was most affected by the Longcross weekend – you were nearer death than any of us. And when Henry . . . died, it hit you hardest. You were closer to him than Nel or me.' I looked down but I didn't deny it – I didn't want to lie to Shafeen. 'And I know you've found it hard to . . . let go of him.'

I hadn't realised he had seen so much. I mean, I knew he'd known that Henry had called me beautiful, and that he'd kissed me once in that crazy movie moment on the Longcross rooftops. But then Henry had died. Just for a moment, I wondered what it was like to be in Shafeen's place. You could front up to a rival who was alive, that was a fair fight, but what about one who was dead? I didn't know what to say, but luckily he changed the subject. He pointed at the play where it lay on the quilt.

'Can I read it tonight?'

'Sure,' I said. What I'd said to Nel hadn't been entirely true. I did trust *some* people. I trusted her and I trusted Shafeen. Completely.

Shafeen put the pages on his desk and threw his glasses on top of them.

He came back and put his arms around me.

'Are you going to tell me if it's suitable?' I teased.

'No,' he said bluntly. 'I'm prepared for the worst. If it was banned, and burned, and they shut down the theatres, I'm imagining it can't exactly be the Barbie movie.'

'It's actually completely tame,' I said. 'I know it says "tragedy" on the title page, so there must have been some bad stuff in there, but on the evidence of the first act, which is all I have, I've got no idea why it was so scary for the Elizabethans.'

'Maybe the really hardcore bits were in the later acts.'

'That's what Abbot Ridley said.'

'But I think you should do it, whatever. I'm all for it.' I was quite surprised that the cautious Shafeen had so few reservations about this mystery play, but he explained at once. 'Ridley's right about how it will help your university admissions.' (I'd told him what I hadn't been able to say to Nel.) 'Even you must admit that until this happened you hadn't been working to full capacity.' He held up both hands, as if in surrender. 'I don't blame you, I don't blame you at all. But if you don't get in to Oxford and I do, what will happen to *us*?'

That shook me. We'd both applied to Oxford – in fact, all three of us had: me and Shafeen and Nel. This wasn't as coincidental as it sounds. STAGS had this dumb, antiquated system where you basically applied to Oxford or Cambridge, the only foundations that were considered medieval enough, or didn't bother with university at all and did something else, like the army or the civil service. We'd all three agreed to apply to Oxford. The three of us were the very best of friends, and we'd been through so much together, it seemed dumb to just chuck that away. And I didn't feel like Shafeen was being big-headed or anything by saying he might get in to Oxford and I might not. One of the things I really liked about him was that he was absolutely honest, and if I was absolutely honest myself, he'd got over the trauma of last year by working and I'd got over the trauma of last year by pissing about.

I didn't even know whether Shafeen and I would be together forever, but I was really happy that he obviously wanted me to work hard enough to get to Oxford. He pulled me on top of him and I began to kiss him extra passionately with relief and thankfulness. It was like movie kissing, swelling-music-on-the-soundtrack kissing. He responded, kissing me harder and harder. I felt the heat of him, and thought, not for the first time, how easy it would be to go further than this, to let the flames burn me up. You weren't supposed to be in the houses of the opposite sex after Commons, and this was obviously why. The house friars patrolled the dormitories, and weren't averse to popping in randomly to people's rooms, even the Medievals. Partly because I was afraid of the house friars, but mainly because I was afraid of myself, I pulled away. I got up and straightened my clothes. 'I better go.'

Shafeen pulled on my deer-leather belt to draw me in for a last kiss. 'Either way,' he said, 'I'm just glad you've found something to get your teeth into.'

As I tiptoed down his staircase I replayed what he'd said. I'd always thought that was a weird expression.

That night it reminded me of a bite, the bite of a dog.

Scene viii

Louis de Warlencourt

Cassandra de Warlencourt

Two names, etched in black, clear as anything.

They'd either been written by the same hand, or their twinnish connection was such that they had identical handwriting. You did hear of such things. Twins can be freaky – the ones on film, certainly. Think of *The Shining*.

I stepped back from the sign-up list as if from a blow. It hadn't occurred to me that I'd be having any more dealings with the de Warlencourt family, beyond seeing the twins around STAGS from time to time. I didn't even know they did drama, as they were in the year below me. But here were their names, on the sheet I'd pinned up on the corkboard outside the Refectory, calling for sixth-form drama students to audition for *The Isle of Dogs*.

I stood staring at those two names, the first and second on the list, marked so confidently in night-black ink. It took me some moments before I could step forward again and read the rest of the list. I recognised some of the other names, and one more stood out, a long way down, written faintly in a round hand in blue Biro.

Tyeesha Morgan

Ty. The first de Warlencourt scholar. The girl I'd befriended when she'd first arrived, but, if I'm honest, had forgotten about since the whole dead-Abbot thing. She'd had what I'd considered to be a lucky escape, when the twins had invited her to Longcross at Justitium, and then the holiday weekend had been postponed out of respect for the old Abbot's passing.

I walked very slowly to the Paulinus well, where Shafeen, Nel and I always gathered after breakfast before the bell went. I must've looked a bit white, because they both immediately asked me what was wrong.

When I told them, Shafeen said, 'Sins of the fathers.'

'What's that supposed to mean?' I shot back, thinking for a mad moment that he was taking a shot at my lovely dad.

'It's from the Bible. Don't you ever listen in there?' he teased, nodding to the chapel.

'Not much.'

'*The sins of the fathers are visited on the sons*. You already hate those twins, even though you don't know them, because of Henry.'

'Not just Henry,' said Nel. 'You read the hunting books. It was Henry, his father, his father's father, and the whole poisonous family tree right the way back to Conrad de Warlencourt and the Crusades.'

'So, because they are from a long line of bad guys, we assume the de Warlencourts are all shits.'

'But they ARE all shits,' I protested.

'So far, yes,' admitted Shafeen. 'But the twins have not actually done anything to you yet except smile. You can't arrest them for smiling.' He peered down the well into the murky depths as if looking into the past. 'They might *not* have been trained to be little hunters, shooters and fishers. I don't think they were even brought up at Longcross, were they? I think they were raised in London. From what you said, I think they just visited Longcross sometimes in the holidays.'

'Henry said they used to skate along the Long Gallery with him in their socks,' I said.

'There you go. Not exactly psychopathic behaviour.'

'I suppose not,' I said, remembering, with a jag of memory, the night when Henry and I had done it too. That was the night he'd kissed me. I looked at Shafeen guiltily through my lashes, hoping he couldn't read my mind. But he'd turned his back on the well and was looking out at the school buildings.

'What if the twins are the ones to break the cycle? What if we can *help* them break the cycle by actually being nice to them and showing them how to be human beings, by example? This *school* has never been bad, not the very stones of it.' He swept his arm wide, taking in all the splendour. 'It's the *people*.'

I couldn't fault his logic. I'd thought something similar myself just a day or two ago.

Shafeen went on: 'And even if they *are* terrible people, what harm can they do you, just being in your play? We're not at Longcross. They can't hurt us here. You need a cast. They are

45

doing drama, just a year behind you. You have to at least let them try out. If you don't, then we are as cliquey as the last bunch of Medievals.'

'But how will they feel about me, about *us*? What if they know what we did?'

Shafeen came to me and took my face in his hands. 'What? What did we do?'

It was hard to say it out loud. 'Murder.'

The crows rose from the winter trees, cawing in protest at the word.

He dropped my face abruptly, as if he couldn't carry my head and all the weight of the guilt inside it. 'Dear God, Greer. We've been over this. You've carried that burden for a *year* now.'

I was silent.

'Listen to me.' Shafeen talked slowly and clearly, as if I was six. 'He committed *suicide*. And no one knows that but *us*. The confession video Nel recorded at Conrad's Force never went online. It is safe in the Saros Orbit storage. As far as the inquest was concerned, Henry's was a death by misadventure. An accident. Why should his cousins hold you – or us – responsible, just because we happened to be at Longcross on the same weekend that he died? As far as they know, we were his friends.'

I was about to protest that I *was* Henry's friend. But I stopped. I didn't really know *what* we were. 'I s'pose.'

'They might be crap actors anyway,' said Nel. 'The twins, I mean.'

'But what if they're good?' I said.

Shafeen shrugged. 'Then you have to cast them. And by the

same token, you can't cast Ty if she's crap, just because she's one of the de Warlencourt scholars.'

'He's right, you know,' said Nel. 'Let's see how the twins perform when they audition. They might be OK. We might all come to be friends. They might even,' she said, 'embrace our Savage ways. The rest of the world is doing it.'

'I guess.' It was hard to believe in a Savage world here, where everything as far as the eye could see was so ancient. For a moment, for a split second of a moment, I felt an indefinable pang. If all this got modernised, would I actually be . . . *sorry?*

Scene ix

When the chapel bell struck one Nel and I were seated in the theatre, with the first act of Ben Jonson's *Isle of Dogs* in front of us.

Abbot Ridley had advised me to transcribe the manuscript for the actors, and since there were no computers at STAGS, I'd stayed up copying out the parts by hand. I'd grumbled a bit about this, but Abbot Ridley, even though he was not nearly as Medieval as the old Abbot, had said that even if there had been photocopiers or scanners at STAGS I wouldn't have been able to use them on such a priceless manuscript, as the light might damage the pages. I thought that after I'd copied the pages out he would have advised me to give the original to Friar Waterlow to keep locked in the Scriptorium, but no – he just told me to keep the play safe in my room. I locked it in the drawer of my desk and wore the key around my neck, tucked under my Tudor coat. At every moment I was expecting *The Isle of Dogs* to be taken away from me – by the Abbot, by Friar Waterlow, by some outside agency (the Government?). But no – for some reason an eighteen-year-old girl was allowed to keep it safe, this precious, priceless thing. It felt quite poetic that I stashed it in the same drawer as my box-fresh, rose-gold, state-of-the-art Saros 8 smartphone.

While copying out the parts, I felt a sense of ownership over the play. I didn't want any one else to have a complete manuscript. Writing it out, scribbling with my ink pen (again, STAGS's preferred writing implement), in the dead of night until my fingers turned inky black, I had almost begun to believe that I was the writer of the play. That Ben Jonson and I, both low-born, scholarship kids, had somehow merged. He was standing at my elbow, sitting at my shoulder, looking out of my eyes. Another ghost to join Henry behind the curtains.

I'd written out an overview of the first act, and the Dramatis Personae, and pinned them up backstage, so the actors would at least know what the hell they were auditioning for. I'd also written out one speech for each main character. Luckily for my right hand, there were very few characters – not millions like in some Shakespeare plays. We were only looking for Cynthia (the queen), Lupo (the dad courtier), Volpone (the son courtier) and Canis (this kind of dumb servant). Apart from that there were just servants and courtiers who had one line, so they would be easy to fill. But those four main parts were the pillars that held up the play. The Earl of Greenwich (the dude the queen wanted to marry) didn't appear in the first act, so we didn't have to worry about him, and nor did the King of El Dorado (the dude everyone else wanted the queen to marry).

I'd picked a peachy speech for each character, and now Nel and I just had to sit back and see what we got.

And the first thing we got was Louis de Warlencourt.

I suppose nine hundred years of inbreeding had narrowed the family genes down to one very definite type. There were the blue eyes, the blond hair, the slim, tall figure. But it was the voice I wasn't ready for. I had never heard Louis speak before, only seen him smile at me once, with Henry's smile. But for him to have the voice too gave me the chills. He sounded *exactly* like Henry. I had to grip my pen to stop myself from making some weird noise. It took me a long time to register what he was actually saying, but when I did I had another realisation. He was *good*.

Watching him stride about the stage, listening to him perform a speech that hadn't been spoken in four centuries, made me shiver again, this time for a different reason.

> *My son, the courtier's skill is no great mystery,*
> *It is no riddle but merely this:*
> *To give the queen her will, but follow mine*
> *To marshal her great wealth, while building ours,*
> *To defend her borders, while hedging our family about,*
> *To fill her coffers and likewise fill our own.*
> *To find an heir for her as you are mine,*
> *To make this land the greatest on the globe,*
> *And our own family the greatest in it.*
> *To be the lapdog but the wolf beneath;*
> *To smile and smile yet not bare the teeth.*

He spoke the speech with confidence and authority. Lupo, the elderly courtier, the most important person at court except the queen, manipulating everyone, running everything, with a God-given assurance that everyone will do exactly what he says. And then, when he doesn't get his way, when he comes up against someone who outranks him, displays twisty-turny cunning and absolute ruthlessness. He was perfect for the part.

Cassandra, next up, was so similar to Louis in appearance, except in her the ashen-blonde hair fell to her flat chest. She was so timid when she announced herself, saying, 'I'll be reading for Volpone,' that she was barely audible. She seemed to have none of her twin's confidence. But when she started to read, the timidity worked really well.

Hereditary showeth in the face;
I hope likewise to imprint my father's grace,
Like a whelp in the litter that follows his sire's path
And plants his footsteps in the prints of those paws
That have gone before.

You could see a young man cowed by his father, desperate to serve his queen, but more desperate still for his father's approval. She brought something really touching to the part – I guess you'd call it pathos – which actually made me feel sympathy for her, something I'd not expected to feel for a de Warlencourt ever again. And, of course, the family resemblance, father for son, would work incredibly well for the play. All we'd have to do would be to give Louis some ageing make-up, shove Cassandra's hair into a hat, and job done. Nel was obviously thinking the same thing. She turned to me, her meticulously shaped dark eyebrows almost at her blonde hairline.

'OK, OK,' I said. 'But there are still plenty of others to see.'

We then sat through forty minutes of Medieval try-hards doing really bad versions of what Louis and Cassandra had already done. We smiled and said *thanks* and *that was really great* and *next*, until there was no one left.

When the last one had gone, Nel looked at me.

'Oh *crap*,' I said, meaning it. I knew what that look meant. It meant, *You have to cast the de Warlencourts*.

'I know. But you've *got* to. They're *good*.'

'Yeah – but you know they've probably had personal drama lessons from Benedict Cumberbatch, and they've probably got their own little mini theatre at whatever stately home they live in, and Daddy probably pays for the cast of *Hamilton* to come and sing them "Happy Birthday".'

Nel slumped back in her chair. 'I know, I *know*. But Shafeen was right. If they are that good, and we *don't* cast them, then what does that make *us*?'

I threw my pen down. 'Oh Jeez. I was hoping we'd get someone else to redress the balance. Ty never turned up, did she?'

Nel checked her watch. 'Let's give her a few more minutes.'

We waited for as long as we could, and as the minutes ticked past I tried to swallow down the tight disappointment that had lodged in the back of my throat. Ty'd bottled it, and I would have a play peopled by pink-and-white privileged people, not exactly what I'd planned when we'd become Medievals. So much for diversity. Nel and I started chatting idly – spinning out the time until the Middle Bell rang – the 2 p.m. chapel chime that meant it was time to start afternoon lessons.

'By the way, why's it called *The Isle of Dogs*?'

'I think Ben Jonson was a big Wes Andersen fan,' I joked. Nel blanked and I rewound. 'No idea. No isles yet, or dogs.'

'Except the names,' said Nel.

'How d'you mean?'

'In Latin *lupo* means wolf, *volpone* means fox and *canis* means dog.' Sometimes, because Nel was so Instagram-pretty, with her nails and her tan and her hair extensions, I was guilty of forgetting how clever she was. I looked at her with respect. 'I guess it's some sort of allegory then. You know, when something represents something else.'

'It's not an allegory,' came a voice. 'It's a place.'

We turned as one towards the stage. Ty stood there. She looked fantastic. The candlelight hit the angular planes of her model-face and her hair had been teased out of its cornrows and stood out from her face in this magnificent Zazie-Beetz-in-*Deadpool-2* afro.

'It's a place,' she said again. 'In London.'

'You sure?'

'I should be. I live there.'

'You *live* on the Isle of Dogs?'

'Yeah.'

'Is it . . . is it posh? I mean, is there a palace there?'

She laughed shortly, almost like a bark. 'No. It's a shithole. But it's *my* shithole.' She sounded quite defensive, and I got that – Arkwright Road was the armpit of Manchester, but even though we'd now (literally) moved up in the world to our penthouse in Salford Quays, I still had love for it.

Ty thawed a bit. 'There used to be a royal palace at Greenwich

53

though, just across the river. *That's* the posh part.' And this time she smiled. 'I'm reading for Queen Cynthia.'

She was spectacular as she strode about the stage like an expensive caged dog. She had real authority and her voice was beautiful, musical and low.

Will nothing sate this appetite of mine?
Tedious jewels, stale coins, gowns and diadems,
I consume the world with my black jaw,
Lick the chops and ask for more.
Gold cannot stave the hunger that gnaws my soul,
And now they offer me a king to match me.
Shall I consume him too and want for more?
Or shall he take my womanhood, queenship, wealth and
*   all,*
And leave me, poor bitch, in litter?
Nay. Greenwich be the only bone to satisfy this cur.
The first meat I have truly desired,
The first to be denied to me.

As soon as she left the stage, Nel and I said, in sync, 'She's hired.'

Nobody came for Poetaster or Canis, the less showy parts.

'Who's going to be them?' worried Nel as the Middle Bell rang.

'You and me, baby,' I said as we packed up to go. 'No one else, is there?'

'Who will be who?'

I *desperately* wanted to be Poetaster. I was sure that the

narrator's sardonic voice was Ben Jonson's and I'd begun to identify with the playwright really strongly.

'I'll be Canis,' said Nel, to my great relief. 'I think he's funny.'

'Cool.' I took a beat. 'I suppose you *can* act, right?'

'Chester Youth Theatre for three years,' she said. 'Oh, and once, my dad did get the cast of *The Lion King* to sing "Happy Birthday" to me.' She vanished with a white grin, like the Cheshire Cat.

That told *me*.

Scene x

The first – and only – act of *The Isle of Dogs* was going really well.

Even though we had only a few scenes, there was plenty of meaty stuff for the actors to, as Shafeen would say, get their teeth into. And I was really enjoying directing, seeing everything take shape. Luckily, the interim Abbot, maybe because he was mostly busy with Abbot-ing, maybe because he genuinely thought I should be given 'creative space', pretty much left me to it. When he was in the theatre, he observed without interfering, only making suggestions when I asked, and in English lessons he even taught us other Renaissance plays to support our drama work on *The Isle of Dogs*. He became known as Abbot Ridley, to differentiate him from the, you know, dead one: who, when we referred to him at all, was simply the Old Abbot. Come to think of it, we'd never even known the Old Abbot's name.

The twins, too, it turned out, were committed to the project – Cassandra in a particularly dedicated way.

One of the weirder things about STAGS was that they had these visiting barbers called Armstrong & Son who came to the school every week. Son was pretty normal, but Armstrong was such an old man I reckoned he must've cut hair in Shafeen's dad's time. Now, we girls didn't really ever bother with haircuts at school – we just got ours done in the holidays, as you only ever had to wait six weeks for the next break. But Armstrong & Son had plenty of business from the boys, who constantly wanted fresh trims, and even, in the sixth form, shaves. Apparently, the ancient Armstrong did a world-class wet-shave and actually used one of those old-fashioned Sweeney Todd cut-throat razors. I wouldn't trust him to hold it steady, myself.

Armstrong & Son would set up shop every week in the boys' changing room, which, as you can imagine, wasn't like a normal scuzzy school changing room, but was all oak panelling and china basins and oars hanging on the wall. Armstrong & Son would pile high hot towels and line up all these little bottles and jars of pomade and shaving soap and hair oil, and in their pristine matching white coats would cut hair all day.

Anyway, the point of all this is that I met Louis de Warlencourt on the stairs of Lightfoot one day when Armstrong & Son had been to the school. I saw the top of his head first as he climbed up towards me in the light from the diamond-paned windows. I noticed his fresh haircut straight away, burnished in the sunlight, cut close around the ears and at the back, longer and shaped and feathered on the top. At the neck the individual blond filaments of almost-shaved hair glittered against the skin, just as I'd seen Henry's hair in close detail in chapel that time. Then he came round the turn of the stair and I saw that it was not Louis but Cassandra. I stopped in amazement. 'Cas-*sandra*!' I exclaimed.

She stopped.

'Your hair!'

'What?' She tugged on the shorn lengths self-consciously. 'Don't you like it?'

I crossed my arms and really looked at her. 'I *love* it,' I said. I really did. 'You look wonderful.' With that long, blonde medieval mane she had always reminded me uncomfortably of those nasty-ass Heathers from last year, Charlotte and Esme and Lara. Now she looked fantastically androgynous and more like Louis – and Henry – than ever.

She smiled shyly. 'Thanks. I thought . . . you know . . . for the play.'

'Wow,' I said. 'You did that for *The Isle of Dogs?*'

She ducked her head. 'Henry always used to say that if something is worth doing, it's jolly well worth doing properly.'

It was a shock to hear his name like that. A) to hear someone speaking of him at all, but B) speaking of him with affection. When my fellow murderers and I spoke of Henry, and that was rarely (as if the very mention of him could put some kind of hoodoo on us), it was always with fear or hate or regret. So I smiled. 'Sounds like him,' I said.

But she didn't smile back. Instead, her face absolutely crumpled with grief. 'I miss him,' she said.

And she ran past me up the stairs and went on her way, leaving me standing there like a deer in the headlights.

The twins cut quite a figure around school after that. Of course, they didn't even have the distinction of the different stockings that us Medievals could wear – Nel's Chanel CC design on shocking pink, my clapperboards or Shafeen's tiger stripes. They had the blood-red, standard-issue STAGS stockings under their Tudor coats like everybody else, and so were almost impossible to tell apart.

Cassandra was so quiet it was hard to consider her a friend, but she was always perfectly nice, and softly spoken, and had an attractive shy smile. She reminded me of Henry in his quieter, more contemplative moments. Louis had the show-off side; the entitled, comfortable anywhere, privileged side. If he was anyone else you'd think he was a prick, but he had such a large slice of the de Warlencourt charm that you couldn't dislike him. He was more flamboyant than Henry, and would wear aftershave and a fancy tooled belt and handmade loafers and product in his hair. Cassandra was less colourful than him, with less of that British ham-pink complexion. Her skin was almost translucent, with a pearly sheen to it, her eyes so slate blue as to be almost grey. But, at the same time, her features were identical to Louis's, so bore a strong similarity to Henry's too. Her resemblance was to a Henry wounded and weakened, Henry on the rooftop talking of a world that had gone away. It made her very appealing, and brought out in me a protective instinct I didn't know I had. For twins who looked so identical, they couldn't have been more different. Louis talked so much, and Cass talked so little, it was as if she and he shared a word count for the day, and because he used the allowance up, there were no words left for her.

But both the twins messed with my head in different ways. Louis's family resemblance to Henry was so strong that once, unguarded, I spoke to him as if he *was* Henry. And when I'd first seen Cass in the chapel, smirking at me on the day I'd sussed that the Abbot was the Grand Master of the hopefully-now-defunct Order of the Stag, I'd thought her the natural successor to those Mean-Girl Medievals. But she was actually nothing like them. She didn't gossip, or giggle, or send bitchy stares my way. And if she spent most of her day in silence, onstage she spoke up and did her part well. She was no Ty, who was a real find, but she interacted with Louis beautifully, allowing his Lupo to crush her utterly, while desperately trying to please him. It seemed to me their parts reflected a little of their own dynamic In Real Life. Cass always knew her lines, as did Louis. They always listened to direction, and to be fair to them never once tried to overrule me with their centuries of privilege, in the theatre that bore their name.

For some reason, this play was important to them.

And because of that, I made friends with them.

And it was a two-way street. They made friends with me, too; with all of us. They seemed to bear no ill will to the trio of people who'd been there at Longcross on the weekend when their cousin Henry had died. It was as if we'd all been best buds and they were carrying on the friendship in his name – we were part of his legacy. As far as I was aware, these London kids knew nothing of the Order of the Stag or the dangerous bloody games that had been played at Longcross for centuries.

The twins were Luke and Leia Skywalker.

They were A New Hope.

Scene xi

It was in this spirit (geddit?) that we all accepted the invitation to a drinks party in Louis's room.

I'd never been to a drinks party before and wasn't exactly sure what we were going to be served. As far as I knew, there was no booze at STAGS beyond the communion wine and the Abbot's sherry, and the twins weren't even eighteen. But since the idea was for all the cast to get to know each other better, I thought we should at least make the effort, especially since the twins invited Shafeen too, knowing how joined at the hip we were. So that Saturday night Nel, Shafeen and I walked across the Honorius quad to Louis's room.

Honorius House was the grandest and most ancient house of the school. I knew that Henry's room had been here, a place I'd never seen. In Honorius the rooms led off a lovely white cloister with these arched windows and delicate stone carvings that looked like they were made of icing sugar. The quad had a cedar tree in the middle that was said to have been a seedling brought back from Jerusalem and planted when the first foundation stone of STAGS was laid. We walked past this stolen tree and it kind of whispered at us as we passed. We wandered through the cloister looking for Room 7, found it, and knocked on the arched oak door.

Louis opened the door with a flourish and beckoned us all in. We shuffled in and stood in this little group, looking round, totally gobsmacked. Louis's rooms were a-MAZING. They were oak panelled, with thick Turkish rugs on the floor, and a lovely old fireplace with a fire burning brightly in the grate. There were two leather armchairs either side of the fire, a painted screen propped against the wall, and paintings that looked so authentic as to be actually genuine hanging on the walls. There was a gramophone, one of those HMV ones with a big golden trumpet, playing some sort of 1930s jazz. There was a huge wooden globe on the desk, as if Louis owned the real thing, and a human skull upended with pencils sticking out of the neckhole. There were doors leading off this main room into at least another two rooms.

This wasn't a bedroom; it was a suite.

And that was what was weird. Since the strange happenings of last year, we three were the only Medievals, and as such, we had suites of rooms, and they were really nice, but not THIS nice. I knew suddenly, with absolute certainty, that these had been Henry's rooms. Louis was the heir apparent, the next in line.

And he certainly was relaxed in his role as king of the evening. He was moving about in a practised way, putting a warm hand on elbows and the smalls of backs, welcoming everyone – the consummate host. I'm here to tell you, drinks parties are *weird*. For a start, everyone *stands up* and chats, no one sits down, and you kind of 'circulate', which means talking to one person and then moving on to another one in a really stilted way. Shafeen and the twins, who'd obviously been to tons of these, seemed to think this was perfectly normal and handled it with ease. Shafeen started chatting with the twins while Ty, Nel and I stood around like doofuses, smiling at each other awkwardly. There was something about that privileged environment that reduced Nel (tech heiress), me (gobby northerner) and Ty (feisty cockney) to silence.

It was Louis who broke the ice. 'Now, ladies, what can I get you to drink?'

Ty had the nuts to speak up. 'What you got?' she said, calling on some Queen Cynthia sass.

'Everything your heart could desire,' Louis said in a mock-cheesy way, carrying her hand to his lips. This olde-worlde gesture seemed to knock Ty's composure a bit. She smiled in a slightly dazed way and said, 'Surprise me.'

'Captain Morgan, I think,' he said with a charming smile. 'Perfect for you. Don't worry' – he clocked her face – 'I'll put loads of Coke in it. You won't even taste the rum.'

I had no clue, so I just asked for a glass of wine to be safe.

He turned to Shafeen. 'What's your poison? Ah – I know just the thing – how about some Bombay Sapphire?'

Shafeen gave a tight smile. 'Fine.'

'Tonic?'

'Of course.'

'Cheeky bastard,' murmured Shafeen out of the side of his mouth as he took the glass.

'Why?' I asked. 'Because he chose you an Indian drink?'

'It's not though. It's like his diabolical cousin's "Punjabi Playboy" thing all over again.'

I was confused. 'But I thought Bombay . . .'

'Yes, *Bombay* is in India. But the Bombay Sapphire, the jewel, came from Sri Lanka. That's somewhere quite different, by the way.' He sipped the offending drink angrily. 'The white man doesn't care where things come from. It's pure cultural appropriation.'

'Oh, give it a rest.' I knew Shafeen in this mood. 'You're so *prickly*. Only you could turn the offer of a drink into a passive-aggressive colonial act.' I led him away from the drinks cabinet. 'D'you think he's going to offer me and Nel a cup of builders' tea because we're from "oop north"? I suppose you think he gave Ty rum because she's West Indian.'

'Yes, actually. He said Captain Morgan would be "perfect for her". It's just offensive. The history of rum is the history of slavery.'

Luckily the twins were in a huddle with Nel, because Shafeen was getting a bit loud.

'As if rum was the only thing she could drink, just because she's –'

'Er . . . I think it's because I'm called Morgan,' put in Ty quietly.

'What?'

'Tyeesha Morgan. Hi.'

I let out a little burst of laughter before I could stop myself, and had to take a sip of my wine to cover it. Shafeen stared but was only wrong-footed for a second. In a moment his manners were back and he extended his hand. 'Shafeen Jadeja,' he said. 'We haven't formally met.'

As Ty took his hand, I was reminded of how bewildered

I'd felt this time last year when Esme shook mine. 'Greer says you're a fantastic actress,' Shafeen said, styling it out, his charm returning.

'And I didn't even tell him to say that,' I quipped. And Ty and I were off, chatting away about her great-uncle who had come over to Britain from Jamaica as a boy on a ship called the *Empire Windrush* in 1948. Shafeen was listening politely, but because I knew him as well as I did, I knew he had tuned out. He was looking fixedly at the corner of the room, seemingly at the wastepaper basket that stood there. I wondered if he, too, was seeing ghosts. When Ty turned to talk to Louis I touched Shafeen's hand. 'You OK?'

He came to, as if I'd woken him. 'There's an elephant in the room.'

'You're damn right there is,' I said grimly. 'Haven't you noticed that no one has mentioned Henry? Even though all of us, except Ty and the twins, were there at Longcross when he died? And even though I'm pretty sure these were his rooms?'

'That's not what I meant. There's an *actual elephant* in the room. Or part of one.' He nodded to the wastepaper basket. I looked at it carefully. It was massive, made of wrinkly grey skin, and round the bottom were these huge discoloured semicircular toenails. I swallowed, feeling suddenly nauseous. The bin was made of a hollowed-out elephant's foot.

'Ew!' I said. 'That's gross.'

'Yes,' he said grimly, sipping his drink, never taking his eyes off the hideous foot-bin.

I looked closer. 'Why has it got that twine round it?' Halfway up the leg, between where the ankle and the knee would be (if elephants in fact have knees and ankles), there was a ratty old piece of thin rope.

Shafeen wiped his mouth with the back of the hand that was still holding the glass. 'It's a tether.' His eyes were glittering dangerously. 'To tie up the elephant. To keep it in its place.'

I looked at the twine dubiously. 'There's no way that little bit of string would hold an elephant that size if it decided to walk off.'

'Ah,' he said. 'That's because they tie the elephant up with that twine when it's just a baby. At that point the rope is strong enough to hold it. The elephant grows up believing it can't get free, because it's been conditioned to captivity. And by the time it is strong enough to escape, it just doesn't try. It learns its place very early on. And it never leaves it.'

I thought about the sadness of it, that even elephants could be institutionalised from an early age. 'You were at prep school with Henry, weren't you?'

'Yes.'

'What was he like back then, before STAGS?'

Shafeen thought for a moment. 'He was a little angel. No trouble. Or rather, nothing you could pin on him. But trouble surrounded him. And it always did. Right till the end.' He took a drink. 'And now there's another one. There's always another one. Henry. Cookson. And now this one.' He jerked his head at Louis.

I sighed. 'You were the one who said to give them a chance. Well, now *I'm* saying it. Give them a chance.'

He shrugged. 'All right, fine.'

'It's not like *he* shot the elephant.'

'No, he didn't.' I didn't even know Cass had been listening,

66

but now she broke in. 'It was our grandfather. Montgomery de Warlencourt. Colonel in the British Army, magistrate at Jaipur during the Raj and all-round *shit*.'

It was the most I'd ever heard her say in one go. Maybe the gin had loosened her tongue. She swung her glass around as she talked, and the crystal-bright liquid sloshed over her hand.

For the first time I saw how beautiful she was. The de Warlencourt looks were just as effective on a girl as on the boys – her choppy gamine hair was just like Jean Seberg's in *À Bout de Souffle*, and her grey-blue eyes bright with drink.

'He was a British magistrate at Jaipur?' exclaimed Shafeen. 'He might have known my family.'

'Probably,' she said, in her clipped upper-class voice, making no effort to be quiet. 'He was probably a prick to them. He was a prick to everyone.'

'Cass,' said Louis, low-voiced, warningly. He'd swapped over with Cassandra – it was her turn to talk; just as I'd never heard her say so much, I'd never heard him just say one word at a time before.

'What?' she protested. 'He was an old bastard. Everybody knows it. He treated the natives app-*all*-ingly.'

Shafeen visibly warmed to her. 'Have you ever been to Rajasthan?'

'Yes. We went out for the old jerk's funeral, two years ago.'

'And what did you think of it?'

'It's the most beautiful place I've ever seen,' she said, with complete, straight-faced honesty. And that was it. Cass talked, Shafeen talked, he laughed, and she drank.

Everyone broke off into pairs and actually sat down. Nel and

I were sharing one armchair, Ty and Louis sat in the other. He'd chivalrously given her the seat, while he reclined on the arm with the same easy, catlike grace that Henry always displayed. Their heads grew closer and closer until her afro began to loll on his shoulder. But I was too mellow to be worried for her. After two drinks I'd begun to feel warm and happy. I was chatting to Nel but doing that thing when you are half listening to other conversations. Shafeen and Cass were in the window seat, next to the offensive wastepaper basket, and I could hear snatches of conversation.

I wasn't jealous. I was glad. This chat was good for both of them – she'd come right out of her shell and he could talk about his beloved homeland. I heard threads of of dialogue – strange and beautiful names that sounded like poetry on his lips: Hawa Mahal, Jantar Mantar, Naharghar. Then the talk wove across the map from Rajasthan to other provinces of India, Cass talking about a temple of Necromancy she'd been to in Orissa where the locals believed you could wake the dead. Her voice fell into one of those sudden silences that happen in the middle of lots of chat – the gramophone had ground to the middle of the record and was doing that wheezy, grindy noise. We all turned to look. Cass'd fallen silent, her mouth a little open, her eyes unfocused.

She looked a strange green colour, like that ill-looking chick from *Guardians of the Galaxy*. Then she leaned over and threw up in the elephant's foot.

Scene xii

'Kerr-ist!' exclaimed Louis, leaping to his feet. 'Every *bloody* time.'

Shafeen, for once, looked a bit lost as to what to do. 'Should I take her to lie down?'

I was a pretty cool girlfriend but not *that* cool. 'I'll do it. You chat to Nel.'

'Yes, of course,' he said, ever the gentleman. 'That would be better. On her side though,' he added – already in doctor mode.

'I know,' I said. 'It's not my first rodeo.' At least two of my friends had thrown up at my last school's prom.

I got Cass's arm over my shoulder and half walked, half dragged her through one of the connecting doors. 'No *way*,' I exclaimed to myself, as I saw the layout. Louis had his own bathroom! I got Cass to the basin and cleaned her face. She was floppy and compliant, and not really heavy at all, so I was able to manoeuvre her to Louis's bed. I put her on her side, undid the buttons of her Tudor coat and loosened the white neckerchief we all wore underneath. I wasn't going to undress her though.

On the side table a bunch of silver-framed photographs

caught my eye. I'd learned at Longcross that the upper classes didn't hang photos on the wall, just paintings. I remembered that there had been dozens of silver-framed photos standing up on the grand piano and it was a bit like that here – lots of pictures of blond relatives, and dogs and horses. There was even one that could have been Good Old Monty de Warlencourt, wearing the white military dress of a viceroy, bristling with medals. At his shoulder stood a boy about Shafeen's age in a white turban, fanning him with this enormous feather fan. Shafeen would do his nut if he saw that.

I looked around a bit, more interested in what wasn't there than what was. There was not one photograph of Henry. Not a single one.

And I couldn't believe Louis had a double bed – *we* didn't get a double bed. This was really unfair. What was Louis, some sort of unofficial head boy? I was about to leave, feeling guilty for snooping, when I noticed there were two pairs of pyjamas neatly folded on the pillows. The pyjamas were exactly the same: a discreet, classy check, with ivory buttons, folded with military precision.

They looked identical.

Except for one thing.

At the back of the neck of each, ironed on absolutely straight, were two regulation STAGS nametapes. One said Louis de Warlencourt; the other, Cassandra de Warlencourt.

When I went back into the living room the elephant's foot was gone. Shafeen was pacing like a new father, and immediately, like the sweetie he was, asked after Cass. Louis was back in the armchair, seemingly totally unconcerned about his sister's fate – not in a callous way so much as an it-happens-all-the-time way. I wondered, having seen that brief glimpse of raw grief on the stairs, whether it was the loss of Henry that made Cass drink.

Louis, however, didn't analyse. 'Never could take her sherbet, old Cass,' he said fondly. 'She'll be right as rain in a bit. Just needs to sleep it off.'

'I'll bring her back to Lightfoot later,' offered Ty quickly. 'I'll stay for a bit, make sure she's OK.'

Nel, Shafeen and I were obviously surplus to requirements, so we let Louis show us to the door. We parted in a friendly way – he and Shafeen even shook hands warmly. As soon as we were in the cloister, I glanced at Shafeen in the moonlight. I expected him to say something like, 'Jesus,' or, 'Thank God that's over.' But instead he said, 'I hope she's OK.'

'Who – Ty?' asked Nel. 'She looked pretty cosy to me.'

'No, not Ty. Cass.'

Now I shot him a proper look, my eyebrows disappearing under my fringe.

'What?' he said. 'You said to give them a chance. I did.'

I had to smile. 'Are you falling for the famous de Warlencourt charm?'

He looked at me sidelong and grinned. 'I wouldn't go *that* far. The jury's still out on him. But I'll admit I was wrong about her.'

We walked across the quad, under the long shadow of the Jerusalem tree, our feet crunching on the frost that had already formed in the shade, our breath smoking.

In the silence I thought how I'd been wrong about her too.

I'd thought Cass was a bit of a drip – a shadow of her brother. But I now thought she had hidden depths. There was one thing for certain – she'd loved Henry, really loved him, and she mourned him, just as I did.

But I'd been wrong about her in another way. I wasn't worried about Cass any more. I was more worried about Ty, as I was pretty sure she would be walking back across this frozen quad alone.

I didn't think Cass lived in Lightfoot at all.

I thought she shared a room – and a bed – with her brother.

Scene xiii

I did tell Nel about the pyjamas-on-the-bed thing, on the way to the theatre the next morning. To my surprise, she took it pretty calmly.

'It's not *that* weird, is it?'

'It's *very* weird.'

'Well, I'm an only child . . .'

'. . . so am I . . .'

'. . . but siblings often share beds, don't they?'

'Yes, when they're *seven*,' I said. 'Not when they're seven*teen*. What if she lives in Honorius, and not in Lightfoot at all?'

'How would she get away with that?'

'Well, let's see,' I said. 'How about by looking *exactly* like her brother, same Tudor coat, same red stockings, same hairdo even.'

Nel stopped in the middle of the Lightfoot quad.

'D'you think that's why she got her hair cut?'

'I think that could be part of it.'

We started walking again.

'What should we do?' she asked.

'Why do we have to do anything?'

'Well, it's against the rules, and we're . . . well, we're *Medievals*.'

'De Warlencourts seems to have their own rules here.'

'Not just here,' said Nel with a shiver of recollection in her voice.

'Let's just leave it,' I decided. 'Medievals aren't unpaid spies for the Friars.'

'I tell you one thing though,' said Nel. 'If she does live in Honorius, she could hardly be your mysterious messenger in Lightfoot. The person who gave you the play, I mean.'

'I s'pose,' I conceded. 'She still has a room there though. She could use it as an HQ.' But to be honest, I didn't give much attention then to the possibility of what *Gone Girl* called 'Twincest'. I had a play to put on.

In the next few days it seemed like nothing could go wrong. Our one and only act of *The Isle of Dogs* really came together. The art students made a beautiful Palace of Placentia set, glossy marble columns, gilded coving and coats-of-arms all designed around dogs. The music department was writing the score, and the chapel choir was going to sing an Elizabethan chant to underlie my prologue. Our production counted as coursework for their Probitiones in art and music too. I felt as if I was getting an awful lot of help. But because everything was so smooth, and easy, and obstacle-free, I didn't even question what was going on, or realise that I was skipping into the forest as innocently as Red Riding Hood in *Hoodwinked*.

Pretty dumb, really.

The first sniff I had that something dark was going on was when I got the *second* act of *The Isle of Dogs*.

ACT TWO

Scene i

'It's about a hunt.'

I'd taken the play – two acts now – down to the Paulinus well first thing in the morning. Shafeen and Nel looked puzzled, as well they might.

'*What's* about a hunt?' asked Shafeen.

'The *play*, dummy. I got the second act last night, after Commons, just like the time before. The same way – pages under my door, delivered by Mr Nobody. And the second act is all about an upcoming *hunt*. Look.' I riffled through the pages and found Act Two, placing the manuscript on the stone surround of the well. 'You remember in Act One, it was that prologue from Poetaster, and then it was Queen Cynthia, and the father and son courtiers, and her wanting to marry the Earl of Greenwich, and a bit of comedy-servant business from Canis. It was all nicey-nicey and we never saw the earl. Well. In Act Two we *do* meet the earl. And the first thing he does is to insult the father and son. He likens them to dogs.'

'The wolf and the fox,' said Nel.

'Exactly. But he's not being nice. He calls them curs, because they are trying to break up him and the queen for their own ends. And they get all mortally insulted, and they devise a plan both to please the queen and to get the earl to fall out of favour, so that the queen will marry this king they've lined up, the King of El Dorado. And guess how they plan to do it?'

They both look at me expectantly, hooked.

'They plan this huge hunt to happen in the dog days of summer – which are apparently in the middle of July, when the dog star Sirius is in the sky. This also coincides with the queen's birthday. Because hunting is her favourite thing in the world, they say it will be this huge birthday hunt, the greatest hunt ever held in the history of England, and the earl will be her guest of honour.' I took a breath. 'Are you following me?'

'Just about,' said Shafeen. 'Go on.'

'OK, so the birthday hunt is going to be held in the Underwood, this big forest near the Palace of Placentia. Lupo and Volpone persuade the queen not to tell the earl about it, saying it should be this big surprise for him. And then they do a creepy thing.'

'What?' Nel asked this time.

'They start to amass this huge pack of dogs, hundreds of them – breeding them and collecting them from other noble houses. And guess where the kennels are?'

'On the Isle of Dogs,' they chorused.

'Yep,' I said grimly.

Shafeen frowned. 'But, how would holding a big dog hunt get rid of the earl?'

'Dunno. That's as far as it goes.'

'You do know,' said Nel softly, her voice shaking a little. 'Come on, we're all thinking it. Surely they are going to turn the dogs on the earl.'

Like they did with you, I thought, remembering Nel at Longcross running from Henry's hounds.

'He's an earl,' said Shafeen, 'but he dares to think that he can be a king. He's trying to climb above his station, and so he has to be stopped.' He looked at us in turn. 'The whole play stinks of the Order.'

'You think they are mixed up in it somewhere?' asked Nel.

'I do, yes. This was Tudor times, remember? The Order has been going since the Crusades, so by the reign of Elizabeth it would be well established.'

'Well, I'm pretty sure Ben Jonson wasn't one of the bad guys,' I said defensively. 'He was a common boy. A bricklayer.' It was one of the things that'd drawn me to him. 'And if we've established anything, it's that the Order is run by posh people – the ruling classes.' I looked at the title page of the play, uncertain. 'But Pembroke's Men might be a different matter.'

'They'd be just actors, surely?' said Nel. 'I think actors were usually low born – not like today with your Tom Hiddlestons and your Eddie Redmaynes.'

'The "men" would be, yes. But the title page says *Pembroke's* men. Men who belong to Pembroke. Pembroke, whoever he was, must've been powerful, to have men.'

I'd been at STAGS long enough to know that if there was a person you needed to look up, you did it the old-school way. Instead of Wikipedia, you looked through the gazillion leather-bound volumes of the *Dictionary of National Biography*.

I bore the other two off to the Scriptorium, where Friar Waterlow pointed us in the direction of the slate-blue and gold-tooled volumes almost at once. We whipped down the

'P' book and took it to one of the carrels. Shafeen clicked on the little light.

'P, P, P,' I said. 'Pembroke, *Earl* of, here we go. I knew he'd be a posh boy.' I stabbed the page with my finger in triumph. The triumph was short-lived. 'Oh. There's about a million of them.'

'Check the dates,' said Nel.

'*Isle of Dogs* was 1597,' I murmured under my breath. 'So it must be . . .' I scanned the page, '*this* one.'

Henry Herbert, 2nd Earl of Pembroke, 1538–1601
He was the son of William Herbert, 1st Earl of Pembroke, and Anne Parr. His aunt was Queen Consort Catherine Parr, last wife of King Henry VIII. In the court intrigues of Elizabeth I's reign, Pembroke was regarded as a partisan of Robert Dudley, 1st Earl of Leicester, and was certainly in very intimate relations with him. During the 1590s, Herbert was patron of Pembroke's Men, a theatre company who were the first group to perform a number of plays, including *The Isle of Dogs* by Ben Jonson. His company included the celebrated actors Robert Shaw and Gabriel Spenser, who played the Earl of Greenwich in Jonson's suppressed play.

Gabriel Spenser.

I stared at that name for a moment. I'd seen it somewhere before. When I suddenly remembered where, I slammed the volume closed, stood up and left the Scriptorium without even putting the book back.

The others, bemused, followed me.

Scene ii

'Look.'

We were standing at the entrance of the De Warlencourt Playhouse, and I was pointing up at the plaque above the timbered door. It said:

THE DE WARLENCOURT PLAYHOUSE
BY KIND DONATION OF THE DE WARLENCOURT
FAMILY
OPENED ON 24th JULY 1969
AND DEDICATED TO
'GABRIEL SPENSER'
PLAYER

'Same guy, see? Gabriel Spenser, Player. It doesn't mean he got loads of women. It means he was an *actor*. He was one of Pembroke's Men.'

'That's funny,' mused Nel. 'I wonder why Gabriel Spenser's name is in inverted com—'

Shafeen cut across her. 'You should get out. Get out now.'

'What are you talking about?'

'Stop doing the play. Stop everything. Choose something else.'

'But *you* were the one who said –'

'I know, I know. But you need to stop. It's too weird. The play turning up in the first place, Ridley getting behind it, Waterlow not knowing a thing about it. The acts being drip-fed week by week – I bet you any money you get Act Three on Sunday night. And then this.' He waved his hands at the timbered structure. 'The theatre that was built in 1969 – that's when my *dad* was here – dedicated to some random actor who it turns out was most probably actually *in The Isle of Dogs*. The whole thing stinks.'

I saw his point, but I also saw that I had no choice. 'I can't quit *now*. We've lost another week. Cassandra's cut her hair and everything. Everyone's really into their parts. Ty's come out of her shell and actually found some confidence, probably for the first time ever.' I did actually feel weirdly responsible for her. She was the first de Warlencourt scholar, here in Henry's memory, and although (maybe because) I'd largely ignored her for the first half-term of her time here, I now felt I owed her something. I wasn't about to take this part away from her. 'You should see her browbeating those twins onstage – it's a total flip of how she is in real life. The sets are being painted by the art Probitio types, and the music Probitio people are writing the music. Plus Justitium's coming up in a couple of weeks, so we lose three days of rehearsal then.' It was true. Abbot Ridley had announced that the postponed Justitium weekend would now be in November. 'And what about the play being my ticket to Oxford? I can't just go in there now and say, *Sorry, we're doing Hamlet*. I wouldn't be able to do it justice. There's no *time*.'

Shafeen held up both his hands. 'All right, all right. But don't say I didn't warn you. And don't expect me to rescue you again.'

That got me mad. 'I don't need *rescuing*. What do you think this is? I'm not a pre-*Frozen* Disney princess. And you are *not* my Prince Charming. In fact, at the moment you're not charming at *all*.'

And he walked off.

He just walked off.

After that I was shaking.

Nel took my arm gently and we walked slowly and soberly across the frosted grass of Bede's Piece to the Refectory. By the time we got there Shafeen was already sitting with a bunch of science types, determinedly eating his breakfast, looking neither left nor right.

Nel and I found a place together on the benches, not far enough away from him to cause comment, but not near enough for conversation. We ate in unhappy silence, until I said, '*You* think I'm right, don't you? You think we should carry on with *The Isle of Dogs?*'

Nel ate a whole mouthful of toast and honey before answering. 'Yes,' she said. 'After all, it is just a play. *Words* can't hurt anyone. Whatever happens to the Earl of Greenwich in the drama, there's nothing to suggest that anyone died in real life.'

I looked sideways at Shafeen, head down, his dark hair flopping in his face.

I thought of what I'd said to him.

Words can't hurt anyone.

I wondered if Nel was right about that.

Scene iii

I had bigger problems than Shafeen right then.

There was another part in *The Isle of Dogs*, and no actor for it.

I had to find an Earl of Greenwich.

I went to talk to Abbot Ridley. It was one of those sparkling autumn days and when I entered his study in Honorius it was pretty dark. He was writing at his desk, as he always seemed to be.

'Just a minute,' he said, and wrote his signature with a flourish. Then he put his pen in its inkwell (yes, really) and said, 'Greer. How can I help?'

Of course, that all made things much easier. I explained about the second act of *The Isle of Dogs*.

'How exciting,' he said.

'Well, it is,' I said, 'except now I need another cast member.'

'Oh, I see.' He breathed in through his nose, banged both hands palms downwards on his desk and stood up. His full height was pretty impressive. 'Let's go for a walk,' he said. 'When I'm stuck I usually find that fresh air sorts me out.'

We went for a walk by the moat. The frosty grass crunched underfoot, the low sun gilded the water and the happy cries of the sports monkeys playing lacrosse on Bede's Piece floated over to us. Friar Ridley shoved each hand in the other sleeve, in a curiously monkish way, and walked along like that.

'Tell me about Act Two,' he said. 'I mean, I assume you'll allow me to read it?'

'Of course.'

'But just give me the elevator pitch.'

I told him about the Earl of Greenwich, shopping for the queen's hand in marriage, insulting the father–son courtiers, and them cooking up a way to punish him with the dog hunt.

'Lovely,' he said. 'So far, so Elizabethan. Couldn't you call someone back from the auditions to play this unfortunate soul?'

I made a throwing-up sound with my mouth, just a second before it occurred to me that it probably wasn't the way to have a conversation with your head teacher. 'Sorry, but all the boys were awful, except for Louis, and we already cast him.'

'What about the girls?'

'The girls?'

'Yes, why not? Cross-dressing has ancient origins in theatre. In Elizabethan times all the players were boys. And in modern pantomime the principal boy is often played by a girl. What else would they do with the alumni of soap operas and reality TV?'

I smiled, and considered then how different he was from the bad old abbot of the bad old days.

'Even in your own production,' he went on, 'you have Cassandra and Chanel playing male characters.'

'I guess,' I admitted. 'But the sad truth is, the girls who auditioned were pretty awful too.'

We walked across the drawbridge and under the shadow

of the gatehouse. 'Isn't there anyone else who could play the earl? Maybe someone who doesn't even do drama?'

Shafeen, I thought. He'd always, whatever I'd just screamed at him, had that princely thing going on. Probably because he sort of *was* a prince, or at least his dad was. But he wasn't an option. One, he was up to his eyes in science revision, and two . . . well, two, we'd just fallen out.

We walked on in silence for a bit, until Abbot Ridley said, 'I'll do it.'

'Really?' I squinted up at him. He was definitely tall and handsome, and certainly looked how I imagined an earl to look. And he wasn't so old (I guessed early thirties?) that it would look weird pairing him with Ty. But still . . .

'Why not? I'm there for all the rehearsals anyway. He just has to turn up and be unpleasant. I'm sure I could manage that.'

I quite dug his dry humour. But . . . 'I don't know,' I said.

He glanced at me, then ahead. 'Why not?'

'I mean, well, you're the *Abbot* and stuff.'

'Interregnum Abbot. And not for long. The governors are appointing a new one. And frankly, I'll be relieved.'

'But won't you be going for the job?'

'I don't think so. It's not really my thing. I prefer teaching to admin, being the figurehead of the school and all that. They only parachuted me in because I'd been head at Ampleforth. But in fact, I *left* Ampleforth because I wanted to teach again.'

We walked on in silence while I considered the prospect of him being in the play. For all I knew, it was quite normal at private schools for teachers to get amongst it on the production side of things. And Abbot Ridley certainly had the potential to be that *Dead Poets Society* inspirational teacher type. By the time we'd got to the theatre I'd pretty much made up my mind, and then I remembered something else I'd meant to ask him. 'O Captain! my Captain?' I said.

I don't know if he got it or not, but he smiled. 'Yes?'

'Have you heard of a guy called Gabriel Spenser?' I'd been back to the Scriptorium to look for him in the *Dictionary of National Biography*, but he wasn't there. Apparently, he was famous enough to have a theatre named after him, but not famous enough to have his own entry in a dusty old book. So I was pretty surprised when the Abbot said: 'Yes.'

'You have?'

'He was an actor. And something of a hothead, by all accounts. Liked getting into fights. Why?'

'Because the De Warlencourt Playhouse was dedicated to him.'

'Really?' He sounded surprised.

'Yes. There's the plaque. Look.' I pointed.

'Well, well,' he said to the plaque. 'So it is. I probably should have known that. But as the new boy I guess there are still some mysteries about STAGS I am yet to uncover.'

That was the understatement of the century, but now wasn't the time to get into the school's darker history. 'I guess he must have been a pretty special actor, to have a dedication like that.'

He shifted his green gaze to me. 'Well, that's just it. He wasn't. He was a journeyman, really. He was tall and he was handsome, he played lots of princes and dukes. But he would be an odd choice, unless he was directly connected with the family. There were much better-known actors. Richard Burbage, for one.'

'Ooh, I love him!' I exclaimed. '*Where Eagles Dare, Who's Afraid of Virginia Woolf?*'

'I said Richard Bur-*bage*, not Richard Bur-*ton*. He was a very famous player in the Elizabethan period. As was Will Kemp. And Ben Jonson.'

'Back up,' I said. 'Ben Jonson was an *actor*?'

'Oh yes. Also in Pembroke's Men.'

'D'you think he would have played Poetaster?' That was the narrator's role, my role. It was suddenly really important that it *had* been Ben Jonson.

'Very probably. It was common for playwrights to act. Look at Shakespeare.'

That decided it. 'Well then,' I said, 'if playwrights acted, I suppose it would be OK for a teacher to have a go.'

He looked amused. 'None taken.'

Abbot Ridley was pretty funny. And it felt weirdly nice walking along with him like that, almost as if he was my friend, not my headmaster. Irrelevantly, as we entered the dark of the theatre, I found myself wondering what his first name was.

Scene iv

Thank Christ, Abbot Ridley could act.

He coped really well with rehearsal, and performed his wooing scenes with Ty, and his arguing scenes with the twins, with skill. He was no Daniel Day-Lewis, but he had good diction, probably from all that headmastering, and a great stage presence too.

Oddly, Abbot Ridley's best bits onstage were between himself and Nel. The Earl of Greenwich and the lowly servant Canis had a really nice little subplot. Canis, tired of the bullying he had to endure from the father–son courtiers and Queen Cynthia, was shopping around for a new master. He got it into his head that the earl would be a perfect new employer and began to follow him around like a little dog, begging to be taken on.

As we rehearsed Act Two I watched them carefully. They had an indefinable *something* when they acted together, that mysterious thing called Chemistry. It was Bogey and Bacall, it was Tom Hanks and Meg Ryan, it was Audrey Hepburn and Cary Grant. There was no romance in their dialogue, as the connection was between a low-born servant and a great earl. But I definitely felt it, in one scene in particular. It was the one where Canis follows the earl from the palace after Greenwich has insulted Lupo and Volpone. Their hatred for those two nobles gives them something in common, and Greenwich decides to reward his new ally.

Greenwich
Come, what will you have? You follow me like my best pointer out hunting. Shall I give thee a bone for thy trouble?

Canis
If it please you, no less than the biggest bone in the body.

Greenwich
Wouldst thou have a skull, my dog?

Canis
Aye, sire, and the skin that covers it. Put orbs in the eyes, and hair on the pate, and a crown on the hair. Then stamp the thing entire upon a disc of gold, and pay it into my palm.

Greenwich
Thou art a clever cur! Here's for thy pains.

(Greenwich throws Canis a coin.)
(Canis kisses his feet.)

I decided that Canis should flip out with joy at being given a coin, and that the little gesture should make him Greenwich's slave forever. Nel and I agreed for his back-story that Canis had never been given a coin before, even though the queen was, according to the play, 'richer than Solomon'.

Because of this I was keen to keep in the bit where Canis kissed Greenwich's feet, A) because Ben Jonson had written it in the stage directions, and B) because it would show Canis's devotion. Greenwich had kissed the queen's hand in the previous scene, and Abbot Ridley told us that kissing in Elizabethan times said a lot about hierarchy and servitude and blah-blah-blah. If you kissed someone's feet you were below them. If you kissed someone's hand you were also below them, but not as much, and if you kissed someone's lips you were an equal. I wondered if Nel would mind doing something as debasing as kissing a guy's feet, but in that first rehearsal in the theatre she got right down, bless her, and kissed Abbot Ridley's size elevens, even though he wasn't even in costume. He looked slightly surprised.

Then she did this thing when she turned her head and laid her cheek on his foot with her eyes closed. It was great. It really conveyed love. But the reality of the gesture unsettled me.

I decided to have a word with Nel on the way back to Lightfoot. 'What were you doing with Abbot Ridley?'

'Er, *acting?*' she sassed me. 'But since you ask, what were *you* doing with Abbot Ridley?'

'What?'

'I saw you having your little chat by the moat.'

'I was casting him in this!'

She turned on me. 'Greer. You had Henry, and now you've got Shafeen, if you don't screw it up. Leave *someone* for other people.'

'By other people you mean *you*, I'm guessing.'

'Why not?'

'Why *not?*' My mind boggled. 'Well, for a start, he's a teacher, you're a schoolgirl. Oh yes, and he's the *head*teacher. He's thirty-odd, you're eighteen.'

She looked around her at the frosty night, watching for eavesdroppers, and pulled me onto the stone bridge that spanned the moat, so we couldn't be overheard. 'Look,' she hissed, 'I'm not saying I'm going to *act* on it. I just think he's nice. And fit.'

I couldn't very well say I'd been thinking the same thing on our moatside walk.

'Are you demented? You're going to be on the news.'

She threw her hands up in the air and started walking again.

'I'm just telling it like it is!' I shouted to her back.

I caught her up and she walked along with me in silence, but not notably sulking. 'What did you mean, if I don't screw it up with Shafeen?'

'Just that you might have to make the first move to patch things up. He's got pride, our Shafeen.' She snapped an icicle off one of the stone trefoils of the bridge and began sucking it like a popsicle. 'You're fond of telling it like it is. Well, now I'm telling *you*.'

Scene v

Even though we had fallen out, I still saw Shafeen every day.

He was in history with me, and the fact that this was the only time I really saw him now was a big part of the reason why I'd really started to enjoy the subject. The rest of the reason was to do with our history friar.

To be fair to the homicidal, cult-running maniac the Old Abbot had been, it seemed he had kept his word and employed a very different set of friars after last year's cull. Abbot Ridley was one example of the new breed, and Friar Camden, our new history teacher, was another. She was very different to Friar Skelton, our last history friar. Friar Skelton was the one we'd called the Punctuation Police. He was the one who had talked to us about the importance of noticing punctuation, and had inadvertently (with his favourite little example about Hannibal and his elephants) put me onto the fact that the Old Abbot was the Grand Master of the Order of the Stag.

Friar Camden, on the other hand, was not a stickler for punctuation. She was all about the bigger picture of the politics of court, and, I suspected, a bit of a feminist on the quiet – something I imagined STAGS hadn't really seen before.

I wondered how she'd got past the stuffy old-white-male governors. (You know in *Mary Poppins* when Jane and Michael go to the bank with their father and we see the board members all with white beards? I imagined the STAGS governors to be very much like that.)

Friar Camden had been teaching us since the beginning of term and we'd chewed through Henry VIII and the Reformation, Edward VI pretty much just opening grammar schools and then promptly dying, and Mary Tudor burning all those Protestants like firewood. And now we'd cycled through womanising dad, sickly half-brother and crazy half-sister, we were onto Queen Elizabeth I of England herself.

The Last Tudor.

Our history classes were held in the Tudor Gallery at the top of Marinius, which had desks set along the polished floor, and stained-glass windows illuminating the long, light room, depicting the lives of the Northumbrian saints, including the ubiquitous Aidan–Stag combo. Every time I stole a glance at Shafeen, which seemed to be a lot, he was bathed in the rainbow light of stained glass, just as he'd been last year when he'd faced off with the Medievals about the Battle of Hattin. The Tudor Gallery was the perfect place to learn about Elizabeth.

At first it was standard that-film-with-Cate-Blanchett stuff. Came to the throne aged twenty-five after her half-sister snuffed it, and went about reversing Mary's Catholic policies. Friar Camden's whole deal was how throughout her life Elizabeth had to outwit lots of enemies who had once been friends. Tudor England was a dog-eat-dog world. Her own half-sister put her in the Tower of London. Then there was her cousin, Mary, Queen of Scots, who plotted Elizabeth's death.

The Mary-Queen-of-Scots bit was really interesting, because it had to do with plots and spies and secret codes and stuff. Apparently, Mary sent secret codes to her co-conspirators from the castle where she was being kept prisoner, hidden in barrels of wine. Elizabeth's spies intercepted them and cracked the codes. We had one really cool lesson when Friar Camden told us all about the code Mary used, called a substitution cipher. We spent a happy hour using the methods that Elizabeth's spymasters would have used to decipher it, looking at the frequency of certain symbols in the code, and how they corresponded to the most common letters in the alphabet. Lots of fun for us, of course, but not so much fun for Mary back in the day; because of all that deciphering, things didn't end well for her. When Elizabeth read those letters she signed her cousin's death warrant, and the Mary-Queen-of-Scots episode ended with a half-cute, half-gross story about Mary's dog, who loved his mistress so much that he stayed under her skirts while her head was being chopped off (apparently it took several goes).

Funny how everything seemed to come back to dogs.

Speaking of which, it was when Friar Camden started talking about the next 'Frenemy' Elizabeth had to deal with that Nel and I really sat up.

'In many ways Elizabeth was a proto-feminist,' the Friar declared, tucking a strand of silver hair behind her ear. 'She realised that marriage would dissipate her own power, so, against the advice of her chief advisors, father–son team William and

Robert Cecil, she refused the hand of Philip II, King of Spain. And it was a costly decision. Philip scorned was an extremely dangerous enemy, and eventually ordered the Spanish Armada to sail against England. But,' the Friar went on, smiling a little, 'this didn't mean that Elizabeth lived a life without love. She certainly had her favourites, even in old age, and chief among these was the young and handsome Earl of Essex. You can imagine how much the Cecils liked *him*.'

It was that nugget of information that had Nel and I looking across the classroom at each other, wide-eyed. And at this point, even Shafeen came out of his sulky bubble and flashed a dark look over at us. *See?* the glance seemed to say. *Too neat. Too coincidental. Too dangerous.*

'So,' I murmured to Nel on the way down the stairs after class, 'Ben Jonson was throwing shade at the queen herself in *The Isle of Dogs*. She's obviously represented by Queen Cynthia.' I thought of all those speeches in the play where the queen was being greedy, lustful, bloodthirsty, spoiled, capricious, childish. Being *human*. It was explosive stuff.

'Not just the queen,' said Nel. 'Lupo and Volpone are clearly William and Robert Cecil. A father–son team running the country. The Earl of Greenwich . . .'

'. . . is the Earl of Essex, her cougar crush,' I broke in. 'And the King of El Dorado in the play is obvs Philip II of Spain. The Cecils wanted Elizabeth to marry Philip. He was perfect on paper, but by the end of her life the Only Way Was Essex for Elizabeth.'

'And,' said Chanel the classicist, 'El Dorado was a fabled land full of gold. Spain had colonised the Americas, and had access to all the gold of the continent. The King of El Dorado is literally the king of gold.'

I stopped on the stairs. 'What the hell was Ben Jonson *doing*?' I mused, half in admiration. 'He's pretty much mocking every significant relationship Elizabeth ever had in one play. No wonder it was banned and he got his ass thrown in jail.'

I would've loved to have talked to Shafeen about it too, and get his take on the whole art-imitates-life thing. Nel was great, of course, but I missed Shafeen. Not just his company, but the touch of him, the feel of him. I missed the kisses and the hand-holds and the arm around my shoulders as we walked somewhere, anywhere. And, if I'm honest, I missed those frightening, exhilarating times when it felt like things were getting out of control.

But he seemed to be getting on just *fine*. I saw him going about with his pet science geeks, which would have been OK, but sometimes I saw him walking around the grounds with Cassandra, which was definitely *not* OK. One time I saw them smiling. That was a smack in the face. How could he *smile*?

I was pretty lonely.

I was pretty hurt.

So I did something pretty dumb.

I went looking for Henry online.

Scene vi

I checked out all Henry's Facebook groups, and Twitter pages, and his Google image page, and his Instagram fan pages – and much good it did me.

There he was, looking out of all the pictures with his direct blue gaze and his white smile. Henry in rugby gear. Henry in white tie and tails. Henry in a top hat. Henry in cricket whites in a punt, for God's sake. When had he ever been in a *punt*?

I just felt worse after my Henry binge. Well, I deserved that.

Out of some muscle memory I checked my own Instagram. I wasn't really expecting any messages, because all my old friends from Bewley Park had pretty much given up on me, as they knew I was off-grid. But in my Instagram, against all odds, there was a new message. The name made my pulse thud:

mrs_de_warlencourt

In the little circle where there was supposed to be a profile photo there was just a little pair of black antlers on a white background. I stared at it for a good few seconds, my heart in my throat. Then I clicked the message. There was no greeting or sign off. It was just one little bald statement:

```
You've seen it before.
```

My thumbs one step ahead of me, I typed:

```
Seen what?
```

I waited, listening to my own heartbeat. It was hopeless. The message was from a few days ago – there was no guarantee **mrs_de_warlencourt**, whoever she was, was even online. But almost immediately another message popped up.

```
The play. You've seen it before.
```

I typed:

```
Where?
```

The answer came back:

```
Think.
```

And then:

```
Gotta go.
```

This seemed pretty final. I stared impotently at the screen

for a moment, sweat bubbling under my fingertips, unsure of what to do. In the end I locked the bright phone back in my drawer, because, for a Medieval, carrying a phone would mean expulsion, and I wasn't about to get chucked out of this school now. I threw on my dressing gown and padded down the corridor in my bare feet to find Nel.

She opened her door dressed in these adorable pyjamas and fluffy slippers. Nel always had really nice jammies. 'What's up?'

In answer I said: 'Gimme your phone.'

Puzzled, she locked the door, and took the bright Saros out of her knicker drawer. I sat down on the bed. Nel's room was really pretty, with lots of pink, her favourite colour, which should have looked wrong with the dark oak Tudor panels but actually looked pretty rocking. But I had no time for the decor right then. I signed in to my Instagram and said, 'Look.'

She sat down beside me and took the phone from my hand, expertly tapping through the thread with her acrylic thumbnail. 'Who the hell's **mrs_de_warlencourt**?'

'No idea.'

'Hmm. Probably some Henry superfan. When I was little I used to call myself Mrs Chanel Jonas Brothers.'

I smiled. 'Well, Henry has plenty of superfans out there.' I neglected to mention that tonight I'd been acting like one of them.

'Do you know what she's talking about? *Have* you seen the play before?'

'Before this term? No. How could I have?'

Now it was her turn to say *Dunno*. She looked at me beadily. 'Are you going to show Shafeen?'

I stuck my chin in the air. 'No. I think I'll let sleeping dogs lie.'

'Greer . . .'

'It's late.' I got up from the bed. 'Better get my head down.'

'Will you think about it then?'

'About where I've seen *The Isle of Dogs* before? Sure. But I'm not sure what good –'

'Well, yes, about that, but about Shafeen too.' She looked at me intently from under her sculpted brows. 'Don't throw him away for a ghost.'

Hand already on the door, I quoted **mrs_de_warlencourt**. 'Gotta go.'

Scene vii

Shafeen was right. Act Three arrived on Sunday evening.

This time I was a bit more prepared . As soon as I heard the rustle of the pages I was up from my desk and straight out the door. I heard running, retreating footsteps, not towards the stairwell this time but back into the belly of Lightfoot House. I saw – or I thought I saw – the tail of a black Tudor coat disappearing round the corner of the oak-panelled passageway. I shot after it and found myself in an empty corridor with a dead end. The rows of doors on either side of me were blank and closed.

There were two possibilities. One, whoever had delivered this manuscript to me must have hidden in one of those rooms. Two, and much more likely, the postie actually *lived* in Lightfoot. I walked back to my room, trailing my fingertips over the studded doors, as if one of them could tell me which of them had just been closed. I looked at the message boards and read the names. Cassandra lived on this corridor – or at least she was supposed to, if she actually slept anywhere else but with Louis. So did Ty. So did Nel. But the tail of that Tudor coat had awakened a memory in me – of last year, when I used to imagine Henry disappearing around every corner, swift and unseen. Was he still haunting me?

Heart thudding, I went back to my room and sat down with Act Three of *The Isle of Dogs*. I was so flustered that I read the first page three times before any of the words registered. Then, like a dark incantation, they drew me into the world of the play.

I was there with Queen Cynthia, all pent up and feverishly excited about her birthday hunt in a fortnight's time. She grants the Earl of Greenwich an audience and teases him with a secret, a great event to take place in the dog days of summer, which she refuses to tell him anything about. Here, Greenwich does that weird thing called an 'aside', which people do in Elizabethan drama, when they talk to the audience *right in front* of another character, as if only the audience can hear what they say. He tells the audience that he believes the queen to be talking about her upcoming marriage to the King of El Dorado, and that she is cruelly toying with him. He leaves the palace, saying he will be there on the appointed day. Then, in a monologue, the queen admits that she fears her impending old age and the loss of her beauty, and that she wants to get herself a magnificent suit of green hunting clothes (which she describes in minute detail) and get all dressed up and made up and hair done, so that she looks amazing for her birthday hunt, when she will confess her love for Greenwich and ask for his hand. I guess that was the Elizabethan equivalent of getting beach-body ready.

Meanwhile, there's a subplot where Lupo and Volpone discover some secret Catholic rebels hiding out on the Isle of Dogs, an area just across the river from the Palace of Placentia.

Pretending they wanted to make peace, father and son arrange to meet the rebels in the Underwood on the day of the great hunt. I was pretty sure how *that* was going to go down. I had a nasty feeling that things weren't going to end so well for the Catholics.

A bit unsettled, and locking the door first, I checked my Instagram. It was almost as though, having done something as Medieval as reading that manuscript, I could allow myself a moment to be Savage. There was a message from **mrs_de_warlencourt**:

Have you remembered yet?

And next to the question mark was a little lightbulb emoji. Frustrated, I replied:

No.

Then I asked her:

Are you in Lightfoot?

But she just replied:

Gotta go.

Scene viii

The more I thought about it, the more I believed that Gabriel Spenser must be the key to this mystery.

Every time I went into the De Warlencourt Playhouse, which was a LOT, I passed under his plaque. He was the one connection between the past and the present. Four hundred years ago, he'd acted in *The Isle of Dogs*. Now we were putting on the same play, and the words he had spoken would be performed in a playhouse dedicated to him. It was Gabriel Spenser who linked the *Isle of Dogs* that Ben Jonson had written, and hidden, to the *Isle of Dogs* that we were performing.

I don't know why it took me so long to ask the twins about him. Of course they would know about him, right? Their family theatre had been dedicated to him. Surely over one of those twelve-course meals at whichever huge house they lived in, Mama or Papa would have mentioned this actor in passing? I decided to ask Louis. Trying to get conversation out of Cassandra was like trying to get blood out of a stone, and if I'm honest I was a bit off Cass because of her buddying up with Shafeen. Louis was the man to give you information; you could barely shut him up. I cornered him backstage after rehearsal. 'Have you heard of an actor called Gabriel Spenser?'

He pursed his lips and shook his head. 'No. Sorry.'

I frowned. 'Really? Your family theatre is dedicated to him. This theatre.'

'Is it?'

For Louis, the answer was surprisingly brief and to the point. And if he didn't know about Spenser, there was no reason to suppose that Cass would, so I sort of left it. But there was something I would have to ask them all about. I gathered my players together in the auditorium, where they sat on the wooden benches. I stood on the stage, hearing my own voice come back to me by that weird trick of acoustics. Those Jacobean builders really knew what they were doing.

'Guys, there's yet another act, so it looks like we are eventually going to get the whole thing. That'll be five acts in total, when we thought at the start we'd be doing just one. This puts quite a squeeze on the rehearsals, and the line learning. Are you all OK with that? You all want to do the whole thing?'

They all nodded, my little band of brothers, their eyes shining, even Cassandra's.

'Great. So my question is, what is everyone doing for Justitium? Because if everyone is staying at school, we could really do with additional rehearsals.'

The twins looked at each other, then at Ty.

'Well . . .' began Louis.

'The thing is . . .' said Ty.

Cassandra, ever the silent one, just bit her lip.

Louis explained. 'We promised Ty a trip to Longcross. She was all ready to come a few weeks ago and it was postponed when the Abbot . . . when the Old Abbot died.' He let a respectful pause fall, then brightened. 'I say, why don't you and Nel come? Then we could at least rehearse. You'd be very welcome.'

I didn't even have to look at Nel. Us going back to Longcross would be like those dumb heroines in horror movies like *Scream* running back into a haunted house instead of getting the hell out of there. 'Oh, no, that's all right,' I said breezily. 'It's your thing. We oldies won't intrude. We'll just have to hit the ground running when you're back.'

The memories of that fateful weekend a year ago did prick my conscience enough for me to have a quiet word with Ty after rehearsal. We walked over Bede's Piece together. 'Are you OK with this Longcross plan, Ty?'

'Are you kidding me?' she said, suddenly very London. 'I ain't never been anywhere like that. I can't wait to see that house.'

'It's not just the house, is it?' I said, suddenly feeling a bit like her mum. 'It's Louis too, isn't it? I saw you at the drinks party.'

The corners of her lips curled in a small, secret smile and she shrugged. My heart sank. How much should I tell her? How could I warn her against the de Warlencourt charm when I had fallen for Henry's myself? How could I tell her to be careful without sounding like a dick? Then I decided to stop beating myself up. It would be no good saying anything anyway. I remembered a white-faced Gemma Delaney warning me, just over a year ago, not to go anywhere near Longcross at Justitium. And had I listened? Of course not.

I changed the subject. There was something else I'd been meaning to ask her. 'So you're from the Isle of Dogs, right?'

'Yeah.'

'Why's it called that?'

'Cos it was where Elizabeth I's royal kennels were. So back then it was literally swarming with dogs.'

'Makes sense.'

'There's this pub called the Ferry House where my uncles used to drink,' she went on, 'and there was a crazy old guy who always used to sit at the bar and say that on frosty nights you could hear those Elizabethan dogs baying across the mudflats.'

I shivered. I was back at Longcross, hearing Henry's dogs barking through the dense fog after Nel's blood. If I was a real friend to Ty, could I really let her go to Longcross alone? Yes, I liked the twins, and no, they weren't Henry. But before I could make up my mind she hurried away, probably to catch up with Louis.

I could've stopped her. I could've called her back. But I said nothing, and my own silence left me feeling a bit sick.

Scene ix

Act Three was taking shape nicely, and Ty was killing it as the ageing queen, desperate to look fit for her birthday hunt. She strode about the stage, calling on the gods to make her beautiful so she could land the Earl of Greenwich.

> *Now, Diana, from thy huntress moon,*
> *Lend me thy beauty for one night,*
> *Bring me a gown the colour of the greenwood,*
> *Bring me arrows keen enough to pierce the hearts of men,*
> *Bring me a net, wrought of gilt, fit to catch dreams,*
> *And a hound with eyes of fire and a thirst for blood,*
> *So I may capture my prey, my love.*

But it occurred to me as we rehearsed that it wasn't Queen Cynthia and the Earl of Greenwich who were the real love story of this play. It was the humble servant Canis and his adored master Greenwich – they were the emotional heart of the drama. The queen and the earl, apart from a bit of courtly compliment-swapping in Act One, spent any stage-time they shared fighting like cat and, well, dog. I wondered then whether

Ben Jonson preferred the company of men to women. But then I remembered what Abbot Ridley had said about his patroness and friend Esmé Stuart. Those two sounded tight. I felt pretty sure there was something romantic going on there.

Meanwhile, I was surer than sure that there was something romantic going on in the present day. Nel was definitely getting seriously into Abbot Ridley, and Abbot Ridley definitely had more chemistry with Nel than he had with Ty, which worked well for the drama – with Nel as the servant boy, whom he didn't want anything from, and with whom he didn't have to pretend, there was a genuine friendship, a connection. Observing the Abbot closely, which I did at every rehearsal, I didn't think he had any inappropriate feelings for *her*. But she certainly had a thumping great crush on *him*.

Watching Nel fall for Abbot Ridley, and Ty fall for Louis, only served to remind me how crap my own love life was. Shafeen hadn't exactly said we were broken up, but it certainly felt like it, especially with Cass sniffing round him. I would have loved to talk to him about everything that was going on with *The Isle of Dogs*, but he just didn't seem approachable at the moment. I'd actually gone to his room one night, hoping to make peace. It occurred to me, as it never had before, that maybe I should knock – we'd lost that closeness that allowed me to just barge in. But as I'd leaned close to the door, knuckles raised, I'd heard laughter from within. Shafeen and . . . Cass. I'd turned and gone straight back down the stairs, cold as stone. There was no reason Shafeen shouldn't have a friend round, and they had some science subjects in common. There was no reason to suppose they were laughing about me. But I supposed it anyway.

I lived for history lessons, as they were about the only time I saw Shafeen. We sat on the adjacent desks we'd picked at the start of the year, too proud to move, trying not to look at each other. The not-exactly-cheerful story of Elizabeth I approaching the end of her life was the backdrop to these encounters.

Friar Camden stood at the blackboard, her silver hair in sharp contrast, telling the end of the tale. 'She'd seen off Mary, Queen of Scots,' said the Friar. 'She'd seen off Philip II of Spain and the Spanish Armada. She'd seen off every count and prince and king who'd petitioned for her hand. But there was another enemy that was slowly besting her. Father Time.' She turned and wrote *Tempus Fugit* on the board, the chalk as white as her hair. 'A bit of garden-centre-sundial wisdom for you there,' she said. 'Time Flies. And Elizabeth was helping it along, ironically, in her efforts to keep herself young. She used toxic lead paint on her face, corrosive vermilion to add red to her cheeks and deadly belladonna to make her eyes shine. She was unknowingly slowly poisoning herself in the name of beauty. And it was in this state, in her old age and her failing health, that she had to face the most hurtful betrayal of all. The betrayal of the Earl of Essex.'

I woke up at this point.

'This is how the romance of the century came to an end,' said the Friar drily. 'There was a rebellion in Ireland and Elizabeth sent Essex to utterly destroy the rebels. Instead, Essex negotiated with their leader and Elizabeth saw this as a treasonous betrayal and demanded his return to court. Essex rode through the night to Elizabeth, arriving early in the morning. He burst into her bedchamber and caught the queen in a state of undress, without her wig or make-up.' Friar Camden waved her chalk at us. 'Imagine her humiliation – to be seen without any artifice by the man she loved – with her thinning grey hair, smallpox scars, every wrinkle on display. She'd always wanted to appear as Gloriana, the ageless queen with immortal youth and fabulous beauty. With his morning visit, Essex had ripped that veil away. Things could never again be as they were; he could never unsee what he had seen. It was the end of them.

'Following the debacle in Ireland and the humiliating episode in her chamber, Elizabeth banished Essex from court and took away his rights to trade in sweet wine, effectively ruining him. Essex raised an army against her in revenge, leaving Elizabeth no choice but to condemn him to death. He was executed at the Tower of London. The queen never recovered from his loss, wished him back alive and by her side every day, and died herself two years later. Time, and the earl, had done for her at last.'

It was pretty depressing, the death of love. Without warning, Henry haunted my thoughts again. He and I had barely begun, we'd shared nothing but a kiss, but I was still trying to come to terms with his death. And I hadn't even loved him, had I? It was certainly not the same as what I felt for Shafeen. Was it possible to love two people in two different ways? I was conscious of Shafeen at the next desk, his long fingers clutching his pencil as they did when he was interested. I tried to remember the last time he'd held my hand.

Time might have been Elizabeth's enemy, but I felt it was

my friend. At Justitium, I'd have three days at a pretty empty school to work things out with Shafeen. I knew he wasn't going back to India because it wasn't worth it for three days, and I wasn't going to Manchester because Dad was away filming. I hoped against hope that we could maybe use the time to get our shit together.

Scene x

On Sunday evening I was pretty jittery.

If the last few weeks were anything to go by, I'd be receiving Act Four of *The Isle of Dogs* that night. And this time I was going to be ready.

At Sunday Commons I could hardly eat – we always had Sunday Commons in the Great Hall, not the Refectory, and it being winter, the stained-glass windows were black with darkness and the room lit with a thousand candles. Above our heads, in the halflands of light between the candles and the vaulted roof, dozens of pairs of stags' antlers were mounted on the walls. In an effect I'd seen a year ago at Longcross, the candles threw multiple shadows; a forest of antlers crowding in upon us like the dense tree cover of a blackthorn wood. All I could think about was that at last I was going to find out what went on in the forest of Underwood in *The Isle of Dogs*.

I knew from all those drama lessons with Abbot Ridley that Elizabethan plays had five acts. So in Act Four, presumably, the drama would really ramp up. I didn't know much about plays, but I did know about film. In Act Four of a screenplay there is usually a challenge that seems impossible to return from – often a death. Think Obi-Wan switching off his lightsabre in *A New Hope*. Han Solo being bagged and tagged in Carbonite in *The Empire Strikes Back*. Or Quint getting munched by Jaws, in, well . . . *Jaws*. Act Four was when things usually got very, very bad for the secondary hero.

I glanced at Shafeen, all the way down the other end of the room near High Table, looking serious and slightly magical in his chapel cape. But I couldn't think about the Shafeen thing tonight. The anticipation was killing me.

When I got back to my room I set myself up to catch the mysterious messenger. This time I didn't sit at the desk, as crossing the room always cost me valuable response time. I moved my desk chair right next to the door and sat facing it. I didn't get myself a book, and definitely not my phone. I didn't want any distractions. I needed to watch and listen. I just looked at that Tudor oak, all the knots and notches and marks, a door that was as old as *The Isle of Dogs*. Lightfoot had been built in 1550 – it was weird to think that my door was here when the play was first performed.

I sat there for what felt like hours, listening to the usual evening chatter of people in the passageway, doors opening and closing, toilets flushing in the bathrooms, and bathwater being run and let out (no showers at STAGS. The school cared more about tradition than the planet). And above it all, marking time, the chapel bell, chiming the quarters and the hour. Eventually everything but the bell fell silent, and my eyes started to droop. Until a sound snapped me awake.

Footsteps.

Light and quick, coming down the passageway. Carefully,

silently, I eased myself off the chair and reached my hand towards the door handle, my fingers hovering above it, poised to turn.

The person outside seemed to be making no effort to be quiet. The pages were stuffed unceremoniously and noisily under my door, and for a split second I wondered why the messenger was being so careless, before I grabbed the handle and turned it, yanking at the door. Then I realised why.

My door was locked.

Frantically I scrabbled in my desk drawer for my own key, but of course it was no good. By the time I was out in the passageway the messenger was long gone.

Cursing myself, I went back into my room and picked up the manuscript pages from the floor. I re-locked the door, leaving the key in the lock, kicking myself again as I fitted the heavy iron key into the oversized keyhole, because if I'd just dropped to my knees as soon as I'd realised the door was locked and looked through it, I probably would've seen who had delivered the pages. It was an uncomfortable feeling that someone had a key to my room, but at least if my key was in the lock, they couldn't gain entry.

I sat at my desk, and even though it was nearly midnight, I began to read the familiar, spidery black hand of Ben Jonson. And what I read sent me straight to Nel's room, midnight or no midnight.

Scene xi

I had to knock quite a few times before Nel answered.

Clearly I'd woken her up, because she opened the door looking unusually rumpled, her hair everywhere, her eyes half closed. But they snapped wide when she saw me. 'Act Four?' she asked.

I nodded grimly.

She grabbed my arm at once and pulled me into her room. She got back into bed and I got in next to her. It was proper winter now and pretty cold in Lightfoot. She clicked on the bedside light and we huddled together under the covers, over the ancient pages on our humped knees. I could've let her read it, but I hadn't the patience. I was gasping to tell the story. 'Get this,' I said. I was whispering, because even Medievals were not supposed to be in each other's rooms after lights out. 'So. Act Four. The Earl of Greenwich is furious at the queen for teasing him about this big event coming up, thinking she's getting married to another. Of course, he has no idea he is the guest of honour at the queen's birthday hunt, where she's going to ask him to marry her. So he bribes her servant, Canis –'

'That's me!' exclaimed Nel.

'– that's you, to get him into the Palace of Placentia early in the morning. He bursts into the queen's bedroom just as she's getting out of bed. She's totally naked, they've just opened the shutters, and he can see her in all her reality, every line and wrinkle.'

'Jeez,' said Nel. 'Poor Ty. D'you think she has to strip off?'

'Wait. Then, the queen gets into this blind rage and screams at him to leave her presence. She calls for the guards to sling him out.'

'So that's it then – she finishes with him?'

'You'd think so, wouldn't you? But no. When he's gone she has this big speech to the audience – you know, like Hamlet does . . .'

'A soliloquy,' Nel supplied.

'That's right, a soliloquy, about how she is two women – the woman in the bedchamber and the great queen with her make-up and jewels and gowns and crowns. He must never see the woman again. But as a queen she still wants him for a husband.'

'Okaaaaay. But I guess the hunt's called off at least?'

'No. She's furiously angry and needs to vent, so she puts on all her finery that she's had made – the magnificent green hunting suit, remember? – and rides out anyway.'

'And what happens to the Earl of Greenwich?'

'Well, he's busy storming off through the palace, but Lupo and Volpone stop him. They've overheard the queen's big speech and they are afraid that she'll take him back. They have to get rid of him once and for all, so they're more determined then ever that he has to die.'

118

'So what do they do?'

'They tell him about the hunt that will take place that evening, and say there is a way that he could beg forgiveness of the queen. They tell him that she was planning to wed him, and that there's a good chance she would take him back.'

'They clearly have a plan, because that's the opposite of what they want.'

'Oh, they've got a plan all right. They tell the earl to disguise himself as a peasant, a peasant called Robert Horne. They tell him to go down to the Underwood at sunset and find the Great Oak, where he will meet some friends.'

'Uh-oh.'

'Yes,' I said grimly. 'Greenwich dresses in humble clothes and styles himself as Robert Horne. He goes down to the Great Oak, and is a bit surprised to find a whole bunch of Catholic rebels meeting there. The hunting horn sounds, and the hounds are released. The queen – well, of course, her blood is up, she's in a rage and she is well up for it. She literally has the best time of her life, never realising that her big birthday treat is to hunt the peasants who have defied her. Her dogs bear down on the Earl of Greenwich, who is not as fast as the other peasants. They corner him in the roots of the Great Oak.' Suddenly it was all real. In that ancient room, in that circle of storytelling light with Nel, I could see it all like a film. The twilit woods, and hundreds upon thousands of hounds being released from their kennels on the Isle of Dogs, streaking through the trees, baying across the marshes just as Ty had said. Nel wasn't looking at the pages now but at me, eyes wide once more, but with fear. It was the opposite of a mum telling her kid a fairy tale – this was a horror story. Too late I remembered how much she hated dogs. 'Then –'

'No!'

'Yes. The dogs tear him to pieces. And every other Catholic rebel too.'

'He dies? The Earl of Greenwich dies?'

I could see that she was thinking of Abbot Ridley, not the Earl of Greenwich. She looked genuinely upset.

I nodded. 'And then Canis is gutted. Not literally – I mean upset. The earl is the only one who ever showed him kindness, so he sits with the body.' I thought that, weirdly, this might cheer her up a bit – she had a really nice scene with the Abbot. But although she perked up a little, her shoulders still drooped.

'God,' she said, 'it's so *sad*.'

'Yes,' I said, 'yes, it is. But it's also a bit familiar, no?'

'How so?'

'Where have you heard this story before? Think.' I was turning into **mrs_de_warlencourt**, but I didn't care. I wanted Nel to make the leap herself. 'Dude sees older chick getting dressed. Chick furious. Dude punished with death.' I couldn't believe she couldn't see it.

'Actaeon and Artemis?' said Nel the classicist.

That stopped me in my tracks. Now *I* was the dumb one. 'God, yes, of *course*. I hadn't even thought of that. Actaeon saw Artemis naked, and she turned him into a stag and had him ripped to pieces. But I was thinking of Elizabeth and Essex. We just learned about it, remember? Friar Camden said that Essex burst in on Elizabeth before she was dressed, and saw her for the first time not as a queen, but as a crumbling old lady. It was the beginning of the end for Essex. When Friar Camden told us that story, I never even *thought* of Actaeon.' I jabbed the last page of Act Four with my finger, forgetting, momentarily, just how precious the manuscript was. 'And now the story turns up in *The Isle of Dogs*. It's almost the same.'

'Greer,' she said patiently, 'it *is* the same. Actaeon is the Earl of Essex who is the Earl of Greenwich. Artemis is Queen Elizabeth who is Queen Cynthia. All these connections. It's . . . spooky.'

'Very spooky,' I agreed. 'But I still don't get why the play was supposed to be so very dangerous. Risky for Ben, yes, but not dangerous.'

Nel turned on me, incredulous. 'You don't think it's dangerous? The depiction of Elizabeth and Essex and the Cecils as bloodthirsty, gold-hungry dogs? You don't think it's at all edgy, showing Elizabeth's favourite, the Earl of Essex, getting ripped apart by hounds? That's political dynamite.'

'I s'pose,' I conceded. I couldn't admit I was a little, well, *disappointed* that there wasn't something more juicy in the text. 'I mean, it's close to the bone, but not *dangerous*. Why burn every copy of the play? Why shut the theatres?'

'Because it's *treason*.'

'But the queen *herself* isn't doing anything wrong in the play. I mean, she doesn't know she's hunting people. She's been tricked by the father-and-son dream team.' Then I remembered what the Abbot had said. 'Ridley talked about *demonic practices and black magic. The full house of Elizabethan sins*, he said. There's nothing like that in here.'

121

'OK. Maybe that comes in Act Five. Would that fit into your story-arc formula?'

'Well . . .' I thought for a second. 'In films, Act Five *is* usually the big kick-off, especially in action movies. Like in *Black Panther* when they have that humongous battle with CGI rhinos that belong to that guy from *Get Out*.'

Nel said incredulously, 'You think there are going to be *rhinos*?'

'No, not that *exactly*. What I'm saying is, there's got to be a Big Finish. When we get Act Five, which should be next Sunday, we might find out, at last, what made the play so damned dangerous.'

Scene xii

Act Four certainly gave me a few headaches as a director – it contained some of the hardest scenes yet in terms of staging.

I had the problem of creating a hunt through a forest, ending with a death. Here the art types really helped me. They made a fantastically chaotic Underwood forest, with trees like tangled antlers and multiple eyeholes cut out of the trunks. When the candles were lit behind the 'eyes' it was pretty effective, giving the impression that unseen creatures were watching from the wood.

For the 'real' attack dogs, played by the rest of the drama class, we'd gone down the *War Horse* route of stylised black dog heads with red glowing eyes like little coals, also made by the art types as part of their Probitio. And they had come up with another brilliant idea – they'd rigged up Abbot Ridley with four rolled-up, enormously long red ribbons, the colour of our school stockings. The four ribbons were tucked one at each wrist and one at each ankle of the Abbot's costume. At the climax of the hunt when the dogs were to attack, they had to pull at the ribbons with their 'jaws', and they would unfurl and spill all over the stage like blood.

Poor Abbot Ridley was doing a bit more acting than he'd bargained for. He now had a major part in the production, including a pretty full-on death scene. But to be fair to him he took it really well. And it didn't hurt that he was good-looking, tall and a reasonable actor. So far, so Henry Cavill.

We tried the death scene in rehearsal and it worked really well – red ribbon pouring out of the Abbot's wrists and ankles. The effect was striking and surprisingly gory. It would work even better when he was in his costume as the Earl-of-Greenwich-disguised-as-the-peasant-Robert-Horne.

After this bit would come Canis's reaction to his beloved master's death. Nel took me aside in the wings. 'You remember that story Friar Camden told us in history – how Mary, Queen of Scots' dog stayed with her under her skirts when she was getting her head chopped off, and then wouldn't leave the body?'

I nodded.

'Well, do you think I could . . . well, you know, *mourn* a bit?'

'Yes, of course,' I said. 'Fill your boots.'

We played the scene. Canis recognised the dead earl and dropped to his knees, cupping the earl's cheek in his hand, feeling his lips for the mist of breath. He sat back with horrible acceptance, facing the fact that his master was dead.

Then Nel did a funny thing. She didn't cry, or wail, or beat her chest, or anything dramatic like I might have expected. She just laid her head on his dead chest, as a dog might lay his head in his master's lap. Then she did the saddest thing. She took the earl's lifeless hand and made it stroke her head, once, twice, three times, making the master pet the servant as he had never done in life.

It was absolutely freaking heartbreaking. No one in the cast moved, offstage or on. We were all frozen with Canis's grief.

Until, from the corner of my eye, I saw a shadow shifting in the upper circle and slipping away. Blinded by the footlight candles, I looked up.

I could've sworn it was Shafeen.

Scene xiii

Since that scene marked the end of the day's rehearsal I packed up as quickly as possible – I wanted to get out of the theatre fast, to see if that really was Shafeen watching.

Nel stayed behind to talk to Abbot Ridley about their scene – her face animated, her eyes shining. I looked at her with a pit of foreboding opening up in my stomach. But I could hardly pull her away from a conversation with, effectively, the headmaster. I left, tucking the precious script carefully in my deer-leather satchel.

Although it was only three o'clock, the weak winter sun was setting and the temperature was dropping. Shafeen, if it had been him, was nowhere to be seen. But a tall figure with cropped blonde hair strode ahead of me, dragon-breath smoking, conjuring up Henry's ghost once again. As usual, you couldn't really tell which twin was which from the back. As I drew level, I could see it was Cass. We smiled guardedly at each other and fell into step. We were heading up the Hundred Stairs, an ancient stone stairway between Bede's Piece and Lightfoot, and we were totally alone. I could ask her, now, about Shafeen. I would never have a better moment. Instead, when I opened my mouth, quite a different question came out.

'Cass, I don't suppose *you* know anything about Gabriel Spenser, do you?'

'Yes,' she said simply.

'You do?'

'Yes. Lots. What do you want to know?'

'Who was he? What was his deal?'

'He didn't exist.'

'Wait, what? Your family's playhouse is dedicated to Mr Nobody?'

'No – I mean, yes. I mean –' She was struggling a little – I imagined because she never got to talk very much. 'Gabriel Spenser wasn't real. It was a . . . what do you call it? A pseudonym.'

'A stage name?'

'Yes.'

'Who for?'

'Nazereth de Warlencourt.'

'Who he?' I was so gripped my grammar went out of the window.

'An ancestor. An Elizabethan one.'

'And he was called Nazereth? As in "Jesus of –"?'

'Except with two Es instead of two As.' We were both getting quite breathless – the Hundred Stairs were tough. 'He fell in love with the London theatre scene, and was desperate to go on the stage. So he did.'

'So he came down all the way from Longcross?'

'Yes. That's when he bought Cumberland Place. The de Warlencourt London residence.'

'Oh.'

'That is, not *exactly* the same house. Our Cumberland Place is Georgian. But it was built on the site of an older medieval house. *That* was the Cumberland Place Nazereth lived in. He was the heir to the Longcross estates; he was presented at court to Elizabeth, tutored in classics and fencing and cosmology and all that stuff. But he got the acting bug.' We kept pace up the stairs, watching our footing as the stone started to frost. 'The family didn't approve of his acting. As he was the heir, they thought he should be managing his estates, and not prancing around on the stage. So he took a stage name.'

'*That's* why the name is in inverted commas on the plaque. I *see*. So why Gabriel?'

'Grandmama used to tell us that it was because of the Angel Gabriel, who first appeared in Nazareth.'

'Clever. And Spenser?'

She gave me an odd look with her light eyes. 'That was the name of his spaniel.'

'His *dog*?'

'Yes.'

Dogs again. So bizarre. But Cass carried on walking calmly up the steps, hands behind her back like Prince Charles, as if there was nothing loop-the-loop *weird* about the whole thing. I honestly believe she was such an odd one that she would've left it there if I hadn't prodded her again.

'You said Grandmama –' I was pretty sure I'd never used that word before – 'used to tell *us*. Does Louis know about Nazereth?'

'Of course.'

'Why didn't he tell me when I asked him?'

'I don't know.'

'I thought you knew everything about him.'

She looked at me with her strange, impassive expression, then her blue-grey eyes slid away. 'Not this.'

She seemed to clam up again, but I had one more burning question. 'Cass, are *you* Mrs de Warlencourt?'

She frowned a little. 'I'm *Miss* de Warlencourt. Actually, I'm the Honorable *Lady* de Warlencourt. But not Mrs. Why would I be a Mrs? I'm not married.'

'No reason. Forget it. Thanks for the info.'

I was pretty convinced. I didn't really think Cass was a good suspect for **mrs_de_warlencourt**. She was a full-on Medieval, and **mrs_de_warlencourt** was a full-on Savage. I doubted Cass even knew how to use Instagram. You couldn't teach an old dog new tricks. She gave me her shy smile and at the top of the steps took the path to Honorius and the science labs. I watched her go, wondering if she would report our conversation to her new crush, Shafeen.

Scene xiv

That Sunday at evensong all I could think about was getting my hands on Act Five of *The Isle of Dogs*.

The choir scored my thoughts with the same hymn they'd sung at the Requiem Mass for the Old Abbot – the one about misery. But that night it couldn't touch me. I was impatient for the service to be over.

After Mass the cast had been invited for 'sherry' in the Abbot's rooms. This was another strange drink-related tradition of STAGS, and one I could really have done without that evening. I just wanted to get back to my room and get those pages. Instead, we all stood around in our chapel capes – me, Nel, Ty and the twins – in the Abbot's study, making small talk and holding teeny-tiny glasses of sweet wine. The only good thing about it was that I could fill the Abbot in about Nazereth de Warlencourt, which I did in a private corner behind his desk.

He was, predictably, properly interested. 'Well,' he said, 'high-born young men wouldn't have been on the stage – it was not considered a noble profession. So I think Nazereth took the only course available for noblemen who wanted to act in those days: to get yourself a new name, a new identity.'

'Hmm,' I said, 'bit easier for noblemen who want to act *these* days.'

'*Are* there noblemen who want to act these days?'

'Well, not noblemen, but come on. Posh boys.'

'For example?

'Well, Tom Hiddleston. Dominic West. Eddie Redmayne. Benedict Cumberbatch. Even Tom Hardy, though he hides it well.'

'Yes,' he said ruefully. 'You make a fair point.'

I'd barely sat down in the Great Hall for Sunday Commons when Nel was all over me. 'What were you talking to Nathaniel about?'

'Who the hell is *Nathaniel?*'

'Abbot Ridley. That's his name.'

I pressed my fingertips into my eye sockets. 'Oh, *Nel.*'

'What? It says it on his MA degree certificate. It was hanging up in his study.'

I took my hands away. I suppose I had wondered what his name was myself. 'I was just telling him about Nazereth de Warlencourt.' Of course I'd told her all about my conversation with Cass earlier in the week.

'Oh.'

I studied her closely. She was carefully, concentratedly forking up her salad leaves, as if a sudden movement would break something.

'Nel,' I said. 'He's the *Abbot.*'

'I know. For now.'

'But even when he isn't the Abbot, he's still your teacher.'

'Until the summer. We leave in six months' time.'

'You actually think you're going to have a *relationship* after STAGS?'

She said nothing.

'Nel?'

'It happens.'

'In *movies*, yes.'

'No,' she said, 'in real life. Some teachers get married to their former pupils. You hear it on the news.'

'Yes, usually when they're reporting a court case.'

'Some of them have kids and everything.'

'You're having *kids* with the Abbot now?'

'No, of course not. Nothing's going on. I'm just saying. It does happen.'

'Does he . . . do you think he likes *you*?'

'Yes,' she said defiantly. 'I think he does.'

'Has he . . . ?'

'No, of *course* not. He's the perfect gentleman. That's probably why I like him.'

I shook my head. I couldn't give my attention to Nel's particular brand of crazy tonight. I was too focused on Act Five. I could barely finish my dinner, I was so impatient to be gone, and I stared at the Abbot as hard as Nel had, willing him to give the Latin blessing that meant Commons was over. Promising Nel that I would come and show her as soon as I had the pages, I practically ran to my room.

Scene xv

When the pages came, I watched them sliding underneath the door and pounced. This time I think, just for an instant, my hand and the messenger's hand were both on the manuscript at the same time. I slammed my face to the keyhole but could just see black – someone's Tudor coat, anyone's Tudor coat. I could feel a slight tug before the unseen hand let go, and for one moment I was worried that the priceless manuscript might rip. But I need not have worried. Something was different this time. There was only one page. It was normal A4 printer paper instead of the usual tea-stain-brown, nibble-edged old manuscript. And it was typewritten.

Something was wrong.

I started to read, heart sinking. I couldn't understand a single word. Printed on the A4 was about a third of a page of what looked like nonsense.

Lorem ipsum dolor sit amet adipiscing elit, risus magnis primis nislquam, odio imperdiet diam montes in ullamcorper phasellus placerat.

Nunc habitant pretium laoreet mauris nostra facilisi ornare integer, magna quisque senectus mollis convallis lacinia nec egestas. Porttitor maecenas magna dictumst lacinia auctor ornare, aenean magnis potenti cursus venenatis libero, egestas molestie metus aptent velit congue. Tempor et sodales eu leo aenean pellentesque nunc aptent, urna convallis sociosqu condimentum magna dis inceptos purus maecenas, risus gravida sagittis integer duis nisi ultrices odio.

Dispirited, I went to find Nel. Although this clearly wasn't Act Five, the paragraph might have a meaning and she was studying Latin, which I was sure this was. She wasn't in bed and opened the door immediately – I got the feeling she'd been pacing the room waiting for me.

'Did you get it?'

'Yes and no.'

I sat down on the bed dejectedly and handed her the sheet of paper. She took it and turned it over.

'Where's the rest of it?

'That's it. That's all there was. But it's Latin, right? I thought you might know what it says. It might be one speech, you know, a soliloquy, which unlocks the last act.' I was reaching, but I couldn't bear the alternative – that it was all over and we'd never know what happened.

She studied the printout, angling her bedside light so it fell directly on the page. 'Well, for a start, it's not a speech; it's placeholder text.'

'How d'you mean?'

'OK, well, you remember in the Savage days of PCs in our old schools? Remember having to use Word and Powerpoint for schoolwork and homework?'

It seemed like a world away, but I did. 'Yes.'

'Well, when the software is trying to show you what different templates or fonts look like, they always use the same chunk of text. This one. *Lorem ipsum.*'

'God,' I said, vaguely remembering those first two words, 'you're absolutely right. But what does it mean? Would it have any connection to *The Isle of Dogs*?'

'I don't know. I've never thought about it – never thought it had any meaning, that is. I thought it was just nonsense – sample text. But I didn't know any Latin then, of course.'

'Could you read it, d'you think?'

'I'll try. But remember, I've only been doing Latin for a year. You'd be better off asking Friar Overbury.'

Friar Overbury was the classics friar. 'No. No friars.'

'Why? You don't think the friars are still mixed up in weird Order of the Stag stuff, do you? Especially not when you think of Nath— . . . Abbot Ridley. You sound like Shafeen.'

'I don't know what to think. But I do know that I want to keep this between us. Will you try?'

She sighed. 'OK. It might take me a while though.'

'Fine. Shall I copy it out for you?'

She patted me on the head. 'Bless you. You're such a Medieval.' She whipped out her phone, expertly snapped a picture and slipped the Saros back in her pyjama pocket. 'I'll get back to you in the morning.'

'Thanks,' I said, a little late. I supposed there was not much more we could do tonight, but I was reluctant to leave the mystery unsolved. 'Can you see anything odd about it?'

'Hmmm,' she studied the text. 'The word endings are a bit strange. Look. There's plenty of room to carry on the sentence but they split it across two lines, see? They do it four times. There's a ma—, mae—, cu— and a temp— just sort of . . . hanging.'

Sure enough, the words were divided in weird places, with the use of a hyphen where they could just have started the word on the next line. I had a brainwave. 'Friar Camden said that in ciphers they shove the plaintext altogether in one block and then split up the words oddly to fool the people trying to decode them, so they don't know how many letters are in the words they are looking for. Do you think this might be a code?'

'No,' said Nel, always straight to the point. 'These are bits of actual words, in an actual language, albeit a dead one. It may not mean much, but it is Latin.'

'Well, whatever it is, it ain't Act Five of *The Isle of Dogs.*'

'So what do we do now?'

'I don't know,' I said. 'I really don't know.'

I went back to my room bitterly disappointed. Had this whole thing been a trick, an elaborate practical joke to make me fail my drama Probitio? But why? To ruin my chances of Oxford? Who would do such a thing? Was this some kind of elaborate revenge for my part in Henry de Warlencourt's literal downfall, off Conrad's Force?

As well as that pretty unsettling thought, I had a more practical problem. What the hell was I going to do about *The*

Isle of Dogs? Doing one act would have been fine, it would have made some kind of sense, just an extract. But to do four acts of a five-act play was nonsensical. The audience would be invested; they would need to know what happened. My mind raced. Maybe we could end on the death of the earl – that might satisfy the audience, but it wouldn't satisfy me. *I* needed to know what happened.

I checked in with **mrs_de_warlencourt** on Instagram. Nothing. This was the first Sunday in a while she'd been silent. I chucked the page onto my desk. Without even getting undressed I lay down on the bed, pissed off, twitchy and wakeful. I couldn't read, and didn't want to go on my phone. I stared up at the ceiling for what seemed like hours. Then I must've gone to sleep eventually.

I know that, because I had a dream.

Scene xvi

I was walking through a dark forest, wearing my pyjamas, like a kid in some fairy tale.

The trees were crowding in on me like stags' antlers and I was afraid, afraid that I would never get out of the wood. Then a female voice said, *You've seen it somewhere before. Think.* And all at once the trees parted and cleared as if they were a stage set, just like the set for the Underwood in the De Warlencourt Playhouse. Through the trees there was a dark, manicured lawn and a pair of glass doors on the other side of it. One of the doors was open and light was streaming across the lawn. I walked over the grass and through the doors. I was in a library. There was a parquet floor, dark-wood shelves reaching up to the immensely high ceiling and a *Beauty and the Beast* chandelier. There, too, was a little staircase leading to the mezzanine. I knew where I had to go. I laid my hand on the banister and my foot on the bottom step, and climbed. In an instant I was up in the gallery where there was a long shelf of books bound in black morocco leather, all with a year stamped in gold on the spine. But I wasn't interested in them this time, those books. I was looking for something else.

I looked through the shelves. The female voice said: *Have you remembered yet?*

I sat bolt upright in bed, eyes wide, breathing fast, just like Sigourney Weaver in *Alien*. I went over to the desk, sat down and clicked on the lamp. In the circle of light, I stared intently at the *Lorem ipsum* page until the letters swam before my eyes.

And this is what I saw:

Lorem ipsum dolor sit amet adipiscing elit, risus magnis primis nislquam,

Odio imperdiet diam montes in ullamcorper phasellus placerat.

Nunc habitant pretium laoreet mauris nostra facilisi ornare integer, ma-

gna quisque senectus mollis convallis lacinia nec egestas. Porttitor mae-

Cenas magna dictumst lacinia auctor ornare, aenean magnis potenti cu-

rsus venenatis libero, egestas molestie metus aptent velit congue. Temp-

Or et sodales eu leo aenean pellentesque nunc aptent, urna convallis

Sociosqu condimentum magna dis inceptos purus maecenas, risus gravida

Sagittis integer duis nisi ultrices odio.

Longcross.

Act Five was at Longcross.

The answer was there, hidden in the letters at the beginning of each line of the *Lorem ipsum* text. That was why the words were divided oddly, to make the acrostic work. And hard on the heels of that realisation came another.

mrs_de_warlencourt was right; I *had* seen the play before.

I'd seen it a year ago when I'd been snooping through Longcross library, up in the mezzanine, and I'd seen all those first editions and original manuscripts. Back then I'd been too intent on what I was looking for to notice some dusty old play.

I'd sworn I'd never go back there, had been – as I'd admitted to myself at the time – too scared to go, even to look after Ty, but now I had been reeled in as surely as the brown trout I'd caught with Henry. It was too late. The whole *Isle of Dogs* thing had netted me. These past four weeks, my mysterious messenger had fed me with fish food, got me hooked and now I couldn't resist taking the final bait.

I had to go to Longcross again, and look in the library. I just had to.

Scene xvii

I couldn't bear to wait until morning. I had to ask Louis now if we could still go.

Luckily I hadn't even taken off my uniform before falling asleep, so I left my room straight away. As I ran down the stone steps of Lightfoot and across the Paulinus quad, the chapel bell struck eleven.

Jeez. It was pretty late. Would Louis still be up?

I needn't have worried. When I got to the Honorius quad I could see the golden light shining out of his diamond-paned windows. I ducked into the cloister, hurried along the stone pavings and knocked at his arched oak door. There was no answer. I put my ear to the wood and could hear music from inside. Maybe he was asleep. I turned the handle and pushed.

I saw Louis straight away, relaxing in one of those big leather armchairs he had, his legs hooked over one arm and his back resting on the other. He had a glass of something amber coloured in his hand and the other was conducting lazily to the music. There was a black vinyl disc revolving on the gramophone, and it was playing that tune that the nurse character plays in *The English Patient*, piano music that is almost like a heartbeat. In front of the roaring fire, between the two leather armchairs, was a chessboard, with white and red pieces arranged as in the middle of a game. Someone had left mid-battle. Who?

It was like I'd stepped back a hundred years. Actually, no – it was like I'd stepped back one year. It could have been Henry sitting there – lolling like an expensive cat. I watched Louis for a moment, the firelight playing in his fair hair and in the facets of the crystal glass, the long fingers waving around to the piano music, the slight grainy sound of the record turning like a wheezy breath.

He opened his eyes to see me standing in the doorway and smiled lazily, almost as if he'd been expecting me. 'Greer.' He said it just like Henry used to, the same lazy upper-class voice, the syllable of my name uttered like a statement, not a question.

I was a bit breathless, as I'd run all the way from Lightfoot. 'Is it too late?'

His eyes snapped fully open. He put his glass down on a side table with a sharp click, swung his feet to the floor and stood up. He came right up to me. 'What do you mean? Why should it be?' For a moment he looked absolutely terrified. I wondered what I'd said.

'I mean, to go to Longcross. Is it too late?'

He visibly relaxed. 'I *beg* your pardon.' He forced a smile. 'Of course it's not too late. I'd – We'd be delighted.'

I narrowed my eyes. 'What did you think I meant? What's too late?'

'Nothing. I don't know.' He laughed suddenly. 'I think I was half asleep. Bach, you know, *Goldberg Variations*. Puts one in a trance almost. Would you like a sherry?'

It's funny how you never hear a word and then suddenly you hear it loads. I looked at the decanter, and the tiny crystal glasses. 'Sure. Why not?'

'Do sit down,' he said as he poured. I took the armchair on the other side of the fire. The fire was lovely. I didn't have a fire, and nor did Shafeen or Nel. And yet we were Medievals. Why did Louis have such a nice set of rooms? And who had laid the fire for him? Some lovely local ladies did the cleaning in the rooms and laid the beds, but I didn't know their duties extended to laying fires.

'What made you change your mind?' asked Louis.

I took a sip of the sherry just to buy time. Some instinct told me not to tell him that I was sure Act Five was at Longcross. Yes, he was in the play, and presumably wanted to perform the last act almost as much as I did. And yes, Longcross was his family's house. But something – the Bach, the fire, the expression of horror when I asked him if it was too late – stopped me.

There was something else, too, that made me feel as if I needed to be in control. After that deadly autumn of conspiracy and danger, it was nice to think I had the upper hand for once. Like the unseen opponent who had been playing chess before the fire, maybe it was my turn to be one move ahead. 'I think it's important that we rehearse. I mean, we've got nearly the whole play now, not just one act.'

He looked at me closely. I thought I had to give him more. 'And it's a beautiful house. The most beautiful house I've ever seen,' I said truthfully.

That convinced him. 'I think so too,' he said in this kind of wistful way, almost yearning. That was a bit weird; presumably he could go there whenever he wanted. 'Do we have to ask your . . . aunt and uncle?'

That was my one big dread – I didn't know how I could meet Henry's parents after what happened a year ago. Of course, they didn't know – no one did – that I was the last person to talk to him alive, or that the three of us were at the top of Conrad's Force when their son fell to his death. But we were still there on that fateful weekend, and I had no wish to meet them.

'No,' said Louis. 'It's not up to them. Since . . . you know.' He didn't mention Henry by name. But then, he never had. It had been Cass who had spoken of him openly. I wondered how Henry's parents felt about being overpowered by two teenage twins. I supposed that even murderers like Rollo de Warlencourt had feelings. Why not? I did myself. At that moment, for example, I felt a profound hope that Henry's parents were not going to be there at the weekend. I'd rather there were no other de Warlencourts in residence except the portraits, the blond, blue-eyed family pictures hanging in the Long Gallery, the same portraits who had watched Henry and I skating along the polished floor in our socks.

And that reminded me.

'Louis?'

'Greer?' he mimicked my tone, teasing.

'Why didn't you tell me about Gabriel Spenser?'

'Who?'

'The actor. The one the De Warlencourt Playhouse is dedicated to.'

'Ah, yes. Well, I told you, I don't know him.'

'You do though. Gabriel Spenser was the stage name of Nazereth de Warlencourt.'

'Really?' If he was faking, it was pretty convincing. '*Gosh*. I mean, I know about Nazereth de Warlencourt, of course. Our Grandmama used to tell us about him. But I didn't know that he had a stage name, nor that it was Gabriel Spenser.' He thought for a minute. 'I suppose that makes sense though, that the theatre was dedicated to a member of the family.'

It sounded very plausible. It was so nearly what Cassandra had said. But I looked into his honest, sky-blue, unwavering gaze and didn't believe a word. Cassandra's shifty grey-blue eyes were much more credible. But I couldn't call Louis a liar when I was trying to get an invite to his family home.

I looked at the closed door to the bedroom. Was Cassandra in there? Wakeful, listening, ear glued to the door? Or had she gone back to Lightfoot to continue the pretence that she didn't share a bed with her brother?

'Who were you playing chess with?' I asked suddenly.

He hesitated just a fraction too long. 'Myself.'

'And who was winning?'

He smiled at my joke.

I twirled my glass in my hand, the sherry warming my stomach. 'Louis. Are you playing chess with *me*?'

'I'd like to,' he said. He drank from his own glass, never taking his eyes off me. He was definitely flirting; poor Ty. 'Maybe at Longcross. We have a set there.'

I held his gaze. 'I *bet* you do. Ivory carved from the tusks of that same poor bastard probably.' I nodded over to the hideous elephant's foot wastepaper basket, with the redundant rope still tethered around it.

He leaned forward in his chair, the flames dancing in his eyes. 'No, you don't understand. In the formal gardens,' he said carefully, 'there are sixty-four squares marked out. In the eighteenth century my ancestors used to play with the servants dressed in red and white.' He ran his finger around the top of his glass until it made a sweet and threatening hum. The hum got louder and louder until I could feel it in my blood.

I leaned forward too, and put my finger on his glass to shut it up.

'Only then?'

He frowned a little, questioningly.

'I mean, you don't play that way *now*, surely?'

His eyes flickered. 'Of course not.'

'I mean, *some* traditions should be left in the past, don't you think?'

'It's arguable.'

'Playing games with people, for instance. That would just be . . . twisted.'

'If they are willing participants, there's no harm.' He smiled a little. 'The fox enjoys the hunt, you know.'

Suddenly I felt we were getting somewhere. Circling a dangerous subject, swirling round and round in an eddying pool, getting drawn irresistibly into dark waters at the centre of the matter.

But Louis set down his glass and broke the spell. 'If you'll forgive me,' he said lightly. 'It's late.'

Ever the gentleman, he waited until I took the hint and stood. 'Of course.'

'I trust,' he said as he walked me to the door, 'that you don't need a formal invitation?'

Could he be joking about last year, and The Invitation to Longcross that had been pushed under my door? Would anybody *joke* about a weekend that had led to the death of a much-loved cousin? Surely I must be mistaken about that. 'No,' I said, but I couldn't let him get away with it entirely. 'The word of a gentleman will be enough.'

For a second, I could see a tiny flash of panic behind the mask of charm and self-assurance. For that split second, I could see he was far, far less confident than Cassandra was. But in a second it was gone. He stooped and kissed my hand, just as his cousin had done. And that told me something. It told me I could never be into him, despite the charm and the trappings and the resemblance to Henry. I didn't really know it till he touched me.

He was no more Henry than Cookson had been.

There was only one Henry.

As I closed the door on him and the chessboard and the music, another filmic memory nudged me. That piece of Bach was the one that Hannibal Lecter played on his harpsichord in *Hannibal*. I'm not sure whether it was that which unsettled me, or the shadow that detached itself from the dark and passed over the far side of the quad.

Someone had seen me leave.

Scene xviii

Shafeen marched into my room without knocking. 'You can't go to Longcross.'

He didn't even say hello.

'What are you – my dad now?'

'No, I'm your . . .' He hesitated.

'What? What exactly *are* you, Shafeen?'

He didn't or couldn't answer, and that made me sadder than anything. A fortnight ago, he would've said, unhesitatingly, *your boyfriend.*

Hackles rising, I said, 'Who told you? Your new buddy Cassandra, I suppose.'

'Yes. She invited me as well.'

'I *bet* she did.'

'Are you going because of Louis?'

'Because of *Louis*?'

'I saw you leaving his room.'

'So that *was* you, sneaking about in the shadows.'

That hit home. I didn't exactly make it sound like gentlemanly behaviour.

But he rallied. 'Do you like him?'

The one answer that occurred to me was that it would be much easier if I did. At least then the de Warlencourt I liked would be alive. But I couldn't exactly say that. I just watched Shafeen pace about my room, like the tiger's son he'd once claimed to be.

'You're treating Louis like a substitute Henry. Like you can finish the fairy tale with *him*.'

This was so ludicrous that I didn't even know how to answer him. What came out of my mouth was quite unexpected. 'Was that you in the theatre too?'

'Yes. I was worried about you. I still *am* worried about you.'

'But not enough to actually hang out with me. You're either revising or coffee-housing with your new *friends*. You know what you are, don't you? You're a dog in a manger.'

'What?' he snapped.

'Well, I've barely seen you for two weeks and now you find out I'm going to Longcross and up you pop again. You're a dog in a manger.'

'I still don't know what you mean.'

I didn't really have a clue what I meant either. It was just something I'd heard my dad say. But I was mad. Mad enough to make shit up. '*You* know. You're like a dog sitting in a manger on the hay, not letting any of the other animals eat the hay because he wants the hay.'

He stared at me. 'But dogs don't even *eat* hay.'

'That's the point! *You* don't want the hay, but you don't want anyone *else* to have the hay.'

'What exactly is the hay in this analogy?'

'Me!' I shouted. 'I'm the hay! I am the hay.' I'd really lost it.

I couldn't quite believe that we'd come to this, me screaming about hay in his face.

Shafeen looked at me as if he didn't even know me. 'Jesus, Greer. There's just no talking to you, is there? You've turned into a proper . . . *Medieval*. Maybe it's spending all your time with the de Warlencourts.'

That did it. 'Well, right back at you, Shafeen.'

His face changed.

'Yeah, you think I don't know about your little evening get-togethers with Cass?' I hissed.

He looked all pious. 'We were *revising*.'

'Oh, that's what it's called, is it? Well, it sounded more like Comedy Central when I came by the other night. I had no idea that chemical formulae were such a hoot.'

'Are you *spying* on me now?'

'Why not? You're spying on *me*.'

He opened his mouth to say something else, and shut it again. Then he just shook his head and slammed out of my room.

Scene xix

Needless to say, I found it pretty hard to sleep that night.

I was raging for a long time, but in the end sheer exhaustion got me and I fell into a deep sleep, in which I didn't dream of Longcross or anything else. The next morning, I went to find Nel at the Paulinus well before breakfast. Shafeen wasn't there. I knew he wouldn't be.

I took out the *Lorem ipsum* page to show Nel what I'd discovered. Before I could speak, she said:

'It's Cicero.'

'It is?'

'Yes. It's from Ciccro's text *De finibus bonorum et malorum – On the Ends of Good and Evil*. It dates from the first century BC. *Lorem ipsum* is from parts of the first book, *Liber Primus*. Although first up I should say that what you've got is a mangled translation. Bits missing, words split. Even "Lorem" isn't a real word. It's part of a longer word "Dolorem". I found the passage it's from though. Here.'

She handed me a handwritten sheet and I read her clear, round writing.

'Nor again is there anyone who loves or hunts or desires to obtain pain of itself, because it is pain, but occasionally circumstances occur in which work – or rather toil and pain – can procure him some great pleasure. To take a trivial example, which of us ever undertakes laborious physical exercise, except to obtain some advantage from it? But who has any right to find fault with a man who chooses to enjoy a pleasure that has no annoying consequences, or one who avoids a pain that produces no resultant pleasure?'

'Well,' I said, handing it back, 'it seems to have absolutely zip to do with the play. Except for the reference to hunting.'

'It's part of a wider discussion on hedonism, if that helps.'

'Well, that's something the old Medievals knew all about,' I said grimly. 'You didn't ask Friar Overbury, did you?'

'No, Amish girl. I asked Friar Google.'

'OK. I mean, thanks. But forget all that –'

'Glad I bothered.'

'No, I mean the meaning doesn't really matter. You were right first time. It was placeholder text.' I jabbed my index finger at the *Lorem ipsum* text. I'd underlined the first letters of each line.

As soon as Nel twigged, she forgot to be pissy.

'Whoa . . .'

'Yes. It's an acrostic, see? Ben Jonson used acrostics all the time at the very beginning of his plays. He used them to set out what he called The Argument. It was basically the story of the play in a few lines. Look at this one from *Volpone*.'

Nel frowned. 'Volpone? That's Cass's part. Is it a sequel?'

'What? No. No, different play. Look, I copied it out.' Now it was my turn to give Nel a handwritten sheet. It read:

V olpone, childless, rich, feigns sick, despairs,
O ffers his state to hopes of several heirs,
L ies languishing: his parasite receives
P resents of all, assures, deludes; then weaves
O ther cross plots, which ope themselves, are told.
N ew tricks for safety are sought; they thrive: when bold,
E ach tempts the other again, and all are sold.

Nel handed the papers back. 'OK, but you're not suggesting that *Ben Jonson* wrote the *Lorem ipsum* page, are you?'

'No, of course not. It was typed. What I'm saying is, it's on message. It's very . . . Jonsonian.'

'Then who did write it?'

I turned my back on the well and watched the long shadows the rising sun was casting over the playing fields. 'My money is on **mrs_de_warlencourt**. I think she's in the school.'

'Or he.'

'Hmm. More likely to be a girl though.'

'Why?' asked Nel.

'Well, because she has been seriously fangirling Henry for a year, if you look at her Instagram.' (I had, a lot.) 'Also, it would be much harder for a guy to creep around in Lightfoot after lights out.'

'Unless,' said Nel, 'he happened to have a girl twin that looked exactly like him.'

'Point taken. But there's no use in guessing.'

'I s'pose. OK then. So *Lorem ipsum* is the major clue. You think Act Five is at Longcross? Where would it be?'

'In the library. Will you come? This weekend?'

She thought for maybe three seconds 'Yes.'

'But I don't want to go in an estate car. I don't want to be driven anywhere by that half-man, half-tree Perfect, if he's still around.'

'*Hell* no,' she agreed. 'I'll drive us in the Mini.'

Nel had brought her eighteenth birthday present to school this year – just one of the other privileges afforded to us new Medievals.

'Great. And this time,' I said, 'we're taking our phones.'

I wasn't about to be the prey again.

ACT THREE

Scene i

Everything was different at Longcross this time, and I was glad.

For a start, Nel and I did drive down in her gold Mini, radio blaring, GPS on. I didn't want to relive the Medieval experience of last year, with a silent and scary Perfect at the wheel, no radio and no conversation. Then it had been night-time, as we'd left school on the Friday evening after Justitium Mass. This year I'd pushed for us all to go on the Saturday morning. As every horror film in history will tell you, nothing bad can happen during the day.

The biggest difference, of course, was no Shafeen. I'd planned that since we would be at school together over the Justitium weekend, alone unless you counted all the other sad acts who couldn't go home, we could maybe see if we could mend things. But after I'd accepted the invitation to Longcross (OK, begged for it), that was out of the window anyway. And now, after we'd fought like cat and dog the night before, a reconciliation seemed out of the question. The only comforting thought was that if he wasn't spending the weekend with me, he wasn't spending it with Cass either, as she too would be at Longcross. I couldn't tell Nel about the row, not just yet; it was too raw and I might easily cry. We bowled along the country lanes on a sparkling winter morning, with the low sun varnishing the frosty fields and the icicles glittering in the hedgerows. We sucked on sweets and I yelled along to stupid songs on the radio, just to show myself I was OK. And at least the dull ache of unhappiness sitting stubbornly somewhere underneath my ribs didn't leave any room for me to be scared.

Even when we caught sight of Longcross, nestling in a dip of a distant valley, I didn't feel a qualm. This time it didn't look like a vast ocean liner, all night and lights. It looked like it was made of gold. For the first time on that journey I thought of *The Isle of Dogs* and the King of El Dorado. This was the kingdom of gold, indeed, and Henry had been its king.

When we arrived we even went in a different door. Last year Perfect had taken me through the side door to the infamous boot room, but this time we went through the grand front entrance into the hall. This time there was no Henry waiting in his weird red jeans, but the twins and Ty arranged in armchairs around a vast and empty stone fireplace in the entrance hall, like they were in a photoshoot. They looked amazing – they so blond and she so dark, still in their black Tudor coats, arranged around the ornate fireplace. Betty was there too, serving tea and cake and tiny triangular sandwiches from a silver tray, and I must admit that the sight of her did give me a bit of a jolt. She looked exactly the same, with maybe one or two more threads of silver in her hair to match the tray. She bobbed a curtsy at us and handed us tea and cake without meeting our eyes. Nel and I, as it seemed to be the done thing, sat down too around the non-existent fire.

While we all made chit-chat about the journey, I looked around me. There was still only Betty in evidence, even though there must have been tons of unseen servants downstairs. No Perfect, thank God. I felt relieved, even though I supposed he must've driven those guys down in the estate car so would be around somewhere. I just wasn't ready for him yet.

I remembered how to talk to Betty – no eye contact, no thank-yous. It felt wrong, but I'd learned my lesson last year. There was nothing to be gained from being nice to her or her Frankenstein's monster of a husband. But her very presence added to our discomfort. There was no doubt about it, our little lunch party was definitely awks. The clatter of our teacups and silver spoons sounded stupidly loud. Our voices echoed in the cold and cavernous place and all us visitors lowered our voices as if we were in a library. The vast stone staircase curved up to the rooms beyond, and far above us, in a domed ceiling, cherubs hid behind fat clouds, listening to us. Welcoming it was not.

Cass obviously thought the same thing. She banged down her teacup. '*God*, this place is dreary,' she exclaimed, in a bored upper-class voice that recalled the deadly Lara from last year. 'Let's get a bloody Christmas tree, brighten the place up. We've got ages until dinner.'

'Ooh yes,' said Nel, clapping her hands. 'It's almost December, so it's not too early.'

'I always thought this would be an amazing Christmas house,' I said, quite truthfully.

'Where would we get one from?' asked Ty shyly. 'We must be pretty far from the nearest Homebase.'

Cass laughed, but not unpleasantly. 'From Longwood, of

course. There are millions of fir trees there. Betty, let's get everyone to their rooms to freshen up and change – we can hardly go like this.' She fingered the dark fabric of her Tudor coat. 'Let's meet back here in an hour.' I stole a look at Louis – he was meekly silent. I'd never seen Cass take the initiative like this before.

'Very good, m'lady,' said Betty in her northern accent, just as if she were in a film. 'And will you be dining in the Great Hall?'

'*Christ* no,' said Cass decidedly. 'It's even more of a mausoleum than this place.' Once again, I felt relieved. Dinner, too, would be different – I'm not sure how I would've coped with the ghosts from those three fateful dinners of a year ago, overlooked by the ghost of Henry and a forest of stag antlers. 'We'll eat in the Queen's Dining Room,' ordered Cass. 'It's much cosier.'

'The Queen's Dining Room, my lady. Very good,' said Betty the maid-bot.

On the way up the stairs, a thought occurred. I caught up with Cass as she strode confidently upward, two stairs at a time, and plucked at her black sleeve. 'Cass,' I murmured, 'who is older? You or Louis?'

'Me,' she said. 'By seventeen minutes.'

Then it clicked. Cass had never been like this at STAGS, but we weren't at STAGS any more.

Here, at Longcross, Cass was the boss.

Scene ii

We all went upstairs together with Betty and were dropped off at our various rooms. Louis had a nice room on a different floor, and we girls were all in the same wing of the house, a part I knew well. I'd half hoped to be given a different room, to really draw a line under the experiences of last year, but it was not to be. I had the same room, Lowther, with same expensive but shabby decor, and on the wall my old friend Jeffrey, the stag's head.

'Hello, Jeffrey,' I said, once I'd closed the door behind me. 'Betcha you weren't expecting to see me back.'

He regarded me with his dark and glassy gaze, but had nothing to say on the matter. With his eyes still on me, I walked to the window to look at the well-remembered view: the ornamental gardens and beyond that the wildness of the forest, which stretched all the way to the tower of Longcross church, the place, I knew, where Henry had been laid to rest. And now I knew that the forest, the de Warlencourts' personal Homebase, where you could just go and get a Christmas tree, had a name: Longwood.

A movement on the drive caught my eye. A guy in a flat

cap and a quilted green waistcoat was leading a dog up to the house on a leash. Then I saw another guy and another dog. Then another, and another. I guessed there must be something going on this weekend – a dog show maybe.

It didn't take me long to unpack. After my experience of last year, I'd only brought what Esme had called 'the foundation garments', as all my clothes would be provided. Sure enough, an outfit deemed suitable for Going to Get a Christmas Tree at a Country House had already been laid out on the bed. I had brought my mum's dress though, and laid it tenderly next to the alien clothes, just to balance things out a bit. Despite what had happened here last year, I still considered it a talisman, a lucky charm.

I took off my uniform and transformed myself into a houseguest in front of the mirror, but I still had a bit of time before I was due to meet the others in the hall, so I decided to look around the house.

Again, this was a very different experience to a year ago. Then, I'd fantasised about being the lady of Longcross. This year the house was a very different place. It seemed to have shut down. I walked through room after room where the priceless furniture was shrouded in big white dustsheets, as if in mourning. Some rooms were in total darkness until I opened some vast shutter a crack. Then a shaft of weak winter light would stream in to reveal the ghostly shapes of hiding chairs and wardrobes, only an elegant golden leg or a curlicued wooden scroll to be seen, peeping from beneath the sheet. Even the carriage clocks remained unwound, their hands drooping like sad moustaches. It was then that I got the strangest, strongest feeling that this was not a house in mourning but a house in waiting. But waiting for what?

Lost, I wandered down a passageway where I'd never been, and saw a thread of light from beneath a door. The light was enough to illuminate the gilded name above the door that all the bedrooms had at Longcross. It said *Alnwick*. Tingling, I pushed open the door.

This room was quite different to the shuttered, sleeping house. This was a room that was lived in. There was a battered Barbour jacket and a tweed flat cap hanging on the back of the door I'd just come through, and a robe slung over the back of a chair as if its owner was just taking a bath. There was even a merry little fire burning in the grate.

I walked to the neatly made bed. There was a carafe and a half-drunk glass of water on the bedside table and the inevitable silver frames of photographs, just as I'd seen in Louis's bedroom at STAGS. But I knew this wasn't Louis's room – I'd seen him go into one on the first floor. Besides, the photographs were different. The first one was of a blond adult couple. From the resemblance, I guessed that they were Henry's parents, the parents I'd never met. Was this their room? Were they actually here this time and I'd have to explain to them why I hadn't saved their little boy from his watery death? Swallowing, I picked up the other frame. This one was of Henry, when he was perhaps eight years old. I remembered asking Shafeen what he'd been like at that age, but it was hard to believe this eager, open smile could mask any inherited evil. I put my finger on his sweet, innocent face, and left a smoky fingerprint. Henry wasn't alone in the photo. He was holding a little girl in his arms, even though she clearly wasn't much younger than him, and she was laughing up at his face, her little star-like hands reaching for him as if he was the only person in the world. Beside them was an identical little boy, who was shading his eyes and looking at the camera with a surly expression. He looked quite apart from the other two. I put down the photo of Henry, Cass and Louis and looked around the rest of the room.

On the dresser there was a little enamel tray covered with the usual male crap. At home my dad had what we jokingly called his 'man drawer', where he'd chuck all the stuff from his pockets. This tray was just like that – coins and receipts and nail clippers. And something that shone out – a little nugget of gold. Uneasy, I picked it up. It was a gold signet ring, to be worn on the pinkie finger, just like the ones that all the Medievals and the friars used to wear in the bad old days.

Just like the one that Henry used to wear.

I slipped it onto my little finger, looking at the tiny pair of antlers etched in the gold. The ring was cold and heavy but warmed to my skin immediately. The heat frightened me. Heart thudding, I took off the ring and dropped it in the tray with a little clatter. I looked at the other things on the table. There was a bottle of posh-looking aftershave, with a label from a shop in St James's, London. I picked it up and sniffed the neck.

And that was what did it. That's when I knew.

This was *Henry's* room.

It was that time-machine thing again, instantly taking you back to a moment and a place. I'd smelled that scent on his tanned throat when he'd waited for me outside my room, in this very house, leaning on the panelling, the black tie loose at his neck. I'd smelled it again when he'd taken my hand to slide along the long gallery in our stockinged feet. And I'd smelled it on the roof when he'd leaned in to kiss me.

I put down the bottle and turned around, 360 degrees. This was *so weird*. They'd kept it, clearly, just as it had been the day he'd died. It was like a shrine. That was *his* robe on the back of the chair, *his* Barbour jacket, *his* flat cap. Had they lit the fire every day, like the flame of the unknown soldier, in memory of him? Had they taken the ring from his cold, dead hand? I remembered seeing David Lean's *Great Expectations*, with that crazy old Miss Havisham who had been jilted on her wedding day. She'd kept everything in her house exactly the same as it had been on that day, growing old in her wedding dress, sitting among the mouldy cake crumbs, trying to cling onto the last time she'd been happy. This room was just like that. It was hard to believe Henry had gone. It was like he'd just popped out and would be back any minute.

Suddenly I could feel an enormous sob ballooning in my chest, closing my throat, stinging my eyes. I knew if I stayed here another second, I would cry. I left the room as quickly as I could, and the house too. I needed some air.

The cold outside was a welcome shock after that weird Dickensian room. I heard the stable clock chime the hour, but I reckoned I had time – I went round the back of the house in the direction of the stable-yard to look for the dogs. Their stupid slobbery faces and waggy tails were what I needed right now. The bright sun cheered me, and so did the sight of these beautiful red roses twining up and around the stone archway into the yard.

But my way was blocked by something quite terrifying.

Under the stable arch, as if he'd been waiting for me, stood Perfect. And he wasn't alone. He had a massive dog, and I mean *massive*. Hound-of-the-Baskervilles massive. My stomach felt like it was going down in a lift. The gamekeeper was just standing there, staring at me, like Hannibal Lecter in his cell in *Silence of the Lambs*. But the dog wasn't nearly that composed. He started baying at me and straining at his leash. His bark was so loud I heard it in my ribs as well as my ears and I jumped about a mile in the air. Trying to style it out, I took a few slow steps backwards, as if I'd never meant to go into the stable- yard anyway, then I turned and practically ran back into the house, to company and safety.

Scene iii

Getting the Christmas tree was lovely.

Perfect was there, but it was actually OK. In the forest he was different to how he'd been in the stable-yard – like his dog, he just needed someone to keep him on the leash. Thinking about it, he'd always been OK when Henry was there – I remembered that last, beautiful day in the fishing boat when Perfect was our ghillie and his behaviour was almost human. I supposed Cass would now keep him in line, taking over from Henry – and sure enough, Perfect deferred to her in everything. Even more interesting was the fact that he all but ignored Louis, to the point of insolence. He was humble and compliant to his mistress, but blanked her brother altogether.

In fact, he spoke to the dog more than he spoke to Louis, calling it to heel in his broad Cumbrian accent. The dog, we quickly learned, was called Brutus. Every five seconds Perfect was calling his name, and the dog would reply with one of his Baskerville barks. Gamekeeper and dog started to sound the same. The exchange got right on my nerves, but that was an improvement. If I was irritated by Perfect that meant I wasn't afraid of him any more, even though he had this kind of pack on his back, bristling with saws and axes, as if he were Braveheart.

The same couldn't be said of Nel. Never a fan of dogs, she was properly freaked out by this one. She tried to keep away from him as much as she could, but of course, probably because he sensed her fear, she would be the one he would almost knock over as he scented a rabbit, or brushed past in a narrow cutting, making her squeal.

Despite this, we all walked along happily enough. The only time I'd been into Longwood was when I'd walked through a corner of it with Lara and Nel, on the way to the shooting lunch a year ago. But as it turned out, that was only a fraction of it. The forest was massive, with thousands and thousands of oak trees (even I knew they were oak trees, because they had those leaves with the wiggly edges). The oaks looked like they'd been there for centuries, which of course they had.

Before we'd gone very far, it started to snow, giving the wood a lovely Narnia vibe. Of course, that set us all off chattering about Christmas and sledging and snowballs and all that stuff, and it all got even more festive as we got to a clearing ringed by massive fir trees. 'Jeeesus,' murmured Ty, her breath smoking. 'They're as big as the ones in Trafalgar Square!' She wasn't wrong. They towered over us, already glittering with snow, holding out their skirts like the Bennett sisters in *Pride and Prejudice*, waiting for someone posh and rich to pick them for the next dance. We picked the tallest, prettiest one – the Rosamund Pike, I guess – and Perfect took all his arsenal off his back and started to arrange the saws and axes and ropes on the ground. He and Louis chose their weapons and began

168

to attack the designated tree. They began with a double saw and, silently, in a very awks atmosphere of mutual dislike, began sawing in a to-me, to-you rhythm. There was a lovely Christmassy smell of pine sap, but I think that was making the saw sticky. Me, Nel, Ty and Cass watched the menfolk struggle.

It didn't feel like stand-back-ladies-let-the-men-do-it; more like Perfect and Louis were Cass's vassals. She stood apart like a queen, the snow on her eyelashes making her look like the White Witch from *The Lion, the Witch and the Wardrobe*, noble and separate and completely in control. I saw Ty watching her, the snowflakes in her afro hair like pearls, adjusting her own stance, raising her own chin, taking notes.

In the male camp, things weren't quite as serene. Perfect and Louis had abandoned the saw and were hacking at different sides of the tree. It was warm work, so they had shed their jackets and their padded waistcoats, and even in shirtsleeves were red in the face. Louis, who'd been getting increasingly irritated, eventually snapped and shouted, 'God damn it, Perfect, you're doing it wrong. Cut out a wedge on one side and then we can knock the bloody thing over.'

Perfect drew himself up to his full (not inconsiderable) height. With one massive paw, he wiped his sweating forehead, pushing back his tweedy gamekeeper cap. He glared at Louis and said, 'You're not the mester here.'

The words, uttered quietly but clearly, seemed to drop to the ground with the snow. It was suddenly utterly, utterly silent, the flakes falling soundlessly, all of us watching, waiting, hardly drawing breath.

Louis straightened up too, axe in hand, and gave Perfect a

look that turned me to ice. It was the same look Henry had given me in the fishing boat last year, when he'd discovered I was wearing a wetsuit. I called it the Ed-Norton-from-*Primal-Fear* look.

'*What* did you say?'

Credit to Perfect, he didn't flinch. He just repeated exactly what he'd said, in exactly the way he'd said it. 'You're not the mester here.'

Louis fixed his blue eyes on Perfect and spat a single word: '*Yet.*' Axe in hand, he looked dangerous, reckless and unpredictable. 'Walk round this tree right now, or by God I'll see that you regret it by Christmas.'

Brutus started to growl, a low, grumbling threat. Perfect, for once, looked a little uncomfortable, and shifted his weight from one great boot to another. Unsure, he slid his piggy little eyes to Cass.

'My lady?'

Cass gave a tiny, almost imperceptible nod. And Perfect walked around the trunk, and began to chop again, furiously. His dumb hound began to bark in time to the strokes as the pale chunks of wood flew everywhere. Louis threw his axe away and stalked into the undergrowth. Ty looked at us, and then followed him.

In a very short time, aided by his own fury, Perfect was able to knock over the tree and it fell with a splintering crash. We left him neatening up the trunk, his oversized mutt dancing around him, barking excitedly at the felled giant. I knew better than to ask if we needed to help him carry it home. There were servants for that.

Scene iv

As we walked back to the house, I caught up with Cass as she was striding through the snow.

Louis and Ty were well ahead, talking intently, so I felt safe to ask. 'What did Louis mean, that he wasn't the master *yet*? What's going on?'

Cass shoved her hands in her pockets. 'Longcross estate is entailed in the male line. D'you know what that means?'

'I think so. It's like Tom Hollander.'

'Who's Tom Hollander? One of the Marlborough Hollanders?'

'God, I don't know about that. He's in the *Pride and Prejudice* film, the Joe Wright one.' She looked at me, puzzled. 'I was just thinking about it,' I explained. 'The Bennett family have five daughters, but the estate is entailed so that when Donald Sutherland (Mr Bennett) dies, their dork of a cousin – Mr Collins, played by Tom Hollander – gets everything and Rosamund Pike and Keira Knightley and the rest of the daughters don't get diddly squat. Have you seen it?'

'No, but I hear it was a book first.' She was mocking me gently, another new side to her, I realised. 'And I've read that.

So yes. Exactly like Mr Collins. That's what Louis meant. He's not the master yet. But he will be one day.'

I looked around me at the wild and snowy wood, the vast formal gardens beyond, and the grand house beyond that. I boggled at her. 'Doesn't that bother you?'

'But I love him,' she said simply. 'Family is everything. Why should it bother me?'

'Because . . .' I thought of what Shafeen had said at Louis's drinks party. 'Because it's a patriarchy – passing power from one male to another. It happens when he's eighteen, right?'

She nodded. 'Just before Christmas. My Uncle Rollo is the owner of Longcross, and Louis will now inherit.' Cass didn't need to elaborate on what that 'now' meant. It meant now that Henry was gone.

I swallowed down the thought. 'So Louis becomes the heir to Longcross on his birthday?'

'Before he's even blown out the candles. All the documents are signed and sealed.'

What else would they be at Longcross? The phrase didn't even sound old-fashioned here. I could almost see the de Warlencourt seal being pressed into blood-red wax. 'It seems a shame.'

'Why?'

I thought of Cass being queen-like in the woods. 'Wouldn't it be quite cool to have a *matriarchy* for a bit?' I wasn't even sure if this word existed, but it sounded likely.

'Well, we will. We are. I mean, until then, I have seniority as the oldest twin. Plus, it might never happen.' I glanced ahead of us, to where Louis was trudging, hangdog, through the snow, angrily kicking up snowballs with his Hunter wellies.

He looked vulnerable, with the snow in his blond hair, like a little sulky boy.

'What do you mean?' I asked. 'Is something going to happen to him?' Suddenly I flipped from being afraid *of* him to being afraid *for* him.

'No,' she said, shocked. 'No. I just meant that a month is a long time.'

I didn't say anything else, but I thought to myself that if Louis was going to be eighteen in just a month, there wasn't much that was going to stop him getting the keys to the kingdom.

We all sat around the roaring fire warming up, watching while Perfect and two stable guys in flat caps, who had appeared from nowhere, winched the tree into place with ropes attached to the balustrade. Even without decorations it looked fabulously Christmassy, glistening with melted snow and nearly reaching up to the cherubs in the dome above. There was a gramophone table, just like the one in Louis's room at STAGS, and Louis dug out a pile of old records, and sorted through them happily for Christmassy music, the tensions of Longwood forgotten. Ty sat with him, their blond and black heads close together as they slid the shiny vinyl from the sleeves eagerly. Louis Medieval-DJed for the rest of the afternoon, sweetly showing Ty how to crank the handle of the gramophone, his hand on hers, true old-school romantic style. The Christmas carols they selected sounded, apart from the scratches and wheezes of the needle, like they could have been sung by the STAGS choir, the notes as clear and pure as icicles soaring up into the dome. Betty served tea, then brought out boxes and boxes of tree decorations – some of them, I was sure, dating from the first years of Christmas trees. The giveaway was these little candleholders that attached to the branches, a fire hazard if ever I saw one. We happily decorated the tree, unwrapping baubles and bells and even deer decorations from their tissue, climbing ladders to reach the highest branches, listening to the carols. Apart from one sour note, it had been a lovely day, even though we hadn't done a scrap of rehearsal and I'd all but forgotten about the play. As we climbed the stairs, turning once to admire the glory of the tree below, I had to caution myself about how seductive Longcross was, how seductive this whole world was.

Scene v

I don't know what Cass meant by *cosy*, but the Queen's Dining Room wasn't it.

Yes, it was smaller than the Great Hall, where we'd dined last year, but not by much. It had standard-issue, stately-home oak panels, which made the room kind of dark. Above our heads, though, was this lovely ceiling, painted a deep, vivid blue, with gold beams crossed like a net, the blue squares studded with golden stars. It looked sort of familiar.

And we didn't shame the room. We'd done that thing I remembered from last year – 'dressing for dinner'. This year I'd decided to start with my mum's dress, the silver grey with the cluster of jet crystals down the front, like someone had spilled the night down me. As it was a lot colder than last year, I'd teamed it with a black jacket, and I was pleased with my overall look. This year I knew who I was; I was coming to Longcross as myself, not some doll they could dress up.

That honour had gone to Ty. They'd put her in a white satin dress, beautifully cut on 1920s lines, teamed with a white fur coat they'd given her to wear about her shoulders. The effect against her skin was beautiful, and the look was topped off with an Art Deco diamond comb in her afro. No wonder Louis was a smitten kitten. The only touch I was pretty sure was Ty's own was a pair of box-fresh, white platform trainers. I guessed this was part of her funky street style, but when I complimented her on them I was wrongfooted.

'Yeah, I wasn't actually *planning* to wear these,' she said a bit sharply. 'I'm not Scary Spice. I brought posh heels from home. But they went missing. Or at least, one of them did.'

'*One* of them?'

'Yeah. Completely gone. So I had no choice but the creps.'

'Well, it works,' I said. It did.

Nel, who'd obviously decided to be herself too, had brought one of her own bodycon dresses in shocking pink, with a pink sequined jacket. Louis, in black tie, looked just like Henry.

It was Cassandra, though, who stole the show. She too had opted to wear black tie, with the full tuxedo and wing-collared shirt. Her hair was parted severely and combed back from her face, and, unusually, she wore a slash of bright-red lipstick. She was only missing a monocle for the full-on *Bright Young Things* effect. She looked fantastic.

The menu was just as grand as last year, and the table crowded with crystal and candles and big pyramids of fruit. Betty came round with some sort of white soup, ladling it into our bowls. But I hardly noticed what we ate. I had a burning question to ask Cass, a question that had occurred to me when I was poking round Henry's room.

I didn't even bother asking Louis. He had shut down since coming to Longcross, and diminished, had changed places with his sister, just as they'd done at the drinks party. Now I knew why – he was in waiting, just as the house had been.

'Cass, where are Henry's parents? Mum and Dad de Warlencourt? I mean, this was their home, wasn't it? Until . . .' Like everyone else, I couldn't bring myself to mention the events of last year.

'They're at Cumberland Place. In London. They live there now.'

'Ah. I suppose they wanted to go? I mean, I guess, the memories of . . . you know. After what happened and all.'

'They didn't really want to,' she said bluntly. 'I made them go.'

Now *this* was interesting. I opened my mouth to ask why, but Ty got in before me with a question of her own.

'Look. What *did* happen last year?' Ty spoke with the confidence that one glass of wine gives you if you're not used to it, as we weren't. 'No, really. Everyone keeps dancing around it, but something huge happened here, right? This time last year? To your . . . cousin, was it? Henry?'

To hear his name, spoken like that, in this house, was like someone had dropped a massive rock into a glassily calm pond.

I held my breath, wondering how the twins would take this. Cass put her glass down, very, very carefully, as if she was afraid of breaking it. 'He was here for the Justitium weekend, with a bunch of friends.' It was her voice, not the glass, that cracked. 'Huntin' shootin' fishin'.' She said it exactly like Henry had, in that clipped, upper-class way that missed off the final 'g'. 'It was the fishing trip, on the last day. He never came home.' She spoke of him so differently to the way she'd spoken of his parents, and I remembered the little girl from the photograph, in Henry's arms although she was really too big to be there, holding her hands to his face as if he was the only person in the world.

You could see that Ty felt awful. 'Oh my God.' Her hands flew to her mouth. 'I'm so sorry. That must have been awful. His poor parents.'

Then Louis spoke up, for the first time. 'They weren't actually here,' he said harshly. 'And nor were we. But Greer was. And Nel. Maybe you should ask them.' It felt like a challenge.

I tried to remember the official line, the story we'd told the police. It was crucial, we'd agreed, that no one knew that we'd *all* been at the top of the waterfall when Henry fell. We'd always maintained that Shafeen and Nel hadn't been anywhere near the fishing trip. It was particularly important that no one knew that they'd been on the packhorse bridge with Nel's phone, waiting to catch Henry in the net of his own confession. So now I said, 'Actually, it was just me there. Nel and Shafeen were back at the house the whole time.'

And Betty dropped the soup ladle with a crash.

It sounded like a thunderclap and we all jumped about a mile in the air. I hadn't even known she was still in the room – she must have been hugging the shadows beyond the candlelight. I shot a look at her. Did she know I was lying? Had she seen Nel and Shafeen leave in the Land Rover to collect me, and seen us all return? She didn't look at me, but mumbled an apology to Cass, who sent her scurrying to the kitchen for the next course with a look.

Of course, this unnerved me even more and I struggled to remember my story. 'I'd got a bit of a ducking in Longmere – I was soaking wet – so I came back to the house to change. Shafeen and Nel were helping me dry out when the Medieva— . . . I mean, the others – came back and Henry wasn't with them. They thought he was with us, we thought he was with them. Turns out he wasn't with any of us. He had . . . drowned.' I swallowed. The story was really hard to tell, even though most of it was a lie. 'After we'd spoken to the police we went to our rooms. I'll never forget the blue lights of the ambulance at the window,' I said truthfully, the trauma of that night returning with full force.

'So you actually saw the body?' It was a really, *really* odd thing to ask, and Cass asked it with such urgency. I looked at her, and then at Louis. They both waited for the answer, their expressions oddly identical. They looked at me as if what I was going to say mattered more than anything in the world. I thought about the question. *Had* I? It was like the bit at the end of *Seven*, when everybody thinks they see a head in a box. But you never actually see anything. And nor had I. I hadn't *seen* Henry's body. None of us had. We'd seen a shape in a body bag on a stretcher, being slid into an ambulance. Having watched that scene again in my head, like some horrid DVD extra, I said, 'No.'

The twins' expressions divided dramatically. Cass looked comforted and Louis looked . . . devastated.

There was an awkward, charged silence. I looked to Nel desperately. We had to change the subject – the terrible, terrible subject. She took the hint.

'Why's this called the Queen's Dining Room?' she blurted out suddenly.

It worked. Cass turned her gaze from me to look at Nel. 'Because of *that*,' she said, nodding at the wall.

We all looked over and there was this giant portrait of Elizabeth I, hanging in pride of place.

I could see that Nel felt like a doofus, but she'd done her job. We were all now looking at the painting, the events of last year forgotten. It was a magnificent thing. The painting was massive, so big that the bottom of the queen's skirts disappeared behind a big dark oak chest that stood in front of the portrait.

'This is the Longcross Portrait of Queen Elizabeth I,' said Cass, exactly like she was a tour guide. 'It's extremely famous, comparable to the Rainbow Portrait and the Ditchley Portrait, and like most paintings of the queen is full of allegorical meaning.'

I got up from my place and went closer to the picture. The flickering candlelight gave the portrait a sense of being alive, almost filmic, animating the queen. She looked out from the canvas straight at me, her direct green gaze all-powerful. Her face was the colour of bone, with a little rose highlight on each cheek. Her red hair was dressed high around her face, with ringlets let loose and rippling over her shoulders. Perched on the side of her head was what I can only describe as a Robin Hood hat, pointy with a feather like the one that Errol Flynn wore in the really old Robin Hood films. Her lips were pursed and blood red. But it was her dress that was really interesting. She was in a green gown covered in oak leaves. The same leaves grew on the trees behind her. She was standing in a forest. In one hand she had a bow with an arrow fitted to the string and in the other hand she held a net made of gold filigree. Behind her skirts, half hidden, was a big unit of a dog, a bit like Brutus, eyes shining with bloodlust. In the sky above her hung a crescent moon.

Ty said, suddenly and forcefully, 'It's the same dress.'

'The same dress as what?' I asked.

'It's the dress from *The Isle of Dogs*.'

It was the first time the play had been mentioned at Longcross, even though we'd supposedly all gone there together to rehearse. Even I had all but forgotten *The Isle of Dogs* – such was the power of Longcross. The memories from last year, and Henry's spectral presence, had crowded it out.

Ty got up from her chair.

'Now, Diana, from thy huntress moon,
Lend me thy beauty for one night,
Bring me a gown the colour of the greenwood,
Bring me arrows keen enough to pierce the hearts of men,
Bring me a net, wrought of gilt, fit to catch dreams,
And a hound, with eyes of fire, and a thirst for blood,
So I may capture my prey, my love.'

She walked theatrically towards the painting, quoting as she walked. She looked amazing in the white gear, and her voice rang out strongly. It was the best she'd ever done it.

I looked again at the portrait and went cold. She was absolutely right.

'She's dressed for hunting.'

'That's exactly what she is,' said Cass. 'This was painted in

1586, just before she executed Mary, Queen of Scots. There'd been a slew of Catholic plots to assassinate Elizabeth. The meaning of this painting was that she would hunt down her enemies, wherever they were hiding. It was a statement of power.' She sounded admiring. 'Now *that* was a matriarchy.'

Betty came in with another course, breaking the spell. I went back to my seat, and so did Ty.

'She actually stayed here, you know,' said Cass, dropping the tour-guide act and sounding much less formal as we all tucked into this nice chicken-y main course. 'Elizabeth, I mean.'

I did know. She'd stayed in the room Shafeen had been in last year. She'd slept in the very bed where we'd all watched YouTube all night as an elegy for Henry.

Shafeen. I suddenly missed him terribly.

'She came here on one of her progresses.'

'Oh yes, we do those in history,' said Nel. 'That's when she used to go round the country in the summer staying with all the nobles. Kind of like a posh Airbnb.'

'Except she didn't pay,' said Cass. 'It was actually a pretty expensive business, having the queen to stay. Nazereth de Warlencourt did up the house for her. This ceiling was made then.'

That's why it looked familiar, I suddenly realised. That heavenly sky was just like the one on the ceiling of the De Warlencourt Playhouse – the same exact period.

'And that's when the portrait was done,' Cass went on. 'It was a great honour for the family to have her here. Especially as we were Catholics, the religion the queen hated. Still are, for that matter.'

'Catholics?'

182

She smiled slightly. 'You seem shocked.'

'No, not at all. I mean, I never even thought about it,' I blustered. 'It doesn't matter. What people are, I mean. I mean, it *matters*, but . . .' *Stop talking, Greer!* 'It doesn't matter to *me*.'

'It mattered back then though,' said Cass. 'Very much. The de Warlencourts were always Catholics, like a lot of the great northern families. And when Protestantism came along, they didn't buy into it. During the reign of Elizabeth, they had to hide and worship in secret.'

'Whoa,' said Nel.

'Yes. Made it a bit tricky when she actually came to visit.'

'I bet,' I said grimly.

'We've got the lot here apparently: priests' holes, false walls, tunnels, you name it.'

'Amazing. Have you ever found any?'

'No. We used to look when we were kids, all the time. There's even a hidden chapel, legend has it.'

'*Cool.*'

'Not so much. It was a dangerous time. Look at Mary, Queen of Scots. Another anointed queen, and Elizabeth's own cousin, but she also happened to be a Catholic conspirator, plotting with Philip II of Spain.'

The King of El Dorado.

'Elizabeth had *her* executed, so she would've thought nothing of chopping off some de Warlencourt heads.'

'And were they ever caught?'

'No.' She smiled, as if to herself more than us. 'This family is pretty good at keeping secrets.'

You can say that again, I thought.

'They rode it out. Carried on doing their thing, in private.'

How very de Warlencourt. 'Then what happened?'

'James I happened. And the patriarchy was restored,' crowed Louis, draining his glass.

Cass had been talking all night. Because Louis had said so little, what he did say now had impact. 'No more women at court after that,' he said, his eyes glittering with alcohol. 'James was very much a man's man.'

I thought about that. Then I remembered what Abbot Ridley had told me when we'd first talked about Ben Jonson. 'I don't know about that,' I said. 'There were still some powerful women kicking around. What about Esmé Stuart?'

'Who?'

'Esmé Stuart. She was Ben Jonson's patroness. And possibly girlfriend. Scottish, like the new king, had a place up north, quite near here. Abbot Ridley thinks she might have hidden *The Isle of Dogs* for Jonson when it was banned.'

'Or Nazereth hid it himself,' said Nel, who had perked up at the mention of her beloved Abbot. 'He played the earl in *The Isle of Dogs*, acted alongside Ben Jonson in his own play. They must have been buds.'

Cass looked a bit odd at that, but didn't confirm or deny. Instead she got to her feet. 'Speaking of Nazereth,' she said, 'I think there's another portrait you might like to see.'

Scene vi

We left the Queen's Dining Room, ignoring the coffee and dessert that Betty was bringing in on the inevitable silver tray, and followed Cass up the stairs.

We climbed and climbed to the top of the house until I recognised the Long Gallery, the room with the polished wooden floor, which stretched the whole length of the top floor of the house. The last time I'd been here was with Henry, when he'd taken me to slide along it the night that he'd kissed me. Back then I'd hardly noticed the gallery of ancestors who'd watched us snootily from the walls. But tonight Cass took us right up to one of the gilt-framed portraits, about halfway along the gallery. Much smaller than the queen's portrait, it featured a man, not a woman. 'Meet Nazereth de Warlencourt,' she said, exactly as if he was alive and standing before us, 'also known as the actor Gabriel Spenser.'

I looked into the face of the man I'd skated past without a glance last year, just as the twins must have done hundreds of times when they were little. He was wearing a gold doublet and a little white ruff at his throat. He had one of those pointy Elizabethan goatee beards and a moustache, and just like the queen in her portrait, a high spot of red colour on each cheek. There was enough of Henry in him to give him a family resemblance, with the de Warlencourt blond hair and blue eyes, but he wasn't what you could call handsome. He looked like one of those expensive dogs you see in hunting tapestries: pale and sleek with a long canine nose, and the dogginess of the portrait was compounded by the fact that his hand rested on the head of a dog. This dog wasn't scary like the one in the queen's picture, or like the one Perfect dragged around with him. This was what I would call a 'nice doggy'. It was white and tan, with floppy ears and cute brown eyes. 'That, I suppose, must be Spenser.'

'Yep,' said Cass. 'Apparently he loved that dog more than any human.'

I studied Nazereth again. His outfit didn't seem particularly significant in the way Elizabeth's was, but he too, it seemed, was in a forest, with young green leaves on the trees. Unlike Elizabeth's portrait though, his had a sun in the sky over Nazereth's golden shoulder. And, right by it, a bright star.

'D'you reckon that's the Bethlehem star?' I said, all pleased with myself. 'Because he was called Nazereth, geddit?'

'No,' said Ty quietly. 'I think it's the Dog Star, cos look – it's really close to the sun. And you can see from the trees around him that it's summer, not Christmas.'

'Oh *yes*. You're absolutely right.'

'Maybe that's a reference to *The Isle of Dogs*,' said Nel. 'Remember in the play, the hunt takes place on the dog days, the middle of July.' She put her head on one side. 'Abbot Ridley would love to see this,' she said softly. A blush crept into her cheeks to match Nazereth's. 'Because, you know, he plays the same part in the play.'

Overexplaining much? Poor Nel. I peered closer at the man who had loved the theatre so much that he had turned his back on his birthright to become Gabriel Spenser, a humble player. But with his shuttered canine face Nazereth de Warlencourt wasn't giving anything away.

Cass turned away from her ancestor and began to walk along the gallery, flinging out her arms dramatically. 'You know, this would be a good rehearsal room,' she announced, as if she was acting on a stage, her voice carrying all the way down the gallery. 'Lots of space, good acoustics.'

I turned around too. 'Fantastic,' I agreed. Talking about the play had got me all jazzed about it again, and the others too.

'Tomorrow, we should get up and rehearse,' said Ty, eyes shining. 'Like, all day.'

'Yes!' agreed Nel.

'So annoying we don't have a fifth act,' moaned Cass.

It was time. 'It's here,' I said. 'Here at Longcross.'

Of course they all surrounded me. Louis was the first to speak, urgently. He'd been so silent that his voice, once again, was a surprise.

'How do you know?'

I glanced at Nel for confirmation, just as Perfect had looked to Cass earlier. Though we weren't mistress and servant, but co-conspirators, Nel gave the same tiny nod.

'Come with me,' I said.

Now I took the lead, down two flights of stairs to my room.

I sat everybody down on my bed and got out my deer-leather school satchel. The satchel that contained the play. I unbuckled it, ignoring their murmured questions, and slid out the last page I'd been given by the mysterious messenger of Lightfoot.

Six pairs of eyes fixed themselves on the printed *Lorem ipsum* page. Five of us were on the bed and Jeffrey watched from the wall as I explained what we had worked out.

Cass, mistress of the house, said, 'So it's here at Longcross. But the question is: where?'

'I think I know that too.' I didn't mention **mrs_de_warlencourt**, and her online clues; I didn't want to show all my cards. But I did recount my dream, and my recollection of going into the library last year. 'I remembered seeing a bunch of original manuscripts on the shelves. Of course I didn't register them then, but one of them could well have been this play. *The Isle of Dogs* by Ben Jonson.'

My cast looked at me, eyes wide, and I looked back at them in turn. As one, we got to our feet.

This time there were no leaders and followers.

We were a pack, and we all knew where we were going.

Scene vii

The library was as dark and mysterious as it had been a year ago when I'd gone there at night to look for the hunting books. But it was a lot less forbidding. This time was different – Perfect wouldn't be lurking around with a shotgun. He was the creature of the de Warlencourts and this time we had them with us. Cass and Louis, the keepers of the kingdom, present and future.

I led everyone up the winding stair to the mezzanine, the place where Shafeen and Nel and I had hidden from Perfect, and the location of my dream. I saw the hunting books at once, black morocco leather decorated with tooled gold, in a row as straight and neat as a rank of soldiers. I noticed, though, that there was no new volume. That, at least, was something. Maybe that dark part of Longcross's history had finally been put to rest. Meanwhile, we were on the trail of another mystery. I looked along the shelves, bypassing all the Lake Poets and the ancient tomes I'd seen last year. I could see the scruffy edges of unbound manuscripts in a dim corner, but, it now being about ten at night, it was too dark to make anything out. 'I can't see a thing,' I whined.

'Hang on,' said Cass. She bent to a low shelf and came up

with a candle on a sort of holder thing. She struck a match and the flame flowered into life. 'It's so people can find things up here at night.'

'Only at Longcross,' I said, 'would you have an open flame in a library.'

'Don't worry,' she said. 'It's a hurricane lamp. Look.' She put a glass cylinder over the flame, so it was protected. She handed it to me. It had a kind of metal handle, like a teacup, to put your forefinger through. I lifted the flame to the shelves and started pulling things out. Some of the manuscripts looked pretty old, and some were quill-written, but they all said things like 'Proceedings of the Moot court of Alnwick', or 'Reflections of a Country Squire'. There were no plays of any sort, never mind plays by Ben Jonson. I could feel the others shuffling behind me with the anticlimax. I'd been so *sure* I'd find Act Five here. Why else would I have been directed to Longcross by the typewritten acrostic? Was it some sort of weird prank? Eventually I straightened up and swung round to the others. It was time to fess up. 'There's nothing here. Maybe –'

I jumped.

The arc of candlelight had illuminated a portrait, hung in the darkest corner of the mezzanine, in a pulse of light so brief it had seemed that the sitter had leaned out of the blackness to scare me. I stepped back, hand on my pounding heart. Then, shaking, I lifted the hurricane lamp high to study the face that had given me such a movie jump-scare.

And that's when I saw the third portrait connected to *The Isle of Dogs* that we were to find at Longcross.

It was the smallest and the strangest of the three.

Unlike in the portraits of Elizabeth and Nazereth, the background to this one was completely black. The sitter was wearing black, too, his doublet and soft hat merging with the background. The only contrast was a stiff white ruff, weirdly at odds with the black, giving the impression that the sitter's head was on a plate. The face was young and male, with sandy red hair, a neat goatee and direct blue eyes. Blond, like Nazereth, and about the same age, but that's where the resemblance ended. There was no trace of the de Warlencourt DNA here. It was the eyes that made me shiver. They looked straight at the viewer – what you'd call 'down the bottle' in the movie world. If I had to identify the expression, I'd say that this fellow held a secret, and he wasn't telling.

'Funny place for a portrait,' I said. 'There aren't any other pictures here in the library. All the other portraits are in the Long Gallery, right?'

Cass nodded.

'So why is this one here?'

'I don't know,' she said. 'I've never actually noticed it before. A whole childhood spent playing in this house and I'm sure I've never clapped eyes on it. Pretty strange, really.'

'No,' said Nel definitely. 'It wasn't meant to be seen. It's up on a mezzanine, in the darkest corner of the library. Even in daylight you'd struggle to see it.'

'Who is he?' asked Ty. 'Does it say?'

'I'll bet my bitcoin it's Ben Jonson,' I said excitedly, suddenly sure. I lowered the lamp to the picture. The guy in the painting watched me, impassive. I moved the light from side to side as if I was sending a signal, and a thread of gold writing sprung out of the dark-wood frame. I read it out slowly, disbelieving:

ESMÉ STUART, 3RD DUKE OF LENNOX,
7TH EARL OF AUBIGNY

I stood back and frowned. 'Duke? Earl? That *can't* be right.'

'Esme's a *girl's* name, isn't it?' said Ty.

'Well, yes,' I said, thinking, as I always did, of Esme Dawson. 'Esmé Stuart was a woman.'

'Maybe you got that wrong?' asked Nel.

'No,' I said, looking at her directly. 'Abbot *Ridley* got it wrong. He distinctly told me that Esmé Stuart was a woman. He said "friend and patron*ess*".'

'Not being funny, Greer,' said Nel defensively, 'but it's more likely that you made the mistake than him. Drama's his subject.'

'Yes, but this isn't drama. This is history.' Although it felt like both. I started to doubt myself. *Had* I misheard him? 'I suppose I could have misheard,' I said, 'but –'

'All right, well, *whatever*,' put in Louis impatiently. 'If this chap was so connected to Ben Jonson, that's good enough for me. Let's try this.' He shoved through the little crowd of us and did something entirely unexpected.

He lifted the painting clean off the wall.

We all stared at the panelling behind it.

What we'd expected to find was a manuscript.

What we found was a door.

Scene viii

We all stood back in a little semicircle. For a moment no one moved. Then Cass stepped forward and laid her hand on the wrought-iron latch. It lifted with an ancient creak.

The mouth of the doorway was blacker than black, and a smell came from inside, an ancient, damp, stoney smell, which told us that the door hadn't been opened for centuries.

Ty was the first to speak. 'Are we going in?'

'Of *course* we're going in,' I said, putting those dumb girls in horror movies firmly out of my mind.

'But shouldn't we wait until morning?' asked Nel a little nervously. 'Bring some more lights?'

'No,' said Cass, with the voice of command she'd been using ever since we'd come to Longcross. 'We go *now.*'

And she took the hurricane lamp from my hand and walked into the dark. Louis followed, just one step behind her, face set as if he were on a mission. Ty went after him, as they seemed joined at the hip these days, and I followed Ty, with Nel bringing up the rear.

Our feet first met a winding staircase, taking us down and down into the bowels of the house. The stone steps were slippery, and when I touched the walls to steady myself they felt damp. At times, Cass would be a turn of the stair away from the rest of us, and the light receded completely for a few terrifying seconds until we caught up. But eventually the passage straightened out into what was clearly a subterranean tunnel. At this point the passage began to smell more earthy than stoney and became more natural, if that makes sense, with crumbly walls of soil and the odd tree root poking out of the ceiling. I would have been afraid of the earth falling in if it wasn't for these strong supporting beams every few feet, ancient timbers but strong as steel, holding up the tunnel.

We trudged along the passageway for ages, and I got so used to it that I almost stopped feeling afraid. We even started to chatter and giggle a little, in staccato, nervous bursts. I was just getting used to the notion that we'd be walking all night when Cass stopped ahead of us. We all barrelled into the back of each other, comically, as if we were in the *Scooby-Doo* movie.

'What's up?'

'Door,' she said succinctly, and we all bunched up to see.

It was a pretty heavy-duty door. With a keyhole. But no key. If I'd had to take a guess, I would say it was made of oak, and it had those wrought-iron studs that the doors had at STAGS. The kind of door that says if someone doesn't want you to get through it, you ain't getting through it. And our way was blocked by something even more sinister: there was no handle on our side of the door. No handle at all, not even a rope, or a hole to put a finger in. The keyhole wasn't big enough to get any leverage, which we tried, and in any case it was blocked by a key inserted from the other side. We tried everything – pushing, pulling, all of us, one of us. But it was no use. 'Great.' I said. 'Now what?'

'Well, we can't get through to wherever it is,' said Cass in a voice of frustration.

'Can you guess where we might be,' I asked, 'from how long we've been walking, and the direction and stuff?'

'Not really,' she said, 'except that the library is in the north tower, so we've probably walked under Longwood. Although it's hard to tell from the twists and turns of the staircase; it might have put us back in quite the other direction.'

'Guess we found one of those old priests' holes then,' said Ty.

'Yes,' said Cass. 'But clearly you had to be let out of this tunnel, by whoever was on the other side of this door. I guess there was some special knock or something.'

'Shall we try it?' asked Nel. 'We might be able to guess the right one.'

'Don't be a dumb bunny,' I said, remembering her crack about Esmé Stuart. 'There's not going to be anyone there *now*. Who d'you think is waiting for us? That crumbly old knight from *Indiana Jones and the Last Crusade*?'

'I dunno, do I?' she said defensively. 'What do you suggest then?'

'We'll just have to go back,' I said, 'and try to figure out where the tunnel goes in the morning. Maybe there are old maps, you know, in that estate room that we –'

Just at that moment I was interrupted by the most chilling sound I think I've ever heard in my life.

It was coming from the tunnel behind us, and it was the unearthly howl of a dog.

Scene ix

The sound was distant but growing louder, echoing down the tunnel.

We froze for a second as the realisation that we were trapped and we couldn't go back reached us all. Then, as one, we turned and started desperately shoving at the door. I had one eye on Nel, as I knew that if I was this terrified, it must be so much worse for her, with her (now very understandable) dog phobia.

'It must be Brutus,' I hissed at Cass as we pushed. 'He's Perfect's dog. Can't you get Perfect to call him off?'

'Yes, Greer, I'll just go back and explain that to Brutus, shall I?' she panted. 'And Perfect's probably not even with him. He does a circuit of the house every night to check it's secure; Brutus probably saw the open door and came down it to follow our scent.'

'*Jesus.*'

Brutus, if it was him, didn't seem now like a huge, slightly scary dog who'd been lolloping along beside Perfect in snowy Longwood. He now seemed like some supernatural hellhound, bent on our destruction. I could see him in my mind's eye, galloping down the tunnel, jaws wide, eyes afire.

Fire. 'We'll just have to break the hurricane lamp in his face when he gets here,' I said, with courage I didn't possess. 'Then we can maybe overpower him.'

And then, of course, the light blew out, snuffed by some unholy draught swirling round the tunnel like demonic breath, probably caused by the movement of a running hound coming for us. We were in total darkness, pushing desperately on a door to nowhere.

Then, over all the row and panic, Nel shouted, 'Look!'

We looked. In the new and total darkness, we could see a narrow band of light glowing under the door.

Someone was on the other side.

As one, we all started hammering and shouting.

'Help!'

'Let us in!'

'Open the door!'

Nel clutched at her neck and started to scream hysterically, a jumble of words about hounds and hunts and Brutus and the fact that he was coming for her and he would tear her throat out. It was horrific. The canine footsteps came closer, and the howl was loud enough to curdle the blood. Now you could actually hear dog claws skittering on the earthen floor. Surely he was just around the next bend.

And then, a miracle.

The door gave way.

Some unseen hand had opened it from the other side.

We all piled through, honour and courage abandoned, pushing and shoving in a desperate scramble, and I fell into the arms of . . .

Shafeen.

Shafeen.

After a one-second embrace of utter relief and delight, he threw me aside and shoved the door shut, locking it at once with the wrought-iron key that at any other moment I'd have found comically large. A moment later, Brutus's mass slammed against the door with a force and a howl that made us all jump back. And even that door, hardcore as it was, bulged inwards with the impact. 'Everyone, hold the door!' yelled Shafeen, and we all – except for Nel, who cringed away, gibbering with fear – pressed our weight against the door. We seemed to be there for eons, waiting for the next terrible bodyslam, but eventually the noise of barking subsided and, with a whimper, the beast turned and padded away.

Shafeen closed his eyes and put his forehead against the door. After a long moment he turned and slid down it until he was sitting on the stone floor, still with his eyes closed. A thousand and one questions crowded my mind. One of them, *ridiculously*, was how did he feel about me? 'Don't take this the wrong way, but what the *hell* are you doing here?'

He opened one eye and smiled, quite the old Shafeen.

'Pleased to see you too, Greer.'

'Of course I'm pleased.' I was. I was really delighted. I'd missed him loads. 'It's just . . . how . . . who . . . when . . . ?

'I invited him,' said Cass.

Of *course*. He'd said as much in our last row. Of course he had. I had forgotten. I turned to look at her.

'He said he couldn't travel with us because he had revision

198

to do, but if I could send a car he would come up after dinner. So I did. And he did.'

I looked back at Shafeen, who had both eyes open now and was watching me with something like amusement. He did jazz hands as if to say *ta-dah*, like he'd performed some magic trick. Cass looked from Shafeen to me. 'I assumed you knew he was coming . . . ?'

There was not much I could say to that without totally letting everyone else know our business. 'Of course I knew he was coming to *Longcross*,' I bluffed. The others all looked at the floor as if they didn't want to intrude on a private conversation. 'I was just wondering what he was doing *here*.'

'I came to pay my respects,' he said sombrely. 'Remember, we were too young to come to Henry's funeral because we weren't eighteen – only the Medievals could go, and the Old Abbot. When I got here it was too late for dinner so I thought I'd stroll over to the church and . . . pay my respects.'

'What do you mean, "pay your respects"?'

He did one of those little nods, which means *look*.

I did a 180 and looked properly at where we'd ended up.

We were in a stone room with a cross-ribbed ceiling, just like the undercroft at STAGS where the choir practised. There were frescoes of saints, little shrines and carved memorial plaques on the walls with the name *De Warlencourt* and dates from centuries ago. Tombs loomed from the ancient shadows and at one end of the room stood a little altar, draped in a cloth of gold, with a silver cross standing on it.

'It's the secret chapel,' I breathed.

Cass set the lamp aside. We didn't need it now, because the

place was a forest of lit candles. 'No,' she said. 'Well – yes, in a way. I guess the priests and the family must have snuck out here to worship in secret. But they were actually hiding in plain sight – this is the crypt of a church. We're in Longcross church.'

It clicked. Pay my respects. *Longcross church.* 'Where Henry was . . .'

She nodded. 'Yes. It's also the family mausoleum.'

That explained the hundreds of white candles. I pointed at them. 'Who lit these?'

'The priest of Longcross. Father Wright. He says Masses for Henry's soul. Told you, didn't I? Catholic to the hilt.'

'For Henry's soul?'

'That's right. He's here.'

She put a hand on the nearest, largest tomb.

When I'd thought about Henry's funeral – and I'd thought about it a *lot* – I'd watched in my head the scene play out in a graveyard, with mourners in black throwing handfuls of earth and red roses onto a hardwood coffin at the bottom of a six-foot hole, like that scene in *The Godfather: Part III*. I hadn't computed that rich people, *really* rich people, have tombs, so they can all live together after death, a jumble of wealthy bones. This tomb was an ornate thing, carved around the sides with running stags. The lid (if that's the right word) had a pair of stone antlers carved into it and a list (if that's also the right word) of names. All of them were de Warlencourts. I recognised some of the Christian names. First on the list, **Conrad**. The penultimate name: **Nazereth**. And newest of all: **Henry**.

I walked forward and bent my head over Henry's silent stone. I hadn't expected to see him again like this. I put my hand on the cold marble. 'Hello,' I said. I moved my fingers across the whole of his carved name, HENRY CHARLES PHILIP ARTHUR GEORGE DE WARLENCOURT 1999–2017. And there was more writing too, across the very bottom of the tomb. It was easy to make out, because of the sunburst of candles. It said:

MISERERE MEI, DEUS, SECUNDUM MAGNAM MISERICORDIAM TUAM

As I murmured the phrase out loud to myself, it seemed vaguely familiar. 'What does it mean?' I asked.

'No idea,' said Cass tightly. And I remembered how much she'd loved Henry too, and so I didn't ask any more. I suddenly felt incredibly sad, and knew in another moment I would cry. It was hard to believe Henry was there, under that cold slab, under my hand.

I was not the only one thinking that.

Louis, demonic in the candlelight, said, in a voice far too loud to be used over a coffin, 'You claimed you never saw the body, didn't you? Let's see it now, shall we?'

Ty laid a hand on his arm 'Louis –'

He shrugged off the hand. 'No. Let's find out once and for all.'

And then, unbelievably, he put all his weight against the lid of the tomb and began to shove it sideways.

I looked at Cass. Everybody looked at Cass. How was she taking this horrific turn of events?

She stood, still as one of the statues, with an unreadable look on her face. Then she did the last thing I would've expected. She put her shoulder to the tomb and pushed. Then Shafeen, *Shafeen*, put his shoulder next to hers and pushed too. Then Ty lined up next to Louis. I looked at Nel, who shrugged and added her weight too. I looked at them all, shoving as if overtaken by some spell, some dark enchantment, and then, led by a strange compulsion beyond my control, I walked forward like I was in a dream. I bent my shoulder to the cold stone and started to shove. I was suddenly seized by a desperate desire to see what was inside. To see *him*.

My strength, puny as it was, was evidently the catalyst. For as soon as I started to push the stone answered, grating a fraction of a centimetre off its alignment with a gravelly, echoing groan. The entire top of the tomb sheared sideways, releasing a triangle of darkness within and a breath of the grave. Dust and decay and a smell I'd never inhaled before, which I realised, with a chill, must be the smell of death. We shoved the tombstone sideways until it almost formed an X with the casket, then stopped before it could fall off.

We all stood back, silent, looking at each other, unable to believe what we'd done. Unable to look. Even Louis, who'd started this madness, hung back. In the end it was me who took a warm candle in my hand, stepped forward and leaned over the dark.

I don't know what I expected to see – Henry, perfect and embalmed as if he slept, some shredded *Dawn-of-the-Dead* zombie or a picked-clean skeleton from *Jason and the Argonauts*. I saw none of those things.

Disbelievingly, I reached in my hand and lifted out the only thing that was in that tomb.

Loosely bound in blood-red ribbon, it was a quill-written manuscript.

ACT FOUR

Scene i

I held the pages high as if they were the baby Lion King, so everyone could see.

Shafeen, Nel and Ty wore treasure hunters' expressions of wide-eyed excitement. But neither of the de Warlencourt twins were looking at the manuscript. They were staring down into the casket, and their expressions couldn't have been more different.

Cass looked incredibly joyful.

Louis's face was a mask of horror.

I couldn't think about their family matters right now, or the implications of what we'd found – or rather not found – in the casket. I was just, A) relieved I didn't have to see Henry's bones, and B) made up to have found, at last, what *must* be Act Five.

Despite my excitement, I slid the blood-red ribbon carefully from the edges of the manuscript, aware of the value of what I was holding.

I looked at the first page, front and back. Then the second. Then the third. Then lost all care and riffled through the rest of the pages like they were cards. 'What the *hell*?' I exclaimed.

'What is it?' asked Nel. 'Is it Act Five?'

'I don't know. It's just a jumble of letters.' I looked up disbelievingly. 'They're in code.'

'We can't see properly here,' said Shafeen. 'Let's go upstairs to the church. There's electric light there.'

I'd forgotten he'd come from upstairs. His idea seemed a good one, so, having replaced the lid of the tomb as respectfully as possible, we went up a stone stairway into the church proper.

At any other time, it would have been a pretty village church. At nearly midnight on a late-November night, it was creepy as hell, even when Louis found the light switch and turned the electric lights full on. The stained-glass windows were blank and black, the air as cold as stone. We all huddled together on one of the pews and looked properly at the pages. They were all gobbledegook. We took a couple each and perused them under the stark light. 'Look for words you can recognise,' I said. Not a single intelligible word was written on any of mine. 'Anyone?' I asked hopefully.

'Nope.'

'Nada.'

'Nothing.'

'Sorry, Greer.'

Louis didn't answer. Instead he thrust his pages back at me impatiently and jumped to his feet. 'I can't waste time with this play tonight. There are bigger things at stake.'

'Where are you going?' asked Ty quickly.

'I'm going to wake Father Wright. I want to know where my cousin's body is.'

'I'm coming with you,' said Cass, getting up too.

'Shall I come?' offered Ty, her voice full of concern.

'No,' said Louis, his face set. 'This is a family matter.'

And she shrank back, like a dog kicked by her beloved master.

As the great door of the church slammed shut, Shafeen put a comforting hand on Ty's shoulder. 'Don't take it to heart,' he said. 'It's quite a big deal, losing your cousin's body. They have to sort it out.'

'They'll never be able to see the priest at this hour though, will they?' asked Nel. 'It must be nearly midnight.'

'They're the de Warlencourts,' I said, 'and he's their priest. They can see him at whatever time they like.'

'I wonder where he is,' mused Ty.

'The priest? There's probably a vicarage quite close to the church.'

'Not the *priest*,' said Ty. 'Henry.'

Again, it was odd her saying his name aloud like that. 'I don't know.' And a little, unwanted hope began to flame inside me like a candle. Might Henry step out of the deep-cut shadows of the nave?

Nel snuffed out my hope-flame almost at once. 'There must be a simple explanation. Probably that tomb downstairs is just for memorial purposes, and the body was buried in the graveyard. Or maybe he was cremated. Maybe you're not allowed to just bung bodies in stone sarcophagi any more.'

My heart started to slow down again. 'Yes. Yes, of course. That's the most logical explanation.' I gave myself a little shake. 'So much for what we didn't find in the tomb. Let's talk about what we did find.' I looked at the pages in my hands. 'It must be Act Five,' I said. 'There are thirteen pages. If it was a message, or a letter, it would just be one page. Thirteen pages is a whole act, I'm sure of it.'

'What's more suggestive to me is that the pages look genuinely period,' said Shafeen, ever the scientist.

'They are. They are exactly the same paper that the rest of the play is on. You can see the stationer's mark, see?' I pointed to a little rune embossed in the top corner of each. 'And the writing is Ben Jonson's. I'd know it anywhere by now.'

'We need to take a proper look at it if we're going to decode it. Back at the house.'

'In the morning though, right?' said Nel nervily.

'*Hell* yes. I've had enough excitement for one night,' I stated firmly, having no idea what was yet to come.

The twins didn't come back for ages. We sort of noodled about the church looking for clues to help us decode the pages, but there wasn't anything. No significant letters hidden in the frescoes, no convenient hymn numbers lined up on the board, no handy ciphers by Ben Jonson hidden in the family Bible. The Good Book lay innocently on a lectern that was shaped like a big brass eagle, open at Psalm 51, with nothing to tell us. I shut the great book with a dull thud. 'It seems the trail's gone cold.'

'Well, that being the case, we can't stay here all night,' said Shafeen. 'The twins are obviously not coming back.'

'Where can they have got to?' wondered Ty plaintively.

Shafeen shrugged. 'Maybe they've had to see the coroner, or the police.'

The police? A jag of fear went through me. I'd been petrified of talking to the police last year. Talking to them, lying to them.

Just then the bells of Longcross church began to chime, sending my heart from nought to sixty again. *One. Two. Three. Four. Five. Six. Seven. Eight. Nine. Ten. Eleven. Twelve.*

Midnight.

Shafeen stood up. 'Let's just go.'

'Go where?' I asked.

'Back to the house.'

'There's no *way* I'm going back in that tunnel,' said Nel, whitefaced.

'No, silly,' said Shafeen. 'Overground.'

'But we don't know the way,' I cautioned.

'I do,' he said. 'I just came from there. You just walk through the woods. It's easy.'

'Through the *woods*?'

'OK, Greer,' he said, 'here's the choice. Would you rather spend the night in a creepy church, with a few dozen de Warlencourt skeletons downstairs, or take a short walk through an (admittedly) creepy wood to comfort and safety?'

I wouldn't exactly describe Longcross as comfort and safety. It was kind of like heading back to the Overlook Hotel. But we didn't have much of a choice. And that's how Shafeen, Nel, Ty and I found ourselves in Longwood at midnight.

Scene ii

At first it was OK.

There was a bright full moon and we found the path pretty easily. 'This is how I got here from Longcross,' said Shafeen confidently. 'Look. Through the clearing you can see the lights of the house. If we just keep making for the lights, we'll be on the right track.'

But soon Longwood began to mess with our heads. If I wasn't such a logical soul, I would say it was bewitched. Quite a few times, having sworn we'd carried on straight, we found ourselves walking back up the path to the church. It was like being in *Inception*, when the whole world folds up on itself and you don't know what the hell is going on. Of course, this was the one time Nel didn't have her phone, as she'd had no idea we would be leaving the house, so we had no torch, no GPS. Soon we lost the path altogether and could no longer see the lights of the house.

We saw other lights though. Beady, burning little lights in pairs, staring at us from the black silhouettes of trees. There were hundreds of them, sort of dotted around in the dark, at waist height.

Eyes.

'Hang on,' I said loudly. 'This is some sort of prank.'

'What are you talking about?' Nel could hardly speak, she was so scared.

'This looks exactly like the Underwood set for *The Isle of Dogs* – it must be a prank,' I explained. 'Very good, guys,' I called out. 'You can show yourselves now.'

There was no answer. No human answer, that is. Just a low, threatening growl.

And then another.

And another.

'Dogs,' whimpered Nel. '*Run.*'

I don't know if you've ever tried running in heels. If you haven't, don't. What gave me Usain Bolt levels of speed was the baying, the horrible baying of the dogs. Of course, in our panic we all scattered. I could see Ty bounding through the undergrowth in her white fur coat. I'd had that glimpse of white fur once before and I remembered where: on the stag hunt a year ago, the snowy tail of the stag bouncing away from us as the dogs hunted him down. And in the dark I saw, or thought I saw, black shadows streaming after her – she definitely had the worst of it. I began to follow her, having totally lost sight of Shafeen and Nel. Then there was a volley of barking in the darkness ahead and I was forced to double back, and the white tail was gone. I began to shout – their names, other people's names, even (and I'm not proud of this) for my dad. I ran desperately, jinking and checking, changing direction constantly like a frightened rabbit trying to shake the hounds. A hand came out of the dark and grabbed mine – I screamed,

211

but it was Shafeen. 'Stay together,' he panted. 'We have to get Ty.'

He practically towed me along as we ran, and from her jagged breathing I could hear Nel on the other side of him. There were now dogs actually swirling around our feet – growling and snapping. In the blackness there was nothing to be seen but eyes and teeth, and the sounds, the terrible sounds, were all around us. Suddenly Ty's white coat was just ahead of us, shining out of the dark. I grabbed at it and took hold of an arm in a furry sleeve. 'Come *on*.'

On we ran, blundering through the dark undergrowth, the greedy branches snatching at our fancy dinner clothes. Until we saw a miracle.

It was a measure of just how frightened we were that the lights of Longcross – *Longcross* – seemed homey and welcoming. But seeing that big cruise liner of a house shining out of the dark almost made me sob with relief. We raced up the drive like we were in the Olympics, the pack of dogs scattering after us on the gravel. We wrenched open the great front doors and slammed them behind us. We ran to the diamond-paned windows to look back at the ravening, swirling pack that had chased us, no doubt now snapping and tearing at the doors, and saw . . . nothing.

Not a single dog was in the driveway.

'What the actual . . . ?'

'Where did they go?'

'Did we imagine it?'

'No,' said Ty. 'Look.' Her white platform trainer was torn at the heel, and I was sure you could see the marks of teeth.

212

'Yes, they seemed to like you in particular,' I said grimly. I remembered what the Medievals had said a year ago, that horrid little fact about hounds being attracted to menstrual blood. But I didn't feel that I knew Ty well enough to ask her if she was on her period, especially not in front of a boy, so I didn't say any more. We all looked at the trainer, in sick horror. Then Ty said, 'Maybe they like the dark meat.'

At that, something peculiar happened: I started to smile.

For a second it was fifty-fifty whether I was going to laugh or sob. Then I began to laugh hysterically, and the others joined in, even Ty, until we were all crying with laughter like at the end of *Sully*. I guess we were releasing tension or something, but it was properly weird. My ribs were actually aching.

Then Betty came into the hall and we stopped as abruptly as if someone had pulled the plug on us. She was in this white nightgown with her greying hair in a plait, just like the off-duty maids you see in films like *Sense and Sensibility* when they are woken at night by a fast-rider with a letter.

She seemed surprised to see us there, as well she might be.

'Betty,' I said, gasping for breath, 'get us something hot to drink, would you?' I tried to sound like Cassandra.

She looked around for the twins, but as there was no one to outrank me, she said, 'Very good, miss.' She hesitated. 'Might I suggest some mulled wine, miss? Won't take a moment on the Aga.'

I was thinking more along the lines of hot chocolate, but actually mulled wine was *exactly* what I needed right then.

Scene iii

So within about ten minutes, we were all drinking mulled wine under the Christmas tree.

We must've looked like a Christmas card, all in our evening clothes round the dying fire, the tree lit up above us. But we were gulping the wine a little too quickly, anaesthetising the shock of what had happened to us. And in the warm glow of the fire and the alcohol, the fear of the dogs in the night gradually abated and we began to relax. And so, despite what Nel had said about waiting until morning, we all, of course, got stuck into some serious decoding of Act Five.

'Let's think logically,' I said. 'Each of these letters must correspond to the letters of the alphabet.'

Apparently all posh houses have notepaper in the bedrooms, and Nel fetched some from hers. We sat on the hearth rug under the tree and tried to figure out the code together.

'All right,' said Shafeen. 'Suppose we take the words –' he thought for a moment – *'knowledge is power.'*

He wrote them on the paper in clear capital letters.

KNOWLEDGE IS POWER

'A substitution cipher would change one letter of the alphabet for another.'

'That's right,' said Nel. 'Friar Camden said cryptographers would sometimes slip the alphabet, so that A represents B and so on. That was the simplest form of cipher.' She wrote:

```
A B C D E F G H I J K L M N O P Q R S T U V W X Y Z
B C D E F G H I J K L M N O P Q R S T U V W X Y Z A
```

'That is really entry level,' I said. 'But let's try it.'

```
KNOWLEDGE IS POWER
LOPXMFEHF JT QPXFS
```

'Then what they'd do is divide up the words in random places, so you couldn't even work out how many letters were in a word.' Shafeen leaned over me and rewrote:

```
LOPX MF EHFJTQP XFS
```

'The more layers in the code to confuse the reader, the better.'

'You're not kidding. The problem with a substitution cipher is that there is no way of knowing which letters have been changed for which,' said Nel. 'There must be thousands of combinations.'

'But,' I said, 'surely you kind of have to make it a *bit* logical, for the person who needs to crack the code. I mean, they wouldn't jumble all the letters up, for example – that would be way too hard to crack, even for the geniuses the Cecils had working for them. You'd have to give them the whole "new" alphabet, written down, and that could be intercepted. It'd be too dangerous.'

'That's right. Friar Camden said that in most instances the letters of the alphabet were kept in sequence, but there was some sort of keyword inserted into the cipher, easy to remember, but made known only to the agent, which would help him crack the code. It was passed on by word of mouth, remembered and never written down.'

'But without the keyword we're stuffed.'

'Correct.'

'OK.' I sighed so gustily that the candle flames on the tree bent and flickered a little. 'What else?'

'Well, the other thing the Friar talked about was a frequency cipher, remember? You work out the frequency of the letters that occur in the code. You start from a known fact, such as that E is the most common letter in the English language, and then you look for the most common letter in the code, and assume that that one is E.'

'All right. Let's look at the real thing.'

The manuscript looked fiendishly complicated, not least because it was closely quill-written, not printed out in Shafeen's neat round hand.

We took a page each and had a good look by the firelight. We were silent for a time, with just the pop and crackle of the logs in the grate to be heard. 'I've got a lot of Rs,' said Nel.

'And I've got a lot of Cs,' said Shafeen.

'It's Ks for me,' said Ty.

'And I've got Gs,' I said. 'Brilliant. Now what?'

No one spoke for a while. Then Ty, who had been very quiet

up until then, spoke up. I guess she felt that we were such an established trio of friends that she was a bit of an outsider. 'How about we look for words that we know must be in there?' she suggested.

'How d'you mean?'

'You know, like Act Five, scene one, scene two, etc. And character names. There must be Cynthia, Greenwich – actually not him, he's dead – Lupo, Volpone, Canis. Even Placentia for the palace, and Underwood for the forest.'

'Ty,' I said, 'that's quite brilliant. Let's look.' We did, and it was a frustrating exercise.

'It's no good,' said Shafeen, at length. 'They've obviously messed with the format. The character names aren't separate, nor are the act or scene headings. They've run the text all together to make it denser. It's hopeless.'

We'd just about given up for the night when the twins walked in. I'm not sure why, but I instinctively shuffled the pages away. Not, I think, that they would've noticed.

The two de Warlencourts, so alike, looked very different at this moment. Cass looked radiant; Louis ashen. They flopped into the two remaining chairs like guests on the worst chat show ever. Cass started to speak.

'Father Wright is convinced there was a body . . .'

'Exactly,' Louis took over. 'There *was* a body.'

'But it isn't there now,' countered Cass.

'Might it not have –' there was no nice way to say it – 'rotted?'

'Not to that extent, not in just a year,' said Louis. 'There would be . . . remains.' I noticed that the power dynamic between the twins had changed yet again. Now they were speaking exactly the same amount, as equals. I'd never seen this version of their relationship before.

'I think we should just leave it,' said Cass. 'He's gone. Does it matter where he is?'

'It matters very much,' said Louis. 'We'll have to speak to the police and the coroner's office in the morning, and the funeral directors too. There must have been a post-mortem, and then they would have released the body to the morticians. I'm going to bed. I have to be sharp for all that.' And he climbed the stairs alone, Ty looking wistfully after him.

Cass stayed on, staring into the flames. Her euphoria gone, she looked dog tired. I put my glass of mulled wine into her hand and she gave me the ghost of a smile.

'Sorry we ditched you at the church. It took longer than we thought.'

'No, no worries. You had bigger fish to fry.' I remembered, suddenly, saying this to Abbot Ridley. *Call me Ishmael.*

'You got back all right though?' She indicated us all with a gesture of her glass. 'Evidently you did.'

'Ish.' We all looked at each other. I was loath to give Cass something else to think about, but I wanted her take on the Curious Incident of the Dogs in the Night-time. 'Actually we were . . . chased . . . through Longwood. By dogs.'

She sat up. 'By Brutus?'

'That's what we thought at first, but no, not him. Dozens, maybe hundreds of dogs. Smaller than Brutus, but loads of them. We *literally* got dogpiled.'

She rolled her head around on her neck in the way really tired people do. 'I think you must have been imagining it.'

'But you have dogs here, don't you? And I saw more coming yesterday from my window.'

'Yes. We're building up a pack.'

'What for?'

'We used to ride to hounds at Longcross, but we haven't done so for many years.'

'What's riding to hounds?'

Shafeen said shortly, 'Foxhunting.'

'Ah.' I frowned. 'Isn't that illegal?'

She shrugged, a shrug that told me something I knew only too well – that on de Warlencourt land, the de Warlencourts made the laws. Thinking back to last year's weekend of blood sports, I supposed I should be grateful that Longcross was lowering the prey down the food chain to just foxes. 'Louis decided to revive it, and we're building up the pack for a Boxing Day meet here at Longcross. We're breeding from Henry's hounds – Arcas, Ladon, Tigris and the rest.' She clicked her fingers smartly. 'Actually, I bet it was foxes who came for you. There's loads of them in the woods. That's why we're bringing back the hunt.'

'Foxes don't hunt *people* though, do they? It's the other way round.'

'What about all those urban foxes chewing kids' arms off in Fulham?'

'That's babies,' I said. 'And besides, this was definitely dogs.'

'But they're all kennelled for the night. They can't get out.'

'Well, I think they *did*.'

She got up wearily. 'Come with me.'

I shot the others a look and followed Cass out into the night.

I stayed very close to her, under her de Warlencourt protection, all the way to the stable-yard. We were literally going to the dogs. When we walked under the stone arch the beautiful red roses were black. We went through to the kennels and looked through the bars of the kennel doors, like we were the ones in jail. But it was the dogs who were firmly locked in. And so many of them. Seriously, it was like *101 Dalmatians* in there. Hundreds upon hundreds of dogs, all curled up cosily, all fast asleep with only the occasional twitch or thump of a tail as they dreamed of chasing rabbits. It was actually super-cute, or it would have been if *we* hadn't been chased through the woods earlier.

'Who has the key?' I asked.

'Perfect. And –' she reached inside her collar and tie – 'me.' She wore a key on a chain, and she dangled it in front of me like a hypnotist. 'And I was with Father Wright.'

'Perfect could have let them out,' I insisted doggedly.

She sighed. 'Let them out, got them all into Longwood to wait for you outside the church, then corralled them all back in again, and got them all to sleep?'

'I know it doesn't seem likely but . . .'

'Greer,' she said, her voice of command back again, 'it's been a long night. Yes, we were chased by Brutus through a tunnel, and of course that made you edgy on the way back. Can we just put it down to an overactive imagination?'

I knew what we'd experienced, but I wasn't about to argue with Cass at one in the morning. She was, after all, the boss. 'Sure. Let's go to bed.'

* * *

We all went up the stairs and dropped the girls off at their rooms. Shafeen was staying in the queen's bedroom again, his old room from last year, and on the doorstep he drew me inside.

'What are you doing?'

'Greer,' he said, 'do you really want to be alone tonight?'

I thought about going back to Lowther, and the scrutiny of Jeffrey's glassy eyes.

'Don't worry,' Shafeen said as he closed the door. 'I'll sleep in the chair. We don't have to be in the bed together.'

I'd missed him so much, and spent all of that evening being so afraid and so relieved in turns that something clicked in me. I'd felt just about every emotion you could name that night. It was time to feel *this*. I put my hand up to his cheek. 'But what if I want to be?' Then I kissed him, and the way he kissed me back told me that I didn't have to worry about Cass any more.

Queen Elizabeth may have slept in that bed.

But we didn't.

Scene iv

Things were just getting interesting when there was a knock at the door.

Shafeen rolled off me. '*Damn.*'

He put the bedside light on, and I blinked at him. 'What time is it?'

'2 a.m.'

I groaned. 'Maybe they'll go away.'

'Greer,' whispered Nel's voice urgently from outside the door.

I threw back the covers, shrugged on a robe, padded to the door and opened it a crack. 'How did you know I was in here?'

'Durrr,' she said. 'Come on. Bring the code pages. And Shafeen.' Her eyes were shining with excitement.

'What is it?'

'I think I might've figured it out.'

'Figured what out?'

'The code, dummy.'

Shafeen and I followed her out of the door. Halfway down the passageway I stopped outside Louis's room. 'Should we get the twins?'

Nel hesitated for a split second, then said, 'No. Not them. They've got enough to process tonight.'

But just as we turned into the wing of the house where we girls were staying, a figure blocked our path.

'Where are you going?'

I must have jumped about a metre in the air. When I came down again I clutched at my heart. '*Jesus*, Ty.'

She stood there, arms crossed, legs slightly apart in a Peter Pan stance. We weren't getting past her.

We all started to bullshit.

'Um . . . I had a bad dream,' I said.

'And I'm taking her to get some water,' put in Nel.

'Me too . . .' said Shafeen lamely.

'Uh-uh,' Ty said. 'No. Enough.' She wagged a forefinger at us. 'It's truth time. You guys are up to something, and I want to know what it is. Whatever it is, you're doing it without the twins,' she narrowed her eyes, 'and I bet you forgot I was even here.'

Shafeen, Nel and I looked at each other guiltily. She was right. We had. We'd consulted on whether to wake the twins, but we hadn't even thought about Ty. Ty had her answer. For a second, she looked unbelievably hurt. Then she raised her chin, every inch Queen Cynthia. 'You know, I'm not some token black character in your little drama. I'm not just here to ask questions and get things wrong, so you can all get them right. I just got chased through a wood by a pack of dogs, same as you. I just sat and tried to decode Act Five, same as you. But you have this little Secret Squirrel trio thing going on, and something happened last year that no one is telling me. So wherever you're going, *I'm* going with you.'

I looked at Shafeen and Nel, my old conspirators from last year. We'd always been a three. But they both nodded.

'Fair enough,' I said. 'Let's go.'

Nel's room was more austere than mine or Shafeen's. It was dark, and furnished in bronzes and chocolate browns, and had a creepy dog head on the wall above the fireplace. Presumably someone's favourite pooch had been rewarded for a lifetime of devotion by having its head chopped off and mounted on a plaque. I remembered that last year Nel had taken the thing down. This year she was stronger.

She led us to her desk. Her light was on and her phone lay on a bunch of papers on the blotter. She sat down in the chair and we all stood around her.

'So I was noodling round on the Internet,' she said, 'looking up codes and stuff. I was interested in that keyword thing. Apparently decryption with a keyword is called a plaintext attack, and it works like this.' She showed us a piece of paper. 'So you have the alphabet, and you have the displacement cipher, just like we said before. You slip the alphabet one place to the right.'

A B C D E F G H I J K L M N O P Q R S T U V W X Y Z
B C D E F G H I J K L M N O P Q R S T U V W X Y Z A

'So far, so simple,' I said.

'Yeah, but then we have to find the right keyword. That's the hard bit,' said Ty.

'That's exactly what I thought,' said Nel. 'But it was simple when I just thought about it.'

She wrote four letters on the paper.

DOGS

She looked up at us. 'Has to be, doesn't it?'

My heart started to beat faster. I bit my lip. She was absolutely right.

'So, I wrote out the key like this with the keyword added:'

```
A B C D E F G H I J K L M N O P Q R S T U V W X Y Z
D O G S A B C D E F G H I J K L M N O P Q R S T U V
```

'But then obviously there are letters that are duplicated – all the letters in DOGS –'

```
A B C D E F G H I J K L M N O P Q R S T U V W X Y Z
D O G S A B C D E F G H I J K L M N O P Q R S T U V
```

'So you leave those out:'

```
A B C D E F G H I J K L M N O P Q R S T U V W X Y Z
D O G S A B C E F H I J K L M N P Q R T U V W X Y Z
```

Nel pointed to the pages in my hand. 'All we need now is to try it. And I'll bet you my dad's jewellery collection that it works.'

I got out the coded manuscript. 'Which bit?'

'Doesn't matter,' said Shafeen. 'If Nel's cracked the cipher, it should all work, whichever line we choose.'

I chose a line at random. Well, not totally at random. I chose a line which had a question mark at the end of it. I'd been intrigued by question marks ever since I'd seen Sherlock Holmes sneaking back from the dead and writing one at the end of Watson's typescript in *A Game of Shadows*. So I isolated the question from the manuscript and wrote it out.

It said:

WMUJSRTIAANDSMCTEDTTUQLASDLSOFTTEAA?

'OK. Here goes.' I leaned over Nel, and, using the key, decoded the first few letters. 'W-O-U-L-D. Would! It's would!' I'd never been so pleased to see a word in my life. 'Nel, you little beauty.' I hugged her hard from behind. The next two letters deflated me a bit though, as they didn't seem to fit.

S-T
WOULDST

'Don't freak out,' said Nel. 'That could just be the beginning of the next word.'

'No,' said Ty, 'It's wouldst, an Elizabethan word. It's the past tense of "will". Carry on.'

I did. And this is what I got:

WOULDSTTHOUKEEPADOGTHATTURNEDANDBITTHEE?

'Split it up,' urged Shafeen excitedly.

'Well, I'll be *damned*,' I breathed.

We stared at the line for a moment. 'OK, chaps,' I said, never moving my eyes from the paper. 'Copy out the key and take a couple of pages each, and then decrypt your pages onto notepaper. Have we got enough pens? Yes? OK, let's get decoding.'

With Shafeen and I on the bed, Ty at the desk and Nel on the floor, we spent a concentrated hour with our heads swimming with letters. We did three pages each and Ty, who seemed quickest of us all, did four. By 3 a.m. we had thirteen pages of handwritten play stacked up on Nel's desk.

Act Five.

I looked at the others. They all looked back at me. We all had a fragment of knowledge, a few pages of the final act in our heads, secrets half revealed. But now we would put them together.

At last we were to find out what was so damned dangerous about *The Isle of Dogs*.

Scene v

'How shall we do this?' I asked. 'Read it in turn?'

Nel shook her head. 'If we do that it will take all night.'

'How about a read-through then?' I said. 'A table read, like they do for movies.'

'But we don't have all the actors,' said Ty. 'Shall we wake the twins now?'

'No,' said Shafeen, so forcefully we all looked at him. 'Not yet.'

'Why not?' I asked, curious.

'Let's see what's in it first.' He looked at me directly. 'Humour me.' He clearly suspected something but I wasn't sure what.

I shrugged. 'If you say so. Then you'll have to read in the parts the twins play.' I indicated in the manuscript. 'Lupo and Volpone.'

'Goddit.'

'And Abbot Ridley's part,' said Nel, blushing even in the lamplight. 'The Earl of Greenwich.'

I shook my head. 'Already dead. He's not exactly going to be making a comeback, is he?'

'I wouldn't be so sure about that,' said Nel, who'd got a later bit of the play to me. But at that moment, all hopped up with excitement, I could have no idea of what we were about to read. We all sat on the four-poster bed, in the light of the dying fire, so we could pass the pages around easily.

It all started innocently enough, with a long speech from the mourning queen. Queen Cynthia was alone in her palace and alone on the stage. It was a speech full of bitter regret, as the queen tried to come to terms with the dreadful birthday hunt in which she'd taken part, ending in her lover the Earl of Greenwich, disguised as the humble peasant Robert Thorne, being torn to death by her own hounds. Ty, despite struggling a little with other people's handwriting, still gave a beautiful reading, her low, musical voice giving life to the words for the first time in hundreds of years. By the firelight, in the midst of Longcross Hall, suddenly what she was saying was all about Henry. The queen wrestled with her own grief, lamenting the lifetime of love she had lost and torturing herself with the thought of what could have been between them if they had had the time to become lovers, and had managed to 'journey beyond a kiss'. But at the same time, she racked herself with the guilt of being an 'unwitting murderer'. Although her situation was massively different to my own, and our fates were separated by centuries, I could feel tears pricking my eyes in sympathy. Shafeen watched me as Ty spoke but said nothing.

He didn't have much to do in the scene because, in this final part, the queen worked alone, acting without the father–son team which had tempted her into the dreadful hunt. In fact, the queen ordered that every hound in the kennels on the Isle of Dogs should be slaughtered. She vowed that she would never hunt again, and decreed that Volpone and Lupo, the counsellors who had tricked her into hunting her own lover, should be banished from court.

Instead, she turned to Canis, the earl's grieving servant, to find her a wise woman from the village for a very dark purpose. And so Shafeen, instead of playing Volpone and Lupo, found himself cast as, for want of a better word, a witch.

And here is where things got really dark. The firelight suddenly became this charmed circle, and beyond that four-poster, the room, with the copper fabrics, the paintings and the dog's head above the mantelpiece – everything went away. I was watching the play as it was being read aloud, as if it were a film. Shafeen was no actor, but his strong clipped voice with just a trace of a Rajasthani accent somehow worked for the enchantress, bargaining for spells with a great queen. So I listened, not to Ty and Shafeen, but to Queen Cynthia visiting a village crone, haggling for the dead.

I listened as the witch told the queen how many years it had taken her to find the incantation that raised the dead, but that in the end, after years of travelling to the Holy Land and back, she had discovered the words in a scroll of the Bible. The queen begged for the secret and the witch named her price but warned her that Greenwich might not come back in a form she could love, or even recognise. The queen, racked with guilt and loss, insisted. The scene ended with the queen paying the crone, counting the price of thirty pieces of silver into her gnarled hand and leaving the hovel with the incantation to raise the dead, a ribbon of paper torn from the Bible, shoved into her bodice next to her heart.

In the dead of night, the queen went into the Underwood, believing she was alone, but followed at a distance by the faithful Canis. By the light of the Dog Star, at the roots of the great oak where Greenwich had been torn apart, she took the incantation from her bodice and, shaking with terror and longing, prepared to speak the secret words aloud into the blood-soaked ground.

'Stop,' I said to Ty.

Our spell was broken, and we were back in Nel's room at Longcross. 'Don't say them. Better not.'

'What arc you *talking* about?' Ty was herself again, a Tower Hamlets girl.

'Don't say the words out loud,' I said, feeling foolish. 'You know, in case you say them in the right way or something.'

Shafeen said, 'What right way could there possibly *be?*'

I looked at him very directly and used his own words back to him. 'Humour me.'

Ty shrugged and missed the lines out. We could all read what they were, but they remained unspoken, for now. We moved on to the next section, which began with a long stage direction. Since I was Poetaster, AKA the narrator, I spoke the instruction aloud.

And this was where the play got even stranger. The stage direction went like this:

(By the arts of the sidesmen, the ground shall be set to bubble and boil, as if it were seething, by use of black fustian or the like cloth, shaken by their hands. From the cloth, as if from the earth, shall rise a player in the form of THE GRAND STAG, a chimera half-man and half-deer. He shall be played by a fellow of more than usual stature, in a riding hood that shall fully obscure his face. He shall have a stag's antlers set upon his brow, to better increase his great height. He shall be a monstrous thing, to strike fear into the watchers, and his entrance shall be marked by the pipe and timbrel, and the drum shall be like to thunder.)

In the following scene, this monstrous thing, this chimera, which was half-man and half-deer, began to speak to the queen. The scene was in prose, with just a couplet of poetry at the end. And what happened in it chilled my very soul.

Queen Cynthia
Who are you?

Grand Stag
Do not you recognise me? Hast known me, in one form or other, these many years.

Queen Cynthia
Art going to kill me?

Grand Stag
Nothing will befall you now. You have our protection.

Queen Cynthia
Who is we?

Grand Stag
The Order.

Queen Cynthia
What Order?

Grand Stag
The Dark Order of the Grand Stag. We protect our own.

Queen Cynthia

Shall I see thee more?

Grand Stag

Every time you hunt.

Queen Cynthia

But I have vowed to hunt no more.

Grand Stag

Each man in his life, and woman too,

Must make this choice as must ye:

Either the hunter, or the hunted be.

'Oh my God,' said Shafeen. 'The Dark Order of the Grand Stag.'

'I know,' I said, feeling sick. 'Stags again. And the Order.'

'Yes,' he said, 'but look at what it's called.' Before I could ask what he meant, he said, 'Who had that page?'

'Me,' said Ty, raising her hand like she was in school.

'Was there anything strange about that part? About how it was written?' he asked.

She looked surprised. 'Yes, actually. There was one word to a line; they were sort of stacked up on top of each other. Let me find it.' She scrambled off the bed and over to the desk, where we'd left the original manuscript. She found the page and showed us.

'Thought so,' said Shafeen. 'Look.'

On the notepaper page, he marked four letters. 'See?'

I looked again.

And then I saw.

The
Dark
Order of the
Grand
Stag

'*DOGS*.' I said. 'And there's the acrostic, at last.'

'How d'you mean, acrostic? What acrostic?' asked Ty.

'I started a few other Jonson dramas while I was trying to choose my play. They all had an acrostic at the beginning, which sums up the play, called "The Argument". That's what put me onto finding the acrostic in the *Lorem ipsum* pages. *The Isle of Dogs* didn't have an Argument at the beginning, it just went straight into the Prologue. I think this is why. DOGS stands for the Dark Order of the Grand Stag. DOGS *is* the acrostic, but of course Jonson couldn't write down his Argument at the beginning of the play. He'd have been arrested before it even started. He kept the message back until the very end of the play.'

'And what is the message?' asked Nel.

'I think I'm starting to guess,' I said with a strange feeling of foreboding, 'but let's find out. Let's let Ben tell us.'

In the final scene, following her dead-of-night conversation with the Grand Stag in the Underwood, Queen Cynthia did a 180. She was happy again, and queenly, and strode about the palace giving orders to Canis, who was back in her employ.

Queen Cynthia

Recall my lord Lupo and his whelp the fox.

Canis

Shall I give the order to slaughter the dogs?

Queen Cynthia

No, by no means. Take this purse of gold and purchase more.
Have my lords and nobles bring them from every shire. And
Canis?
(He turns)
Bring me my bow. A-hunting I shall go.

That was the last line of the actual play. *'A-hunting I shall go.'*

After that, Poetaster (me) spoke an Epilogue, standing with
his head in a noose. Which, although not the weirdest thing
in the play, was still plenty bizarre.

When we'd finished the whole thing there was a long, long
silence.

I broke it. 'Well,' I said, 'I guess now we know.' I didn't need
to explain. I meant we knew why Ben Jonson had been thrown
in jail for writing this play, why not just his theatre but every
theatre in London had been closed, and why every copy of
the play had been burned.

Every copy except one.

'Yep,' said Shafeen. 'That would do it. Witchcraft. The
corruption of a verse from the Bible. And necromancy – raising
the dead.'

'Not just *anyone* doing it. But the queen herself. Ben was taking a shot at Elizabeth as a sorceress who uses black magic.'

'Which is why,' said Ty, 'when he kept just one copy of the play, he wrote the last act in code. Because it was so dangerous.'

'And now we're supposed to perform it,' boggled Nel. 'In three weeks.'

'But we can't *now*,' I said. 'Can we?'

'You must,' said Shafeen. 'How can you not? This is your chance to be part of history.'

I looked at him disbelievingly. 'You know what? This is *just* like the *X-Files* movie.'

'How,' said Shafeen wearily, 'is this like the *X-Files* movie?'

'Mulder and Scully, you know, two agents investigating the paranormal? Mulder believes in aliens, Scully doesn't, and then they swap over?' He folded his arms and listened, used to me by now. 'You were the one actively encouraging me to do this play, and to buddy up with the de Warlencourts. Then you were all like, *no, no, this is too weird*. As soon as you knew about the hunting, you were all, *pull back, you can't do it, the hoofprints of the Order of the Stag are all over it*. Now you think there's this big historical significance and you think we should get stuck in again. Make up your mind.'

'But, Greer,' he said, taking my hands, eyes shining, 'could you *really* stop now?'

With Shafeen's hands warm over mine, I didn't even bother to reply.

The answer was in my eyes.

Scene vi

Dog tired, we codebreakers all slept pretty late.

When we eventually got down to breakfast, the twins were already there. Breakfast was in the Morning Room, with its long windows looking out onto grounds bathed in winter sunshine. Cass, grey-faced, was nursing a cup of black coffee and staring into space. Louis, head down, was shovelling up a full English. I'd gone into breakfast ready to blurt out what was in Act Five, but with one look at them I remembered where they'd been that morning.

'Did you talk to the police and the coroner?'

'Yes,' said Louis. 'We've asked for the report into Henry's death, but that will take a little while, probably till after we've gone back to school. But it doesn't matter anyway,' he said with a beatific smile. 'Turns out Henry was *cremated* after the inquest, and interred in the family bone house. That's why we didn't see the old chap when we opened the tomb. He was a pile of snuff.'

There was something pretty uncomfortable about the way Louis talked about his dead cousin. It was a nasty combo of creepiness and downright disrespect. He seemed to relish the thought of Henry's ashes as much as he relished the Cumberland sausage he popped into his mouth.

'Ah,' said Shafeen. 'I suppose that explains it.' He bent to Cass's ear as he passed her to take his seat. 'I'm really very sorry,' he said quietly, and my heart sort of blossomed – he was showing Louis how the gentleman thing was done. Cass continued to stare ahead, saying nothing.

We all helped ourselves to a sort of buffet of breakfast-type foods underneath these big silver domes. We waited until Betty had been round with the tea and coffee, in equally big and silver pots, then told the twins about Act Five.

Louis was suitably enthusiastic, and seemed to buy the fact that we hadn't wanted to wake them because of where they had to go this morning, but Cass barely seemed to react. Until we got to the bit about the village wise woman, and the dark bargain with the queen to bring back the Earl of Greenwich, and then she seemed to perk up. Something about the resurrection part seemed to interest her strangely.

Encouraged by this, I ventured, 'I don't know how you feel about this, in the light of . . . but I was thinking that we could maybe rehearse this morning.' I looked at the clock – it said noon. 'This afternoon in the Long Gallery, like you suggested, Cass? I mean, it might take your mind off . . .' I tailed off.

'Doesn't matter to me, m'dear,' said Louis, wiping his mouth and standing up. 'I'm happy to do anything.' As he passed her chair, he stunned us all by grabbing Ty and kissing her, joyfully, full on the lips. 'We can rehearse all day if you like.'

And that's exactly what we did.

It was not the easiest, blocking the scene in the Long Gallery, as it was hard to get the atmosphere of the crone's house and the midnight forest with the winter sun pouring into that glorious gilded room. But there was something pretty cool about rehearsing that final, dangerous act for the first time in four hundred years.

Shafeen was going to be pretty busy – as the only one without a part, he was not only cast as the crone but was all set to fill in as the Grand Stag. The twins were occupied with their scenes at the beginning and the end of the act, and of course Ty and Nel were onstage pretty much all the way through. Even Henry was forgotten – but not for long.

When Ty got to the part where she had to say the Biblical incantation to raise the dead, I stopped her again. I laughed at myself. 'Call it superstition,' I said.

'Why not now?' asked Cass. She seemed keen to say the incantation, bordering on the insistent. 'Let me see it?' I showed her the page, pointing out the line with my forefinger.

'Seems pretty harmless.'

'Hmm,' I said. 'I mean, we'll say it on the night, but no need to tempt fate, eh?'

'What do you mean?'

'Well, it's a corruption of a Bible verse. I thought you lot were the Catholic posse?'

'We are. But –'

'Look,' I said, conscious of everyone's eyes on me. 'It's like the Scottish play. Isn't that a thing, that you're not meant to mention it in a theatre?'

'That's right,' said Nel. 'And if you do you've got to spit

over your shoulder and go out of the dressing room and knock three times and all that.'

'Exactly,' I said. 'It just feels like this play doesn't need any more bad luck.'

'I'll just skip it,' said Ty, 'and carry on.'

Cass stamped her foot on the floor. 'Well, I think you're all being jolly silly. I don't believe in superstition. *Macbeth, Macbeth, Macbeth!*' She had real tears in her eyes.

We all went still with shock. Then Louis came right up to his twin and spoke more softly than I'd ever heard him. 'Leave it alone, Cass. It's not like it's going to bring him back.'

Her tears spilled over and she ran, wrenching open the little Alice-in-Wonderland door in the wall, which Henry had taken me through last year, and bounding up the little staircase.

Shafeen made as if to follow her, but I stopped him. 'No. I'll go. You lot take a break.' And I ran after Cass.

I had something very particular to ask her.

Up on the roof it was stunning, the acres of silvery, mismatched levels like some medieval platform game, and the sun setting beyond the park and sinking into Longwood like a red eye closing. The grounds of Longcross were perfect, bathed in the rose-gold light. I had vowed not to set foot outside since we were chased through Longwood by a pack of hounds, but this didn't count. This was the way to see the gardens, and the woods, not at ground level with dogs snapping at your heels. Whatever Cass said, I was still convinced that had happened. We couldn't have *collectively* imagined it, could we?

Just as I thought of Cass, I saw her, hunched on the roof at the front of the house, exactly where Henry and I had sat last year. She could have *been* Henry, with her barley-blonde hair ruffling in the bitter wind, and her shirtsleeves and waistcoat.

I sat down beside her.

'Was he right?'

She turned to me, eyes and the tip of her nose red.

'Was Louis right? Did you think *The Isle of Dogs* could bring Henry back?'

'I *know* it can.' She spoke in the present tense, with absolute conviction in her voice.

'So you don't believe in superstition, but you do believe in necromancy?' I sighed. 'I think, Cass . . . I don't know you very well, but I think you have to let him go.'

'What makes you think that?' she said harshly. 'How could you possibly know?'

I sighed. 'Because I think I need to let him go too.' I thought of Shafeen, and of what had nearly happened between us the night before. It was time to draw a line.

'You?' She turned to me.

'Yes.'

She looked back over the park, and the lawn where Henry and I had seen the midnight vixen last year, frozen in her tracks by the sound of our voices. 'I *knew* you loved him.'

I didn't know if I'd call it that, even to myself, but at that moment it didn't seem right to contradict her. She'd just found out that her beloved cousin had ended up in a jar, and if I was having a hard time dealing with it, that could be nothing compared to what she was feeling.

'He's gone,' I said gently. 'And nothing's going to bring him

241

back. Not keeping his room like a shrine. Not a police report. And certainly not a 400-year-old play.'

She sniffed and scrubbed the back of her hand over her eyes and nose. 'You don't know that.'

'Yes,' I said. 'I do.'

It was the second time I'd felt sorry for a de Warlencourt on this roof. I put my arms around her shoulders. She was shivering like a whippet. 'Come on,' I said. 'It's getting late. We should dress for dinner.'

She half smiled. 'I say,' she said. 'You're getting the hang of this Medieval life.'

I smiled back. 'I know,' I said. 'Sad, isn't it?'

Back in the room I hadn't slept in, I packed my stuff, as we were planning an early getaway in the morning to be back for Monday-morning lessons. I had no intention of returning to Longcross ever again. 'With any luck,' I said to Jeffrey as I left Lowther to put my case in Shafeen's room, 'this really is goodbye.'

He looked at me in that knowing, glassy way he had, and said nothing.

Scene vii

Dinner, once again in the Queen's Dining Room under the queen's eye, had an odd atmosphere right from the off.

We were all super-smart once again. I was wearing a teal dress, the colour of peacock feathers, which I'd found laid out on my bed, complete with accessories. Ty was in a bronzey orange and Nel, the pastel queen, was in baby blue. Cass, red eyed, drank heavily from the start. Like the boys, she was wearing white tie. I used to hear this and think that guys were wearing just a white tie and nothing else, but from my Medieval experience of last year I knew that white tie meant a white dress shirt, white bow tie, black trousers and black tail coat. She looked fantastic, and slightly dangerous.

Louis, looking almost identical to her, except he had his blond hair parted on the other side, like a mirror image, was at his most charming. Tonight, by some unspoken arrangement, he sat at the head of the table, and Cass right down at the foot, where he'd been the night before. Louis was firmly the king in waiting, the knowledge that Henry was a little pile of grey ashes giving him the certainty that he would inherit the earth in approximately four weeks.

For the first few courses no one talked about the play. Two nameless, interchangeable footmen revolved around us in the half-dark, putting down full plates, clearing empty ones and filling glasses in a seamless, fluid dance. We all politely chit-chatted about Christmas and what we were doing (de Warlencourts: Longcross then skiing; everyone else: normal family stuff) and our exams, and what we Medievals were hoping to do next year, etc. But as the night grew later and the candles burned lower, inevitably we began to talk about the play.

'I can't believe he got away with it,' said Nel as Betty cleared the plates and one of the anonymous footmen (so if you follow the rules of *Galaxy Quest*, they'd be the first to die in a gun fight) came round and refilled the glasses. 'Ben Jonson, I mean. He insulted William and Robert Cecil, the father–son team who were running the country, calling them Catholic-hunting dogs. He insulted the Earl of Essex, the queen's favourite. I mean, the earl is the nicest person in the play, but he's still pretty shallow and gold-digging. And Ben even throws shade at the queen, saying she took part in a death-hunt (even though she was, technically, an innocent party) *and* was a sorceress who raised the dead.'

'I don't think he *did* get away with it,' I said. 'Abbot Ridley said he was thrown in jail.'

'And they closed the theatres. Not just the one the play was in, but all the theatres. He pretty much got them all shut down.'

'That happened to Shakespeare too,' said Ty. 'With *Macbeth*. They were worried that Shakespeare got the witches' spells from, well, real witches, and that they were real spells and would make bad shit happen. That's why the play is considered so unlucky, even to this day. That's why they do all that crazy stuff we were discussing earlier.'

She looked at Cass quickly, uncomfortably, remembering that this discussion had led to Cass storming off. 'I mean,' she tailed off, 'I'm not saying that actually happened.'

'It did,' said Cass. 'That's exactly what happened.'

'What, with *Macbeth*?'

'No. Well, maybe. I don't know about that. But it certainly happened with *The Isle of Dogs*. That's why they shut the thing down.' We all fell silent, listening. 'Not the slander, or even the treason. The necromancy. The raising of the dead.' The candles flickered in a sudden draught, lending even more of a ghost-story vibe to her speech. 'They found that the play was making weird stuff happen.'

'Like what?' asked Nel, interested.

'When it was performed in London, people would go home and find their lost loved ones alive. A woman who had died two days before came back to life when her husband got home and spoke to him. A mother whose stillborn child started to move in its cot. A grandmother laid out for burial, who woke up not understanding why there were coins on her eyes. Everyone thought it was witchcraft, but it was the play.'

'Crap,' said Louis. 'Back then they didn't understand things like comas. That's why there are scratches inside coffins. People would wake up buried.'

Cass pointed at Louis with a white finger. 'You know *nothing* about it, Louis.'

He sat back in his chair and took a drink of his wine, fully in control of the situation. 'Then why don't you educate me?'

'Ben Jonson was acquainted with this fellow called Dr Dee, who was all mixed up in the occult. Years later, he – Jonson, I mean – wrote a play called *The Alchemist*, and everyone thought the main character was based on Dee. Apparently Jonson got his wise woman's incantation for *The Isle of Dogs* from Dee, who knew all about the Witch of Endor. His wise woman is based on the Witch of Endor.'

'Who the hell,' said Louis, spitting the words, 'was the Witch of Endor?'

'She,' said Cass, her eyes glittering, 'is the only witch in the Bible. A necromancer. She spoke an incantation to raise the dead. They are the words in the play, the words you lot wouldn't let Ty speak.'

'If you think –' began Louis.

But I cut across him. 'How come you know so much about the play?' I asked. So far as I knew, the first time Cass had heard about *The Isle of Dogs* was when I'd brought it to that first drama class at STAGS. 'I thought —'

'*What* a load of old shit,' interrupted Louis in his turn. 'If you're going to go on about this – witches and spells and all that bollocks – I'm going to bed.' And he got up from the table so suddenly that the cutlery in front of him jumped. We all jumped too.

Cass stood up, a lot more slowly and a lot less steadily. The two twins were facing each other across the table, their clothes, and their opposite-parted hair, made them look like reflections of each other. No – not a reflection – Cass looked much the worse for wear by this point. She looked like the dodgy painting of Ben Barnes in *Dorian Gray*.

'It's happened before,' she said, in a suddenly sober, low voice – a voice that sounded exactly like Louis's, as if he'd thrown it across the room like a ventriloquist. It was chilling. I looked from one to the other. 'You don't know,' she warned. 'You've no idea.'

Louis threw down his napkin, a gesture I've only ever seen in movies, and strode down the table past her to the door. She clutched at his sleeve to stop him. 'I tell you,' she protested, louder now. 'It's happened before.'

'You're *drunk*,' he said, with the utmost contempt.

Then Cass did a weird thing. She pulled Louis to her by the sleeve she held, and kissed him on the lips.

It wasn't a snog or anything. It wasn't like there were tongues. But it was still weird to see a sister kiss a brother like that.

For a moment he let it happen, then he pulled away. Cass collapsed in her chair, distraught.

Louis looked equally upset. 'For God's sake. I can't do this any more.' He turned back.

'Ty, you coming?'

Ty looked at him and then at us, torn. Then she seemed to make a decision. 'Yes,' she said. 'I am.'

I couldn't let this play out. I got up and followed her into the hall. I held her sleeve just as Cass had done to Louis, who had gone ahead, stalking up the stairs. As she turned back I said what I'd wished someone had said to me this time last year.

'Ty, you can't seriously be thinking of a future with Louis.'

'Why not? Things are changing. Look at Meghan Markle.' She put her hands on her hips and cocked her head on one side, in what I was coming to learn was Ty-in-defiant-mode. 'You think I'm not good enough for him?'

'No, of *course* not that. Quite the other way around. You've got to admit he's a little . . . off. Look at how he was about Henry's ashes.'

'Greer,' Ty lowered her voice, 'my mum cleans hotels during the day and offices at night. She has to feed four kids and a smart meter. She pays off one loan shark with another. So *yes*, I'm thinking of a future with Louis.' She looked up the stairs after him. 'Gotta go.'

I thought about this. I was from a middle-class background with a dad in the media. I'd never been short of anything and *I'd* been knocked sideways by the prospect of being mistress of Longcross. Who was I to judge Ty?

I let go of her sleeve and watched her bound up the stairs after Louis, graceful as a deer.

Scene viii

When I went back into the Queen's Dining Room we all clustered around Cass.

Nel and I took the chairs either side of her and Shafeen sat half on the table, like one of those casual newsreaders. 'Cass,' I said gently, 'what did you mean, that it's happened before? What has?'

She had her head on the table now. She looked up, unsteadily, then plonked her chin on her hand. She looked at me as if she'd never seen me before and smiled. It was so *weird*. At that point Betty came into the room, saw us all crowded around Cass and started to back out.

'Betty,' said Shafeen with the command that he and the Medievals seemed to have been born with, 'bring some coffee. Strong and black.' She went at once, closing the door again.

It was just us, in the Queen's Dining Room. Just us and the queen. Elizabeth I watched us with her hooded green eyes – but it didn't matter if she heard our secrets; she couldn't tell.

'Are you saying that the play has raised someone from the dead?'

She nodded, her great eyes fixed on me.

A chill travelled all the way down my spine. 'How do you know?'

She put her forefinger unsteadily to her lips, squashing them unnaturally into a duck's bill.

Nel said, 'Do you mean those people in London? The ones who came alive after their loved ones had seen the play?'

She shook her head, finger still on her lips, then took the finger away. She held it up, a centimetre away from her thumb. 'Someone a *little* closer to home.'

She leaned in close to my ear and said, in this massively loud stage whisper that everyone heard, 'It was *Nazereth de Warlencourt.*'

I closed my eyes, and spoke with them closed. 'Are you *actually saying* that this play raised your ancestor from the dead?'

'Yes. Yes. Yes.' She nodded, so many times and so rhythmically that I thought she would put herself to sleep – literally nod off.

'But Nazereth de Warlencourt was Gabriel Spenser.'

'Yes.'

'And Gabriel Spenser was *in the play.*'

'Yes.'

'So he wasn't dead *then.*'

She started to laugh, in this odd, shaky way. 'Obviously.'

I was getting nowhere. Shafeen had a try.

'Cassandra?' he barked. Her head snapped round, and I wondered if she'd been told off using her full name as a child, the little girl I'd seen in Henry's arms. 'When did Gabriel . . . Nazereth . . . die?'

'He was killed in a duel after the play closed.'

'And if the play closed, how did it bring him back?'

'It was a very special performance.'

'By whom?'

She looked at us, wide eyed. 'Ben Jonson, of course. Who else?'

The three of us looked at each other. 'Ben Jonson brought Gabriel Spenser back to life?'

'Yes.'

'But . . . why?'

'Because he was the one who killed him.'

At that moment Betty came in with the coffee on one of those huge silver trays. She placed it before Cass in such a practised way that it hardly made a sound on the polished oak table. She vanished just as soundlessly, in that way she had.

We could barely wait for the door to close this time. Cass looked at me, and I looked back at her, trying to process the fact that Ben Jonson might be a murderer too.

'Ben Jonson killed him? How?'

'In the duel.'

'What were they duelling about?'

'Nazereth felt that *The Isle of Dogs* insulted the queen. The queen had been his guest at this house, and after the play was performed our family fell out of favour at court. As you might imagine.'

'No shit,' I said.

'Jonson had been in the army, in the Low Countries, so he could really fight. He killed Nazereth – or Gabriel as he was known – in Hogsden Fields in London.'

'And then what?'

'He was thrown in jail for the second time in his life. But this time it was serious. He was going to hang.' She flapped her hand at me. 'That's why there's a rope at the end of the play. Remember? There is a noose hanging down and Poetaster . . . Ben Jonson . . . *you* . . . puts his head in it to speak the Epilogue.'

'Maybe he knew what was coming down the track if he put on this play,' I said with a shiver.

Then Nel said, 'But it was a *duel*. They both must've agreed to fight. Aren't the rules different in that case?'

Cass shook her head as if she would shake it off. 'Doesn't matter. Even if he didn't *mean* to kill Nazereth, he still killed him. He was still a murderer. And that's what should happen if you murder someone, isn't it? Trial and punishment.' Her eyes were boring into me. It definitely felt at that moment like she knew how much I (we) had to do with her beloved cousin's death.

'So what happened?'

'He . . . he dodged the noose somehow and was freed with the help of Esmé Stuart. Jonson was mortified, racked with guilt. He couldn't countenance the idea of being a murderer. He brought the play to Longcross and performed it over Nazereth, and raised him up. It was said that Nazereth spent the rest of his life here at Longcross.'

The chill spread – now I was shivering.

'Didn't anyone realise?' asked Shafeen.

'How?' said Cass. 'There were no photographs then, no – what is it called . . . what is it called . . . what is it called?' She banged her hand on the table, making us all jump. '*Social media*. Nobody really knew what anyone looked like, unless they'd met them. There was no one to put together Nazereth de Warlencourt, Lord in the North, and Gabriel Spenser, a penny player on the London stage.'

'So he just lived happily ever after?'

She wagged her forefinger again, in front of my face. 'Not quite. He was changed, evil. He began to hunt. But not just deer.' She lowered her voice to a whisper. 'The legend goes that he started to hunt, well . . . peasants, if you can imagine something so horrid.'

I looked at the other two. 'It just so happens that we *can* imagine that.'

'According to the legend, he styled himself the Grand Stag,' said Cass, in her stride now. 'The hunting continued, and the play remained in the library here all these years. Except the fifth act, which stayed in the family tomb where Nazereth had been laid. The tomb was supposed to be opened last year to lay Henry to rest, but now I don't think it was. Now I think that it has remained closed all this time, with the last act kept safely buried. I think Jonson left it there so no one could do what he did ever again.'

'Then why didn't Jonson burn it or something if he was so worried?' asked Nel.

She gave a small smile. 'He was a playwright. When it came to the crunch I imagine he couldn't bear to destroy it. I guess he thought that some of the writing was good. You know: *Either the hunter, or the hunted be,'* she quoted sleepily, her head beginning to loll onto her shoulder.

'What did she say?' I prompted.

'*Either the hunter, or the hunted be,*' repeated Shafeen.

'It's from the play,' said Nel softly.

'I know,' I said.

'I know *you* know,' said Nel, not taking her eyes from Cass. 'But how does *she* know?'

'Well . . . the rehearsal . . .'

'No,' said Shafeen slowly. 'We stopped when she ran out onto the roof. We never got to that bit. I never got to play the Grand Stag. That line is the last line in the play, bar the Epilogue.'

'Cass.' I'm not proud of this, but I did shake her a little bit. Nel lifted the coffee to her lips. 'Cass, how did you know that line of the play?'

She snapped awake. 'I don't. I didn't,' she said. 'I never.' She looked to all of us in turn, a deer surrounded. Now *she* looked afraid, at bay.

'Cassandra,' I said softly, 'you were the messenger, weren't you?' I put my hand on her shoulder. 'You gave me the play in Lightfoot. It's OK. You can tell us.'

She breathed out as if she'd been holding her breath for a long, long time.

'Yes,' she said. 'I found the play in the library, last year when we were here for the funeral. There were only four acts, and I didn't know where the fifth was. I knew it was somewhere here, but not where, and then, last night, we found it. And now it's complete and everything is ready.'

'Ready for what? Why give it to me in the first place?'

She was drunk enough to be honest. She looked at me with huge blue-grey unfocused eyes. 'Because it has to be *performed*,' she said, as if it was the most obvious thing in the world. 'I told you. That's part of the ritual.'

The word *ritual*, over and above the strangeness of what she was saying, made me more afraid than anything.

'But *you* could have put it on. With your brother and family.'

'No, you don't understand. A person can only be brought back by the person that killed them. That's why the queen in the play brings back the Earl of Greenwich. That's why Ben Jonson brought back Gabriel Spenser. And that's why –' she pointed her finger at me unsteadily and actually touched my nose – '*you* have to bring back Henry.'

I recoiled as if she'd hit me.

'Is that what you think?' I whispered. 'That I killed your cousin?' It was the first time I'd actually said it out loud.

'Didn't you?'

'*No*. What makes you think that?' I looked at the others. Now it was our turn to be afraid. How much did she know about that night at the top of the waterfall? How could she possibly know?

'I just do. I know you were all here that weekend. And I know you were the last one to see him. I just got a feeling.'

I started to breathe again.

'I know you didn't mean to and I know you're sorry. And I know you loved him.' In that moment I couldn't look at Shafeen. 'And that's why you're going to help me.'

I felt really sad then. There was something very wrong with Cass if she actually thought that the play could bring Henry back. I said, very gently, as if she might break: 'But this is just a legend, a spooky family tale. Admittedly it's a good one, but it's still a ghost story. Surely you can see that.'

'Can *you*? Do you believe in ghosts, Greer?'

Suddenly everyone's eyes were on me. And the queen, bone white and luminous, stared too from the Longcross Portrait.

'If you don't believe, why did you make Ty skip that line?'

I couldn't answer that, especially under the dark gaze of Shafeen. But luckily I didn't have to. Cass crossed her arms on the table and dropped her golden head onto them. She was asleep.

'We won't get any more out of her tonight,' said Shafeen. 'Let's get her safely up to bed, and then hit the hay.'

Between us we bundled Cass up the stairs, pausing at the top. 'Where do we take her?'

We all knew that Cass and Louis had been sharing a room at STAGS, and they'd probably been doing the same at Longcross. But now Ty was with Louis, what happened? In the end we took Cass down the passageway to a room called Fenwick, the one she'd gone into the afternoon before. The bed was pristine, and there was no luggage on the floor or clutter on the dressing table. I'd have bet this was the first time she'd been on this bed. Because there were no night clothes to put her in, Shafeen politely stepped outside while Nel and I took off her jacket, tie and trousers. We rolled her onto her side – 'Recovery position,' said Nel. I put a wastepaper basket by the side of her bed, just in case, and filled a glass of water from the carafe to put by her.

I smoothed a lock of hair from her forehead and felt, suddenly, enormously sorry for her. She looked like one of the Lost Boys.

Before we left her, I drew the curtains against the dark.

Scene ix

Just as we'd done the year before, the three of us went back to the Queen's Chamber (Shafeen's room) with more questions than answers. But this time we weren't going to discuss someone dying. We were going to discuss someone coming alive again.

And, just as we'd done the year before, we all sat on the four-poster bed, the bed that Elizabeth I had slept in. Then we had watched all the crap that the Internet had to offer, bathed in the blue light from the ambulance on the drive outside. This time, it was lightning that illuminated the room. There was the mother of all storms brewing outside.

'God,' I said as I climbed up on the bed. 'Where to start?'

'I've got one,' said Shafeen, loosening his tie. 'I wonder how Cass knew that line from the play.'

'Because she'd read it. We established she was the messenger.'

'But we also established that she never had the last act. She needed us to help her find it.'

'And it was us who decoded it,' added Nel. 'She wasn't there. And when we rehearsed it, we never got that far. She ran out onto the roof.'

'Could Ty have told her?'

'No. They're not close, have you noticed?' said Nel. 'It's some sort of tussle over Louis.'

'Ty might have told Louis,' said Shafeen. 'I wonder how much *Louis* knew about the play.'

'They share everything,' said Nel.

'They *used* to,' I replied. '*I* wonder how Cass found out all this stuff about Ben Jonson and *The Isle of Dogs* since Henry died. Who told her?'

'All this wondering,' broke in Nel, 'is dumb.'

She snapped open her sparkly clutch bag decisively.

'What are you doing?'

'What we should have done in the first place. Googling Ben Jonson.' She fished in her bag and got out her shiny rose-gold Saros 8S smartphone. I knew Nel's phone would be, A) close to hand, and B) charged – she was much more of a Savage than me. Smartphones were her birthright and she found it much harder than me or Shafeen to stay Medieval. I remembered a time, of course, when I'd been very glad that she hadn't been able to leave tech behind: when I saw the torch of the Saros shining out above Longmere Lake. Then she'd searched for ciphers and found out how to crack the coded Act Five. It looked like tech might be saving the day again.

'Ooh, there's a notification. It's for you. That is, it's your Instagram.'

'I must still be signed in,' I said. 'Give it here.' My thumbs a little out of practice, I clicked the little paper aeroplane for direct messages. The message was from **mrs_de_warlencourt** – I'd all but forgotten about her. It read:

I think you might find this Quite Interesting.

And underneath it was a URL:

https://www.youtube.com/watch?v=GMWsKtaJoG8

And a number:

15:24

'What's 1524?' Nel said. 'A date? That would be Tudor, right?'

'No,' I said, ever the film nerd. 'Look at the colon. It's not a date. It's a *timecode*.'

Shafeen leaned into my shoulder. 'Click it then!' he urged. But I already had.

The URL directed me to YouTube, and an episode of a quiz show I vaguely knew of, called *QI*. There was this woman host, that funny one from *Bake Off*, and a panel with two comedians on each team. When the clip began, the host asked a question about something called the 'neck verse' and then played a piece of beautiful choral music, which seemed very familiar. We all barely breathed through it, until one of the comics made a joke and broke the tension. 'What's this got to do with anything?' whispered Nel. 'What's that song?'

'Wait,' I said, clutching her arm. Because I'd just heard something that grabbed me. *Ben Jonson the playwright* . . .

I scrolled back along the timeline a little, and this time we listened intently. And this is what we heard:

Woman host

Ben Jonson the playwright, in 1598, avoided being hanged for killing an actor in a duel, an actor called Gabriel Spenser, by pleading Benefit of the Clergy.

Scottish beardy comedian

(Cutting across her) I know a bit about Ben Jonson. He murdered someone that he acted in a play with, the play was called *The Isle of Dogs*, and it was so offensive that it was suppressed so completely that nobody's ever worked out what it was about.

Woman host

We don't even have a record of the script or anything.

(Clip ends)

'Yes, we do,' Nel said grimly into the sudden silence.

'Let's watch it again,' I said, and we did.

'OK,' I said, 'so Ben Jonson got out of being hanged, just as Cass said – and that was a year *after The Isle of Dogs*.'

'It must have been,' said Shafeen. 'Like you said to Cass, Spenser was in the play.'

'I'm getting in a muddle with the timeline. Let's Google Ben anyway.'

'Where do we start?'

'Where does everyone start?' I said. 'Wikipedia.'

'OK.' Nel expertly tapped away, no clumsy thumb syndrome for her. 'The entry's pretty long.'

'Just give us the bare bones,' said Shafeen, 'until you get to the meaty bits.'

'All right,' said Nel. 'Here we go. *Early Life:* son of a bricklayer. Westminster School. Supposed to go to Cambridge but didn't. Fought as a soldier in Flanders. Became an actor. *Career:* ah, here we go. Look.'

We all huddled together around the shining screen of the Saros 8S. And this is what we read:

In 1597 his play *The Isle of Dogs* was suppressed after causing great offence. An arrest warrant for Jonson was issued by Queen Elizabeth I. Jonson was jailed in Marshalsea Prison and charged with 'Leude and mutynous behaviour'. Two of the actors, Gabriel Spenser and Robert Shaw, were also imprisoned. A year later, Jonson was again briefly imprisoned, this time in Newgate Prison, for killing Spenser in a duel on 22 September 1598 in Hogsden Fields (today part of Hoxton). Tried on a charge of manslaughter, Jonson pleaded guilty but was released by benefit of clergy, a legal ploy through which he gained leniency by reciting a brief bible verse (the neck-verse), forfeiting his 'goods and chattels' and being branded on his left thumb with an M for manslayer.

One bit jumped out at me straight away. 'There's the neck verse again!'

'There's a hyperlink,' said Nel.

'Punch it, Chewie.'

Nel did, and by the flickering of her eyes we could see her speed-reading the text. 'OK, so here's the deal,' she announced.

'Apparently if you were literate and condemned to hang, you could save your life by speaking a verse from the Bible. If you could do that, in Latin, that meant you could be tried in a church court instead of a normal one, as a clergyman – you know, a vicar or a priest. The loophole was known as "benefit of the clergy".'

'Even if you *weren't* a clergyman?'

'Yes. You just had to read this one verse from the Bible, and that was what was known as the "neck verse".'

'And what's the verse?'

'Let's see. It says:

The biblical passage traditionally used for the literacy test was Psalm 51, *Miserere mei, Deus, secundum magnam misericordiam tuam* ('O God, have mercy upon me, according to thine heartfelt mercifulness'). Thus, an illiterate person who had memorised the appropriate psalm could also claim the benefit of clergy, and Psalm 51 became known as the 'neck verse'.

'Read it again,' I demanded suddenly.

'All that? Can't you –?'

'No,' I said urgently. 'Just the Latin bit.'

Miserere mei, Deus, secundum magnam misericordiam tuam.

I had to take a beat. 'It was on the family tomb,' I whispered.

'How d'you mean, on the tomb?'

'Nazereth's tomb. Henry's tomb. Those words were carved into the stone over the names. Remember?'

'Oh yes!' exclaimed Shafeen.

'But . . .' I frowned. 'Why *that* one?'

'Why that one what?'

'The psalm that saved Jonson's life carved onto the tomb of the man he killed. Isn't it a bit of a coincidence?'

'Well, it's a psalm, isn't it?' said Nel. 'A verse of the Bible. There are always verses of the Bible on tombs, aren't there?'

'I don't know – are there?' I said. 'It seems a bit neat.'

Shafeen looked over Nel's shoulder at the verse. 'It's very short, isn't it? The neck verse, I mean. Surely anyone could just memorise it and save their lives.'

'Well, that's exactly what happened, according to this,' said Nel, 'so in the 1700s they closed the loophole. But Ben Jonson wasn't one of those people. He wasn't just gaming the system. He was highly literate.'

'So reading gave him his life back. He was literally saved by the book.'

'Yes. *But* remember he lost all his money and property, and was branded on the thumb with an M for manslayer.'

'Ouch.'

'Yes. But I imagine more than the pain would be the disgrace. For the rest of his days, everyone would know he took a life. If you're *literally* branded a killer, it must make it that bit harder to climb up the social ladder.'

'But it can't have affected him *that* much,' I said. 'He wrote all his most famous plays after his trial, and made his fortune. In his lifetime he was more famous than Shakespeare.' Not for the first time, I felt a warm admiration for Ben Jonson. 'Abbot Ridley said he became Court Poet under James I.'

'Hmm,' said Shafeen doubtfully. 'If Abbot Ridley said it, maybe we should look that up for ourselves.'

'What do you mean?' demanded Nel defensively.

'Well,' I said, 'he did say that Esmé Stuart was a woman.'

'Are you saying he was deliberately misleading you? Because I –'

'Calm down. I'm just saying maybe he knows more about drama than history. Now, thanks to this lovely little puppy –' I tapped the Saros 8S smartly with my fingernail – 'we can look stuff up ourselves.' This convinced Nel. She had always been an advocate of Savagery. 'You always made the point that being Medieval is all very well, but it limits your access to information,' I reminded her.

'And that's why they do it,' said Nel. 'Look at China. It's got two great walls. The first one you can see from space, but the other you can't see at all. It's a firewall, stopping social media and censoring the Internet. Because people with information can rise up and rebel. STAGS,' she said, 'is China.'

'Exactly. We could've found this out in five minutes, right back when this all started,' I said. 'But we didn't. Why?'

'I guess we're institutionalised,' admitted Shafeen.

'Like the baby elephants,' I murmured.

Shafeen nodded. 'We were tethered and never learned to break free.'

'What?' asked Nel.

'Nothing. Let's get searching. The Friars can't stop us now.'

On that ancient bed, the storm now howling outside, we went, once again, on an Internet binge. We were drunk with our ability to search anything – the world, once again, was at our fingertips. With the light from the phone illuminating our faces, and the lightning outside intermittently lighting the room, we went down a rabbit hole of Ben Jonson-ness.

We looked up his childhood, his schooling, his military record. We looked up his friends, his plays and all his poems. Then we looked up his trial, his eleventh-hour escape from the noose. And the neck verse. We watched a million different versions of the psalm, set to music by someone called Allegri. It was the same haunting piece that was in the clip from *QI*, sung by choristers from King's College, Cambridge, to Cambridge, Indiana. There was even a video of these American college kids all doing the neck verse. One even rapped it.

Then Shafeen said, 'Hey, why don't we search up Longcross? It would be interesting to see if there's any presence at all online, or if it's too Medieval for that.'

Nel tapped in the search term. 'Well, there's a village in Surrey called Longcross. And a film studio. But as far as *this* Longcross goes . . . Oh, actually there's quite a few results – loads actually – but they all relate to Henry's death. They're all the news reports from last year, or those creepy fan sites.' She scrolled away. 'Hang on – here's something different. Oh. It's just the "Longcross Portrait" of Queen Elizabeth I.'

'Let me see.' Shafeen grabbed the phone. 'Painted in 1586,' he read, 'artist unknown. Oil on canvas . . . oh, here's a photo.'

He clicked the picture and did that reverse-pinch thing that you do to make things bigger.

Then his eyes widened and he dropped the phone on the bed.

He leaped up, wrenched open the door and propelled himself through it. Nel and I looked at each other and followed him.

Scene x

At first, we didn't know where Shafeen had gone.

We were trying to be as quiet as possible and obviously didn't want to put any lights on. The last thing we wanted was to run into Perfect and his hellhound doing the security sweep before bed. From down here we could hear that the storm was sending the dogs in the stable-yard mad. Every time there was a peal of thunder or a flash of lightning, they howled. It was properly eerie. And you could hear, now, just how many of them there were. It sounded like there were hundreds. This was quite different to the Disney-esque, cute 'n' cuddly pile of pups that we'd seen in the kennels. These dogs sounded serious. They were baying for blood. I couldn't speak for Nel, but I was ready to run back up the stairs, when the lightning lit up the atrium and we could see Shafeen's back disappearing into the Queen's Dining Room.

Nel and I followed him and found him lighting all the candles in one of the silver candelabras on the dining table.

'Shafeen?'

He didn't answer.

Nel tried. 'Shafeen? What's going on?'

The candles warmed the room into light.

Shafeen said, 'Help me.'

He went over to the Longcross Portrait and began to heave at the huge dark-wood chest that was covering the bottom of the frame. Nel and I exchanged glances. 'Come *on*!' he hissed.

We leaped forward and began to pull too. For a time, it seemed like the chest just wouldn't move, but eventually we felt a bit of give and were able to pull it forward. It made quite a row as it scraped over the floor, but luckily the thunder covered the noise. Eventually we managed to angle it to the side, so the whole picture frame was revealed.

Shafeen snatched up the candelabra and held it to the painting. There was Elizabeth, enormously powerful, staring out of the frame in her green hunting gown. Red hair the colour of blood, jade eyes as direct as an arrow, skin white as bone. Shafeen moved the candelabra down to the bottom of the queen's skirts.

And what he revealed I still have a hard time believing to this day.

It was a pair of feet. But not dainty female feet shod in satin as you might expect.

They were the cloven hooves of a stag.

We stood back as if stunned. None of us even spoke for probably a whole minute. You couldn't call it silence though – with the storm howling outside and the dogs howling in reply.

'How did you know?' I said at last.

'You can see the stag feet on the photo online. And look – there's something else.'

He moved the candlestick a little to illuminate the ground between the queen's deer feet. There on the forest floor were words tooled in gold. They read:

'*That's* where Cass got it from.'

'Yes. She must've grown up with this picture.'

'I wonder when they decided to put the chest in front of it.'

'I'm guessing Friday night,' said Shafeen darkly. He carried the candelabra over to the end of the dining table and sat down. We sat across from him.

He put his hands palms down on the table, fingers spread. 'Here's what I think went down: Jonson got wind of the death hunts happening at court, using the hounds kept on the Isle of Dogs. A way for nobles to have some jolly fun while getting rid of undesirables in society. He wrote a thinly veiled play about it. Then Gabriel Spenser, an actor in the play, blamed him for ruining the family's relationship with the queen, who had been a guest at Longcross. Spenser challenged Jonson to a duel. But Spenser was really Nazereth, a foppish, airy-fairy noble, and Jonson was an ex-bricklayer and ex-soldier and tough as shit. So Jonson killed Nazereth.'

'And then what?' I asked. 'Raised Gabriel Spenser – AKA Nazereth de Warlencourt – up from the grave?'

'The bringing-back-from-the-dead thing I don't buy,' said Shafeen. 'That's just wishful thinking on Cass's part – she's grieving, and damaged by some fairly major brother issues, and reaching for any scraps of comfort that she can find. She's turned an old family myth into gospel.'

'But do we think that Nazereth and Gabriel Spenser were the same person?' asked Nel.

'I'm prepared to believe that Nazereth had an alias,' I said.

'It was the only way a young nobleman could go on the London stage. People did it all the time. Some scholars even think Shakespeare was an alias for the Earl of Oxford, don't they? But I don't think Jonson came here and did some sort of comeback show in the crypt for one night only and brought forth a dead man.'

'Then how did the play get to Longcross?'

'If Jonson wasn't ever here then it could've been Nazereth's own copy,' suggested Shafeen. 'Maybe from the London house. Or perhaps Esmé Stuart brought it here – if there is a painting of Stuart in the library, he might well have been a family friend. If he knew Jonson, he surely must've known Spenser/Nazereth.'

'And how, Einstein, did the fifth act get into the tomb?'

He paused. 'That I don't know. Perhaps the family buried it with him. People do get buried with letters or personal effects, don't they?'

'Yes, but usually lockets and stuff,' I said, 'Not pages of code.'

'Or,' said Nel, 'maybe the family thought it was something secret and dangerous that had to be literally buried. It was in code, remember. And they wouldn't know it was an act of a play. It was just gobbledegook.'

'Maybe. That whole play thing is a bit of a mystery. I can't get my head around it,' admitted Shafeen. 'But the painting is a different matter. That's tangible evidence. In a time when pictures were stuffed with allegory, it is very suggestive that Elizabeth was implicated in the death hunts, and worse.'

'What,' Nel asked, incredulous, 'could be worse?'

Slowly, hairs rising on the back of my neck, I said, 'That Elizabeth I was the Grand Stag herself.'

Scene xi

'Are you actually saying,' asked Nel, 'that the Queen of England was the head of the Dark Order of the Grand Stag?'

'That's what the painting is saying,' said Shafeen. 'That's what Ben Jonson is saying.'

'But what even *is* the Order?' asked Nel. 'Why's it got a different name to the one Henry told us about? That was just the plain old Order of the Stag.'

'I think I might know this one,' I said. 'You know how Scientology has all these levels, and Tom Cruise and John Travolta are up at the very top?' I got all animated. 'I think DOGS is the ruling order of the Order of the Stag. It's an order *just* made up of the Grand Masters: the guys – or gals – in *charge* of the Order of the Stag. Cass said Nazereth used the title. And it passes down from one dude to the next, like the Dread Pirate Roberts.'

'Who the hell is the Dread Pirate Roberts?'

'You know, in *The Princess Bride*.'

'I never saw it.'

'You never saw *The Princess Bride*? Nel, it's –'

'Greer,' she said, 'focus.'

I did. 'OK, OK. In *The Princess Bride*, there's this character called the Dread Pirate Roberts. He's this fearsome pirate, but it turns out that he isn't one person. He's *lots* of people.'

'You mean, like a team?'

'No. It's a title, and it passes down from one Dread Pirate Roberts to another. They keep the name, because everyone already dreads it and the new guy doesn't have to build up a reputation from the start. The *outgoing* Dread Pirate Roberts elects the *next* Dread Pirate Roberts.'

'You established that the Old Abbot was the Grand Master, or the Grand Stag as he'd have been known in Elizabethan times,' said Shafeen. 'But who is it now?'

'Why does it have to be anyone?' I said. 'What if it really is all over? Henry died, then the Abbot died. There was no new hunting book in the library, remember? And you can't assume the twins are guilty by association, you said so yourself. Maybe that's it. End. *Finito*.'

Shafeen looked doubtful. 'It was Henry himself who said the Order would carry on. They were his last words.'

Nel said, 'But if what you're saying is true, and the Grand Stag is a title that is passed on only after death, it wouldn't be an Order, would it? Because there wouldn't be more than one Grand Stag at a time. I think the meetings would be pretty boring.'

'Hang on a second,' I said. 'In *The Princess Bride* –' They both started to groan theatrically, making the candles flicker. 'No, wait, wait: the Dread Pirate Roberts *doesn't* die. He retires. He passes his title on to the hero, Westley, and goes off into the sunset to enjoy his wealth. What if you are Grand Stag for a fixed term, like being President? Then you hand it on

271

to a successor. But all the living ones come to the meetings, like a ruling council.'

'Yes, but the Old Abbot *did* die . . .'

'Or so we *thought*,' said Shafeen.

'Oh Jeez,' I said. 'This isn't another resurrection theory, is it? I thought you didn't believe in the whole raising-from-the-dead thing?'

'I don't. But who told us that he died?'

'Abbot Ridley. He got a phone call. We were there.'

'But we only heard *his side*. You're the film buff. Please tell me you've seen movies where someone is talking to no one on the phone.'

I had – a whole bunch. It happened in Hitchcock all the time.

'And that time when we all went in to the Scriptorium to look up Pembroke's Men,' went on Shafeen, 'Friar Waterlow would've known about the play by then. Why didn't he say, *Well, my dear, I hear you've made something of a discovery?*'

'Maybe he never leaves the Scriptorium. He *looks* like he never leaves the Scriptorium. He's practically got cobwebs on him.'

'Yes, but still. Surely he goes somewhere to eat, and to sleep. Surely word would have reached him that you were staging the play, especially as he's head librarian. Surely someone would've said, *I say, old boy, you'll never guess what*. He must've been told. But he didn't say a word to us. He just pointed us to the *Dictionary of National Biography*, nice as pie. And Ridley – why didn't he take the pages off you as soon as you showed him *The Isle of Dogs* and call the British Library or wherever? But he didn't. It's ludicrous that he left a schoolgirl to look after something so priceless.'

'Thanks very much.'

'You know what I mean. This whole thing has been *facilitated* by them – the friars. They are all in on it – they must be.'

'But in on *what*? What's the plan?'

'That's just it,' he said. 'I don't know. All I know is, even if they didn't give you the play, they certainly want you to put it on. *Why* is the mystery.'

'This is all dogshit.' Nel appealed to me. '*You* don't think Abbot Ridley's in on this, do you?'

I thought for a moment. 'No. If there is a Grand Stag now, and it's a big, massive, giant IF, I don't think it's him.'

'Well, whoever the Grand Stag is now,' said Shafeen, 'I think we can all agree who it was *then*.' He lifted the candelabra again towards the painting.

I looked back at the portrait. '*Christ*. It can't be true, can it?'

'Yes. There's your matriarchy. But not quite the one you would wish for.'

And that was when I'd had enough. I looked again at those deer feet sticking out of the queen's silken skirt, greasy, gristly, every hair detailed with the thinnest brush, a dark, threatening sheen on each cloven hoof. Of all the things we'd seen and heard that weekend at Longcross, those feet were more scary than anything. Something about them well and truly spooked me. 'Let's go,' I said. 'Let's go *now*.'

'What are you talking about?'

'Just get our stuff, get in Nel's car and *leave*.'

'How?' said Nel. 'It's blowing a gale. I don't want a tree on top of my Mini.'

'Also, we can't just leave without a word. It's just . . . it's just not *done*,' said Shafeen, as always the guardian of good manners. 'And also, what about Cass?' Not for the first time, I thought he liked her. I didn't think it was romantic any more, I was secure enough for that, but I thought he wanted to kind of protect her. 'She was in a pretty bad way.'

I calmed down a bit. I knew, when I really thought about it, that we couldn't actually go, but it was not for any of the reasons they'd said. 'No. It's Ty we can't leave.' Even if she was in love with Louis, there was no way I was leaving her at Longcross, overnight, on her own. There was a pause while we listened to the storm and the dogs howling outside. I said, 'We'll go tomorrow first thing. We were going then anyway.'

Shafeen looked at his watch. 'It's pretty late now, so it's just a matter of hours. Let's get some sleep. But we stay together,' he said, 'all three of us.'

No one slept much in the Queen's Chamber, so we were able to leave quite early in the morning. We all crept downstairs in our uniforms and took our stuff to the car. I had to briefly break my vow not to set foot outside the house again during my stay, but I practically ran the few steps to the Mini. Thankfully, there was no sign of Perfect or Brutus. I kept my eyes ahead as we bowled up the drive, literally leaving without a backwards glance.

I had no wish to say my goodbyes.

This time I was convinced that I would never see Longcross again.

ACT FIVE

Scene i

It was a sparkling winter morning as we drove back through the gates of STAGS.

In the sunshine it was hard to believe in last night's storm. With the daylight, the idea of our whispered candlelit conference in front of that demonic painting seemed unbelievable. The portrait that had turned a queen into a chimera, the priest's hole, the tomb, the neck verse, were like a fever dream. In the cold light of day all the events of that weekend at Longcross retreated like a nightmare into the shadows. STAGS looked amazing; it was England's top independent school, and we were all privileged to be there. I wouldn't have believed in any of the weekend, except for one thing. I had the coded manuscript, the cipher and our transcription of Act Five beside me in my deer-leather satchel.

We all went into the Refectory to catch the end of breakfast. Louis and Ty, who had followed us in one of the estate cars, sat with us. They were wrapped around each other, looking radiantly happy. I had a feeling their little sleepover the night before had gone pretty well. Cass, who had travelled with them, was, not surprisingly, feeling 'unwell', and had gone straight to her room.

We agreed that, as the director of *The Isle of Dogs*, I'd see the Abbot alone to tell him we had found the missing act – little point in all of us piling in there and barking at him at once. So as soon as the chapel bell had struck nine, I took my satchel and walked through the grounds to the Abbot's study. STAGS looked fantastically beautiful that morning, and as I walked up the Hundred Stairs to the drawbridge and over the moat, I thought it looked peacefully benign after the dog-ridden, lightning-shot Gothic-ness of Longcross. I fell into the trap, once again, of thinking nothing bad could happen here.

I knocked on the door of the Abbot's study and went in when bidden. The Abbot was sitting behind the huge mahogany desk, but even though the thing was massive, his height made it look the right size for him. He was writing something and looked up when I came in.

'Write of the devil and she shall appear.'

I'd literally never been greeted like that before.

'Eh?'

He indicated the form he was writing. 'I'm just in the middle of writing your supporting statement for Oxford.'

'All good, I hope,' I joked weakly.

'Oh yes,' he said. 'And I've got my old tutor, Professor Jennifer Nashe, to agree to attend our production of *The Isle of Dogs*. In fact, she can't wait. She's a world-famous Jonsonian scholar, so you can imagine, this is like Christmas for her.'

I'd forgotten his good looks, his straight gaze, his slightly northern accent. That, and the fact that he was in the middle of doing me a huge favour, convinced me once and for all that he was nothing to do with the Order of the Stag, Grand or otherwise.

He screwed the cap on his fountain pen – I suppose the nearest practical pen to a quill STAGS could issue – and used it to indicate the chair opposite him. 'Did you have a good weekend?'

'Ish,' I said, sitting down in the chair.

He put the pen down on my form and clasped his hands. 'Problem?'

'I don't honestly know,' I said. 'But what I do know is that we found Act Five.'

He almost shot out of his chair. 'Where?'

I decided to edit the story slightly. 'In the library at Longcross.' And then, in case he didn't know, 'The de Warlencourt twins' house.'

'Good Lord. May I?'

I snapped open my satchel and gave him the decoded pages. 'We had to decrypt them,' I said. 'Sorry about the pick 'n' mix handwriting.'

You can be sure I watched him very carefully as he read. If this was part of some grand scheme, he would somehow know what to expect from Act Five and be a bit of a cool customer about it. But whatever Shafeen's conspiracy theories, I knew from the way the Abbot's green eyes widened, his nostrils flared and his cheeks began to flush a little that he'd never seen this bit of the play before, had no inkling of what was going to be in it. He showed no more emotion than pure, uncut excitement. His hands even started to shake a little.

When he put the pages down, very carefully on the desk, he

let his fingertips rest on the paper for a moment. 'No wonder,' he said softly, 'it was considered to be so dangerous.'

'I know, right?'

He looked up. 'How exciting, Greer. How exciting for you. To perform this thing in front of your peers, the friars and Professor Nashe too. And there's a good chance that, once we give it to the British Library, they'll call it the Greer MacDonald Manuscript.'

I squirmed a bit. That sounded amazing, but I couldn't take the credit. Plus, I wasn't actually sure I wanted to be associated with such a dark text for the rest of my days. 'Actually it should really be called the Cassandra de Warlencourt Manuscript. It turns out Cass found it first. At Longcross.'

He raised his eyebrows. 'Your honesty does you credit. Although if it was found at Longcross, it may well end up being called the Longcross Manuscript. Things are often called after where they are found – the Dead Sea Scrolls and so on. Still, it's going to be amazing for you – you'll be the first person to direct it since Jonson himself.'

That was actually quite cool. 'A bit more work for you though, if you don't mind,' I said, a bit hesitantly – it felt weird bossing around your head teacher.

'How's that?'

'Well, you'll be . . . if you don't mind, that is . . . playing the Grand Stag. Because your character is, you know, dead. And, the stag is a kind of mutant Earl of Greenwich. Also, you're the tallest person in the play. The tallest person I know, actually.'

He rubbed his clean-shaven chin, thinking. 'Well, if you put it like that.'

He leafed through the pages, written out in our different scruffy handwritings. 'Well, I suppose it's really just that one big scene with the queen in the Underwood.' He grinned. 'And, to be frank, I would wrestle it out of the hands of anyone else.' He shook the pages excitedly. 'This will make history, Greer.'

At that moment, he didn't seem much older than me. Which I guess he wasn't, really.

'Can I see the cipher?' he asked. I handed it to him, with the original coded pages. He looked from one to the other, following what we'd done. He nodded as he read. 'A plaintext attack,' he said. 'Very clever. And this is the keyword?'

'DOGS,' I confirmed. 'What else?'

'Ah,' he said. 'Well, Jonson was very much of his time. A cipher like this one was used in the Lopez Plot, just a few years before he wrote this play.'

'Cool,' I said.

'All right then.' He picked up his pen again. 'So I'll get back to your statement and I'll see you for drama at noon. In the theatre for rehearsal, I presume?'

'Yes. Thanks.'

Then I took a beat. I'd never heard of the Lopez Plot, even though I was doing history. But Abbot Ridley had. He did seem very clued up about history, not just drama. So why had he made that one crucial, howling mistake?

I was going to let it drop. I really was. I was actually on the way to the door. But my big mouth wouldn't let me. I blurted: 'Abbot Ridley?'

'Mmm?'

'When I was asking you about Ben Jonson, the first time, d'you remember we talked about Esmé Stuart?'

He'd already gone back to his paperwork – my paperwork – and spoke to the page in his hand. 'Yes? What about him?'

'Him?'

'Yes.' He put his pen down. 'Are you talking about Esmé Stuart, 3rd Duke of Lennox, 7th Earl of Aubigny? Ben Jonson's friend and patron?'

I couldn't remember all the titles, but I was sure about the last bit. 'Yes. I distinctly remember you said he was a woman. You said "friend and *patroness*".'

He frowned. 'Are you sure? You didn't mishear? Perhaps you were confused because Esme is traditionally a girl's name.'

I had thought that, because of the deadly Esme Dawson. But he'd *definitely* said she was a woman.

'I'm a hundred per cent sure,' I said.

'Oh. Oh. Well, if I did, it was a slip of the tongue. Of course Esmé was a man. He and Jonson were very close, and Jonson didn't like women much, I'm afraid. He said, "Women are but men's shadows".'

'Huh,' I said. Then I just stood there, eyes unfocused, thinking. *Had* I been mistaken? I was *sure* not. I'd even talked about Esmé being a woman to the others.

'Was there anything else? I'm engaged in something terribly important.' It was said with great charm, as he waved the Oxford form at me.

He was totally gaslighting me. I remembered what he'd said. I wasn't going crazy. But he literally had my supporting statement for Oxford in his hand, half written. I wasn't about to piss him off. So I just said, 'Oh, OK. And thanks.' I opened the door to go out.

'Greer,' he called after me. He had a smile in his voice. 'History's not carved in stone, you know.'

I thought that was an odd thing to say then, and I still do, if I'm honest. History might not be carved in stone, but surely whether or not a person from the past was a man or a woman was pretty, well . . . *binary*.

I was still thinking about what he'd said as I crossed back over the moat. Then I dismissed it as something that a freewheeling drama teacher would say, but a history teacher like Friar Camden wouldn't say in a million years.

Still, I'm glad I remembered it.

Because it saved my life.

Scene ii

We all had a study period before drama, in which, technically, we should have been revising. But I went to see Cass.

I hadn't seen her properly since – was it only the night before? – we'd put her to bed at Longcross. She was in a very shabby state then, so I expected to find her looking pretty green this morning.

Halfway across the Honorius Quad, I stopped next to the Jerusalem tree. It occurred to me that I didn't actually know *where* to find her. It was an open secret among us Medievals that she'd been living in Louis's room, but now I wasn't so sure. Louis and Ty's relationship seemed to have taken a big leap forward at Longcross, so I wasn't sure Cass's silken PJs would be on Louis's bed any more.

I turned around and went back to Lightfoot, to Cass's official room. I'd never known her be home, but as I lifted my fist to knock I thought, *She must have used this room occasionally in the last few weeks*. Specifically on Sunday nights when she was drip-feeding the play to me. Now I knew why I could never catch my mysterious messenger in the passageway. Cass was just a few doors down from me – she could have dropped the pages and been back in her bed before I'd even left my room.

I was surprised to hear quite a cheery, 'Come in!'

I did. Cass was over by the windows, with a letter in her hand. She looked pretty well, considering. In fact, she looked *very* well. Her hair was shining in the winter light, her skin was clear and glowing and when she looked up her blue-grey eyes were shining. She waved the letter at me.

'There was no body,' she said. This was the second strange greeting I'd had today.

'What do you mean?'

She waved the letter at me. I could see it was actually a document, quite a few pages stapled together. 'The police report. They sent it here. *Missing, presumed dead*,' she read. '*Body never recovered.*'

'But . . . I saw an ambulance. With someone in it.'

'But you said yourself. You didn't see *him*. You saw a body bag.'

This much was true. 'And you went to the funeral. There *must've* been a body.'

'There was a coffin. But that's not quite the same thing, is it?'

It wasn't. 'Didn't you see the coroner? On the Sunday morning? And didn't he tell you Henry was –' it wasn't easy to say – 'cremated?'

'Yes, but it was a new chap. Not the one who was in charge of Henry's case.'

'Where's *he* gone?'

'No one knows.'

'What d'you mean?'

'They've got a new chap, but the old chap disappeared.'

'*What?*'

'Well, not quite. He retired and moved abroad with his wife. Spain, they think. But no one can get hold of him.'

'And what about the police inspector?

'Same.'

'He moved to Spain with the coroner's wife?'

'No. He's vanished too. And no record of his registration with the police force.'

'Wow.'

'Yes. They are pursuing things with the mortuary, and trying to trace the paramedics who came with the ambulance. But that will take a bit of time.'

Ever seen a film called *Catch-22*? It's about these airmen at a Mediterranean airbase in the Second World War. They had to fly eighty of these really dangerous missions before they were rotated out of duty, and that was the 'catch' of the title. The squadron's doctor explains that you would have to be crazy to ask to fly more missions, but if you refused, that proved you were sane, and therefore fit to fly. My Catch-22 was this: I was as sure as I could be that Henry de Warlencourt was dead, because I had seen him die. In fact, I was the last one to see him alive as his hand had slipped from my grip. I had climbed that waterfall, with him in pursuit, and I, and only I, knew how Reichenbach-high they were. They must have been a good few hundred feet, with razor-sharp rocks all the way down. So no, I didn't think he could possibly be alive.

BUT.

I couldn't say that to Cassandra without giving myself away. I'd lied my ass off at Longcross, first a year ago to that nice inspector who had since mysteriously disappeared, and secondly to all the houseguests this year, saying I'd fallen in Longmere and then come back to Shafeen and Nel at the house. So now there was nothing else I could say without contradicting myself. I was stuck.

I looked back at Cassandra, and thought of the film again. She was either insane or giving a very good impression of it. 'It's a win-win,' she said brightly. 'Henry's either still alive, or he's dead and we bring him back with the play.' She gave me a dazzling smile. This was a different Cass once again – the Day-One-at-Longcross Cass. She'd arrived at the house acting like a queen, and left as the underdog, crushed below the foot of her twin. Now she was on top of the world again.

I sank down on her bed, closed my eyes and pinched the bridge of my nose between my thumb and forefinger. In that moment I made the decision. I had to.

'This is crazy town. We can't do this play.' With a pang I mentally kissed goodbye to a good mark in my drama Probitio, and potentially to Oxford, but I wasn't selfish enough to exploit a grieving girl who clearly had major issues.

Cass knelt by the bed, took my hand away from my face and gripped it, as if she was about to propose.

'But I *want* to. I do.'

'Even though you know it's hopeless?'

'Yes. If we do it, then I'll know.'

'And then you'll drop this . . . this crazy resurrection thing?'

'Yes.'

I took a breath. 'Last year, after Henry . . . passed –' I used the horrible jargon – 'the Old Abbot put me on to this woman

287

called Sheila. She was pretty crap, but she was someone to talk to. She might know about . . . grief counselling or whatever.'

Cass got up slowly, walked to the window and started fiddling with the clasp. 'I don't know, Greer.'

'But you will get help?'

'If it works, I won't need it.'

'And if it doesn't?'

'The same. He'll still be gone, and I'll just have to deal with it.'

I looked at her for a long time. Then I got up too and said, 'OK. Well, it's your funeral.'

Of all the incredibly dumb things to say at that moment, I'd somehow found the dumbest.

Scene iii

I made it down to the theatre at a quarter to midday.

Nel was already there, lighting candles on the stage, and Shafeen was helping her. We'd already arranged that since this was one of his study periods, he could watch the play for the first time in its entirety. And I was glad we had, because I had some pretty deep stuff to tell them. 'Any one else here?'

'Not yet.'

'Good. You might want to sit down for this.'

We all sat on the stage while I told them about my meeting with Cass and the police report. In that circle of candles, we were more like conspirators than ever. The fact that we spoke in hurried whispers, because we were expecting the rest of the cast any minute, only added to the impression.

'Henry *can't* still be alive,' said Shafeen. 'We saw him die. We all did.'

'I know. But I couldn't exactly tell *her* that.'

'And to be fair, we didn't see him *die*, we saw him *fall*,' said Nel. 'My question would be: if he's still alive, where is he?'

I had my own theory about this. I told them about the 'Havisham' room at Longcross, the room that looked as if

Henry had just left it. 'It had his clothes, his scent, his ring, everything. At first, I thought it had just been kept as a shrine to him, you know, like grieving families do? But it definitely looked very lived in. Then again, if he was still there, the twins would know. And they clearly don't. They have such different attitudes to Henry, and neither one would have behaved in the way they have if they knew he was alive.'

'How d'you mean?' asked Shafeen.

'Remember the attitude of the twins to the tragedy, and how very different they were? Even from that first conversation in the Queen's Dining Room, Louis wanted to know if we'd seen Henry's body. He was bummed out that we hadn't; Cass was glad. In the crypt, Louis wanted to look in the family tomb, Cass didn't. And conversely, when we *didn't* find Henry's body, Cass was delighted, and Louis devastated. When we were rehearsing the play, Louis didn't want to say the incantation, Cass did. It all comes from their very different relationship with their cousin. In the picture in "Henry's" room, Cass is embracing him, Louis is scowling. I think Louis hated Henry, but Cass loved him and just can't accept that he is gone.'

'And – even creepier – wants him back,' said Nel.

'But for Louis, the stakes are much higher,' said Shafeen slowly. 'The stakes are Longcross.'

'If Henry is dead, he becomes the heir the minute he turns eighteen.'

'If Henry is alive, he gets nada.'

'He's dead,' said a voice from the wings. Ty walked out from the shadows into the light.

She sat down on the stage with us, joining, uninvited, the

charmed circle. 'When Louis and I went back to his room after breakfast there was a letter waiting for him. He read the letter over by the window. He looked so . . . happy.'

I could see it all in my mind's eye, playing like a movie, because I'd seen it before. A figure in a black Tudor coat, with close-cropped blond hair, reading a letter by a window, and looking up from it with a beaming smile. I'd seen that scene play out only that morning, but with Cass instead of Louis.

'What was in the letter?'

'His cousin's death certificate. From the police.'

'Henry de Warlencourt's death certificate?'

'Yes. The covering letter said that further to the twins' enquiries at the weekend, they were enclosing the death certificate, and they hoped this would be the end of the matter.'

I gaped at Nel and Shafeen. This was nuts. The twin who'd wanted Henry dead was sent a death certificate, and the one who wanted him alive was sent a police report saying that no body had ever been found. Ty was watching us, measuring our response, but I didn't really know what to say.

I wasn't sure how much she had heard of our earlier discussion, but I did know she was totally in Louis's camp. I didn't feel it was up to me to tell Ty what Cass had been sent. At the same time, to be fair to her, Ty had decided to share a discovery with us.

'What do you think of that?' she asked, clearly a bit freaked by the lack of response.

In the end I found something totally truthful to say. 'I think that after centuries of them messing with everyone else, someone's messing with the de Warlencourts.'

And whoever was messing with their heads was messing with mine. I couldn't tell the other three about the doubt – or was it the hope? – that had started to seep into my soul since Cass had told me what was in the police report. A question mark, that tiny, innocent piece of punctuation, suddenly assumed an enormous significance. That single character – a little squiggle and a dot, which meant that something wasn't quite settled, that a case wasn't closed, that an answer wasn't definite – loomed large in my mind and prompted me to think the unthinkable:

I might not *be a murderer.*

The chapel bell struck twelve, snapping me out of my daydream. 'They'll be here in a minute. Whatever the truth of all this, we have a play to perform.'

Nel said, 'Did you show Act Five to Nathani— Abbot Ridley?'

'Yes.'

'Was he surprised? Or did he look like it's all part of the Grand Plan of the Grand Stag?'

'His gob couldn't have been more smacked. I'm with you here – I don't think Ridley is the Grand Stag. He was just mega excited at the idea of putting on the play. He's got his old tutor coming from Oxford and everything. So –' I got to my feet and brushed down my Tudor coat – 'the show must go on.'

Ty got up too. 'What about the lines?'

'Which lines?'

'The incantation. We've never yet read the words out loud. Do I say them today or not?'

I groaned. 'Oh Jesus.'

'No, but really.'

I thought for a minute. And in that minute, the theatre doors opened and Cass herself came in with Louis. They walked in tandem, shoulder to shoulder, no one ahead and no one behind. For the first time they looked like total equals, neither one having the upper hand. They looked more alike than they had ever looked, and for a very particular reason. They were both happy – shiningly, joyfully happy. I wasn't about to upset that particular cart of apples. I turned to Ty and whispered hurriedly, 'Don't say the words properly. Change the order or something. I don't want Cass freaking out at every rehearsal, expecting to see Henry popping up out of the shadows. It would be impossibly cruel.'

She nodded and everyone found their places for Act One, Scene One.

The art types gathered in the wings to do the scenery and the music types tuned up in the minstrels' gallery. Abbot Ridley, after greeting Nel so fondly that she blushed, vaulted easily onto the stage. He said the teachers' catchphrase – 'Settle down everyone' – then went on: 'There's some exciting news about the performance, but I'll let Greer share that. My only role in this – apart from the earl' – people laughed politely, as you do when teachers make jokes – 'is to remind you that this play constitutes two-thirds of your drama Probitio, with the other third being the written exam. So let's see some concentrated effort. And now I'll hand you over to your director. Greer?'

'Right,' I said. 'The good news is, we have Act Five.' I waited for the little ripple of surprise to die down. 'The bad news is, we have just over two weeks left to rehearse. So,' I said, 'no pun intended, we're going to have to work like *dogs*.'

Scene iv

The day itself had arrived.

We'd had all the usual end-of-term stuff like the carol service and the Christmas lunch (goose and all the trimmings – turkey was considered too newfangled and, even worse, American). And now it was time for the end-of-term play. Our play. Ben Jonson's play. *The Isle of Dogs.*

We had indeed worked like dogs since our return from Longcross. The craziness of that weekend had been mostly forgotten in the hectic schedule of the play. As far as I knew, neither Cass nor Louis had heard any more about Henry's case from the police. I never asked – there was too much to do.

We rehearsed over and over until we were sick of the play and knew every line, but there was one section that no one had ever heard out loud. The incantation, a mere couplet of lines, read by all of us but spoken by none, remained the only unsaid part of the play, a little isle of silence amid all the words. For every rehearsal Ty had swapped the real words with the same thing. There had been some chat about what should replace the incantation, and it was Nel who had the idea. '*Lorem ipsum*, of course. The standard replacement text.'

So Ty, instead of the words of power, said, each time: *Lorem ipsum dolor sit amet, consectetur adipiscing elit.*

Then came the day when we first did the play in costume, and the whole production, miraculously, woke up. Having the right clothes and the right props breathed life into something that had become stale and mechanical. It made such a difference for us all to be in our authentic period costumes, shipped in specially from the oldest costumier in London (of course – this was STAGS). My costume was one of the least showy – a plain black doublet and hose and my black poet's cape – but some of the others looked fantastic. Ty looked beautiful, particularly in the green hunting dress, which seemed spookily to bear a very close resemblance to the one in the Longcross Portrait. Abbot Ridley did, I have to admit, look very dashing in his gold doublet and ruff, but it was his costume as the Grand Stag that really made an impression. The first time he came onstage in antlers and a red hooded cowl, I actually felt genuinely scared. The antlers gave him such height, and the cowl so perfectly shaded his face that there could have been any monster lurking beneath that hood. It was not until he spoke that I could actually relax.

We did our own hair and make-up, as there was nothing so modern as a beauty school at STAGS. I was just me, and my black bob was deemed fine for a sixteenth-century male poet (I tried not to be offended by that). The twins' blond hair looked great with their black courtier clothes, and Louis aged himself with some talcum powder in his hair and a few lines round his eyes. We tried a beard on him too, but it fell off with such predictable regularity that I was convinced it wouldn't survive the performance, so we ditched it. In the end, with his white-blond hair and the fine lines around his eyes and mouth, he looked like my fantasy version of Henry's father, Rollo, a man I'd never met and now never would. Ty took the prize as the Elizabethan period's Next Top Model though. She teased out her afro and set it with white pearls in a fantastic up-do that really set her apart.

Props were another thing to get used to – we had some unintentionally hilarious mishaps with people's swords whacking other actors if they turned around too fast, or cups being empty when they were supposed to be full, or full when they were supposed to be empty, or the ribbons of blood not falling properly from the Earl of Greenwich's cuffs as he died. But eventually the play came together, we got used to our costumes and props, and we were as ready as we were ever going to be.

The night before the play I don't think I slept at all. The dress rehearsal had been disastrous – everything that could go wrong did and no amount of people (and there were a lot) telling me this was a 'good sign' could comfort me. On the day itself I got up, grey-faced, went to breakfast, had one slice of dry toast and just made it to the bathroom in time before I threw it up. People wishing me luck made me feel sick. Just looking at the theatre in the distance made me feel sick. Catching sight of one of the many playbills that had been posted up around the school, featuring a stylised black dog's head with red eyes, also made me feel sick. In the end I retreated to my room. That whole day there were no lessons; the students were just packing anyway, as most people were going home for Christmas the following day. Some, who had parents coming to the play, were leaving that night. I wasn't leaving until Sunday, but as I looked from my window down the drive I wished I was going home right that minute. My dad was away in Madagascar filming until just before Christmas, so I was going to stay with Nel. Nel, at breakfast, had been as grey as me. Only Shafeen, who had nothing to do with the play except as an audience member, was chipper. 'This time tomorrow it will all be over,' he said. But for once I found that reliable old cliché of absolutely no use. And it was also, as it turned out, wholly inaccurate.

The day crawled by, and it seemed impossible that seven o'clock would ever come. But of course it did, and I found myself, along with my very jittery fellow cast members, huddling in the wings of the De Warlencourt Playhouse. Abbot Ridley, looking proper in his Earl of Greenwich gear, walked out to centre stage. The theatre looked completely different, and completely terrifying. All the candles were lit, and the familiar smell of warm beeswax filled my nose. But the really different thing was the audience. I'd never seen the theatre full before, and the concept of an audience was utterly horrifying. And not just any audience, but the very well-heeled, tweed-and-pearls audience made up of mega-rich STAGS parents. The thought of them judging me made my heart sink into my black deer-leather boots. I almost didn't hear the first bit of Abbot Ridley's speech.

'It's not often that we get to be part of history,' he began, 'but those of us on this stage this evening have that chance. For tonight, for the first time in four hundred years, we'll be performing *The Isle of Dogs*, a play by playwright, court poet and contemporary of Shakespeare, Ben Jonson. The play was performed only once, in 1597, after which it was immediately supressed, and every copy destroyed. Every copy,' he said, 'except one.' You could feel that he had the audience in the palm of his hand. No one breathed. 'The sole remaining copy was found at Longcross Hall by one of our students, Cassandra de Warlencourt, who is a descendant of one of the play's original cast members, Gabriel Spenser, to whom this theatre is dedicated.' I looked sideways at Cass – I hadn't warned her that she'd be getting credit for this. She looked pink and pleased. 'The play is directed by another one of our drama students, Greer MacDonald, who first brought the play to the school's attention. I'm also delighted to say that we are joined tonight by Professor Jennifer Nashe, of the University of Oxford.' He indicated a kindly-looking woman with merry eyes and grey hair in a bun, sitting in the front row. 'Along with her impeccable credentials as the world's foremost Jonsonian scholar, she also possesses the much more dubious distinction of having been my tutor at Christ Church. I can't tell you how many times she had to deal with my pathetic excuses for late essays.'

The lady with the friendly face smiled, nodded and rolled her eyes in a way that made everyone laugh.

'I won't try your patience any longer, but instead will let the play speak for itself. Considered seditious, treasonous and even demonic, you must judge Jonson's work for yourselves. I'll just say the words that no one thought they would ever say again – it's my honour to present *The Isle of Dogs*, by Ben Jonson.'

Under the cover of applause, I grabbed Ty's sleeve. The

Abbot's speech had really got to me. For the first time I was really getting how significant this was – I was the first person to direct this play since Ben Jonson, and I had to do it right. And that meant word for word.

Every word.

Ty turned to me, her eyes wide with excitement. 'What?'

'The lines. The incantation. Remember to say it properly. Tonight's the night.'

'Are you sure? No *Lorem ipsum*?'

'No.'

'You're certain?'

'Yes.' And then I said another of those really dumb things. 'What's the worst that could happen?'

Scene v

And then it was time for my entrance.

The candelabras were winched to the ceiling by the backstage dudes, with only one left hanging to light my Prologue. I honestly don't think I've ever been so scared as I was then, walking out onto the stage in my black poet's cloak, in the character of Poetaster, ready to speak the Prologue to *The Isle of Dogs*. I know this will sound weird when you remember that I was fished out of Longmere lake the year before, and then chased through a priest's hole by a hellhound two weekends ago, and then through Longwood by a pack of dogs. But this – looking out at all those white blobs of faces, and hearing the supressed coughing and shuffling and rustling of programmes all fall still, and the expectant, endless silence – was far, far worse.

I opened my mouth and nothing came out. I tried again and made just a very little trembly sound. Then, in all those white faces I saw one, just one, brown one. Shafeen. He put up two thumbs and smiled. And on my third try, I could speak.

On the Isle of Dogs
In days of old
Lies a palace made of gold.
The great queen who resides there
Is pursued like a hind,
For privilege, office, titles, land;
All princes chase her for her hand.
Who shall catch her?
The lapdogs who live upon her chairs,
Or the common hounds,
Baying from distant shires?

I'd done it. I'd got through the first speech. And halfway through, I'd begun to sense something new – that a play is changed by an audience. I stopped being afraid of them and talked to them like a friend. Now they seemed benign, friendly, shoring me up and willing me on. And when I'd finished, something weird happened. They started to clap. Of course, I hadn't expected that, and we hadn't rehearsed for it. In the end I just bowed with a flourish, flung my cape over one shoulder and turned to make my exit, hoping the candle guys wouldn't lower the candles for Ty's entrance too fast. Luckily I just about got off the stage before the musicians began to play the queen's fanfare. I was back in the wings. I drank about a gallon of water and turned to watch Ty.

And that's when I knew it was going to be all right. She was fantastic. Wonderful, marvellous, beautiful Ty – I blessed her in the name of St Aidan and every other saint I could think of. She was being utterly brilliant. She got through her first soliloquy as well as she'd ever done it. In fact, better. She too was changed by the audience. They were making her even better. I felt like she was a proper actress – the rest of us were only playing at it.

I was really proud of the staging in Act One – the art types had done a great job with the scenery backdrops of a gilded palace, and all the drama-class extras looked great in their Tudor gear. Blocking-wise, I'd done something I thought was quite clever – whenever Queen Cynthia spoke one of her 'asides' to the audience, all the crowd actors would freeze in their positions, mid-conversation, with a goblet halfway to their lips, or in the middle of a dance, hands clasped high. At the end of the soliloquy, the crowd would come back to life and move around the queen, her courtiers once more.

When Ty was done being beautiful and bored, it was time for the twins' entrance. They played the scene really well, trying to get Queen Cynthia to look favourably on a marriage proposal from the King of El Dorado, and in return promising her diversion in the form of her favourite pastime, hunting. I watched the twins scheming, planning to build up the pack of dogs on the isle, and for a moment I left the world of the play and was back at Longcross. Which one of these two had built up the pack of dogs in the stable-yard, those dozens, maybe a hundred dogs that had chased us through Longwood and howled at the storm?

The scene changed and I was on again, introducing the Earl of Greenwich. Abbot Ridley made his entrance and he and Ty were off, playing well against each other as they always had. Then came the part when he insulted father and son Lupo and

Volpone, calling them curs, and they made their dastardly plan to destroy him. Watching them plotting together was chilling. I had an uneasy feeling in my stomach. We'd assumed that the twins were pitted against each other just because they didn't share a room any more and they didn't share an opinion about their cousin. But what if they were working together?

They'd be invincible.

Scene vi

Act Three belonged to Nel.

She was by turns funny and touching as Canis, and the way she played her devotion to the earl, following Abbot Ridley around like a little dog, made me scared. Nel was a good actress, but not that good. She was feeling this for real.

Then came the part when Queen Cynthia and the earl row because she won't tell him the secret she is keeping. The earl thinks she is being unfaithful, but actually she is planning the birthday hunt at which he is to be guest of honour. Then we were on to the bit where Volpone and Lupo meet with the leader of the Catholic rebels – five more of our drama class, in peasants' rags – and arrange to meet them in the Underwood on the night of the birthday hunt. That done, we were into Act Four, and I couldn't believe how fast the play was going. I actually started to feel sorry, sorry that, although I was sure others would perform *The Isle of Dogs*, maybe the National Theatre, maybe even the RSC, the likelihood was that I would never be in it again. This was quite a flip from earlier that day, when I would have given anything to drive away from the school and home for Christmas, skipping the play altogether.

Act Four had always been the most challenging act in terms of staging, as the action took us from the palace to the Underwood. The act opened with Queen Cynthia alone, lying in the middle of the stage under a coverlet. This was the first scene after the interval, and it made a pretty great contrast to the scene before, with the glory of the Palace of Placentia and all the elegant courtiers.

Ty moved a little, sat up and stretched her arms above her head, as if she had just woken up in the morning. Her afro was combed out and she was wearing an all-in-one body suit the colour of her flesh. For a moment it did really look like she was naked. The audience audibly gasped, until they twigged that she was actually perfectly decently dressed. I had a lot of time for Ty in that moment. That girl had nerves of steel to be that exposed in front of all those people.

As the queen stood, her ladies-in-waiting came in bearing her gown, ready to dress her. But before they could, Greenwich burst in demanding an audience. The ladies all screamed and tried to cover the queen's nakedness. Cynthia lost it and banished Greenwich from her presence.

After the bedroom scene came another bit of staging I was quite proud of. The Earl of Greenwich stormed out of the palace by jumping off the stage and into the auditorium, up the aisle actually between the audience. It was there that Volpone and Lupo accosted him and told him there was a way for him to see the queen again, by disguising himself as Robert Thorne and meeting her in the Underwood by the great oak. The big advantage of all this stuff taking place in the audience was that it left room for the pretty major bit of scene shifting to be done to take us to the Underwood and the meeting with the Catholic rebels.

The art types put the forest backdrop into place, and the audience started applauding again, this time for the scenery. It was pretty impressive, with the twisting blackthorn trees and green leaf cover, created in three different perspectives to give it a spooky depth of field. I swelled a little bit with pride in the art guys. *You wait*, I mentally told the audience. *If you like the daytime Underwood, you'll love the night-time one*.

The twins were now back onstage, meeting with the Catholic rebels, and I knew that Abbot Ridley would be out the back of the theatre, frantically changing into his peasant's rags. He re-emerged at the end of the scene, striding down the central aisle as Robert Thorne. Then he did the other thing I was quite smug about – he slowed his walk right down as he approached the stage. There was no one else but him and the forest. I wanted to give an idea of foreboding, and was always a bit worried he would look like Superman doing the slo-mo power walk, especially with his Henry Cavill resemblance. But in the moment it really worked – the candelabras were winched slowly up to the ceiling to simulate nightfall, and the musicians struck up this mournful, minor piece, and it all added to the feeling of dread.

We saw 'Robert Thorne' climb onto the stage, and then, like zombies, the Catholic rebels appeared from the trees. Then, and this was the really cool bit, the backlit eyes appeared in the branches. First one pair, then another, then hundreds, those little red burning coals. The audience clapped again, but I didn't so much feel proud that time as afraid – it was too much like our night in Longwood. Even more so when the dogs came out, in their black bodysuits and the fantastic stylised black masks with red eyes that the art students had created. The Catholic rebels scattered and the dogs leaped on Robert Thorne, nine or ten of them carrying him shoulder high, tearing at him. This was the bit that almost never worked in rehearsal, when the dog actors had to release the red ribbons from Abbot Ridley's wrists and ankles so that the coils unfurled down to the stage like blood. Luckily it all worked perfectly this time. Then came the sound of horses offstage and Queen Cynthia entered. Recognising her lover, she knelt in the blood, cradling his head, sobbing, *You are my Actaeon, I your Artemis*.

Much more gutting, though, was Canis's reaction. Nel crawled up to her new master – we'd decided that she should be on all fours like Mary, Queen of Scots' dog after her execution – and laid her head on the dead earl's chest. I felt a prickle at the back of my eyes, and I swear I actually heard someone in the audience sob.

Then, unbelievably, we were into Act Five, the final, darkest act, appropriately for a finale that had been found in a tomb. It began in the Palace of Placentia, with Queen Cynthia wailing and tearing at her clothes, demented with guilt and grief. She banished Lupo and Volpone, saying, *Wouldst thou keep a dog that turned and bit thee?* and ordered the slaughter of all of her hunting hounds. Then, disguised in a battered travel cloak, Cynthia charged Canis to take her to the wise woman in the village, to purchase a spell to bring back her love.

The scene-shifters quickly put in place the props for the wise woman's hovel, and Cass, shrouded in grey cowled rags, rocked rapidly in a wooden chair. Since we couldn't exactly co-opt science major Shafeen into the play, we'd decided that Cass, who'd been banished at the beginning of the act, could throw the costume over her courtier's clothes and play the witch.

The whole interaction was lit by a single candelabra overhead, throwing crazy shadows through the hovel from the creepy objects the witch collected around her – a stuffed crow, a skull, a mammet made of sticks. The scene was playing well, but too fast for me. The transaction was made – spell for money – and the queen tucked the scroll into her bodice. We were rapidly coming up on the incantation, the moment when the apparently 'genuine' spell that Jonson had bought from Dr Dee, the spell of the Witch of Endor, who had lived in the days of the Bible, would be spoken. Every word we'd painstakingly decoded at Longcross brought us closer, closer, until we arrived at the moment itself. After I spoke the introduction to the Underwood, I caught Ty's eye as I passed her in the wings.

This was it.

Scene vii

Ty, as Queen Cynthia, was alone in the Underwood.

The single candelabra had been lowered to the ground, where it sat like a fire. The queen was a silhouette, clothed in darkness. She felt in her bodice for the scrap of paper the witch had given her in exchange for thirty pieces of silver.

Ty unfurled the little scroll and, for the first time in four centuries, a human voice spoke the incantation, culled from the Bible, the words of the Witch of Endor:

> *Thou shalt speak out of the ground, and thy speech shall*
> *be low out of the dust, and thy voice shall be, as of one*
> *that hath a familiar spirit, out of the ground, and thy*
> *speech shall whisper out of the dust. And thou shalt be*
> *brought up.*

Ty spoke the lines beautifully, considering she'd never said them before. They rolled about the round theatre, power in every syllable. Ty closed her eyes and conjured the spirit out of the ground with her hands, and the last word – 'up' – was almost a shout.

I held my breath. I looked at Cass in the wings, hands clasped like she was praying, her face white and pinched, her top teeth biting her bottom lip. I could see she expected, really expected, Henry to come walking down the central aisle of the audience.

And at that moment, so did I.

But nothing happened. No angels crying, no thunderclap, no creature birthed from the bowels of the earth. The moment passed with nothing but a heartbeat of silence before the music from the minstrels struck up to herald the entrance of the Grand Stag.

After the anticlimax of that moment, I felt like it was all downhill. The rest of the play would be easy, even the transformation of the Earl of Greenwich to the Grand Stag. And it was – Abbot Ridley and Ty smashed it. His entrance, in the red robe and cowl with the stag horns on his head, drew gasps from the audience, and Ty got just the right mix of fear and longing as she talked to her lost, changed love. The Grand Stag's cold, deathly voice as he convinced his queen to become a killer in order to preserve herself was chilling. He uttered the infamous words, *Either the hunter, or the hunted be*, and she held his gaze for a moment, nodded once, then turned and left the forest.

The Grand Stag stepped back into the trees. The light below him was extinguished, and by a trick of the staging, and the branch-like design of his antlers, he disappeared, becoming one with the trees.

The scene changed again, back to the Palace of Placentia. But this time the gilt was dimmed, the queen looked old and evil, the courtiers all lined up in their robes, now tattered, the gold frogging coming off their sleeves, their jewels tarnished, their white ruffs soiled. They all faced away from the audience, the queen alone looking forward. She reinstated Lupo and Volpone, and father and son came in grovelling. She ordered Canis to save the dogs and feed them the meat meant for her courtiers. She told him to bring her hunting outfit, uttering the final line, *A-hunting we will go*. That was the moment that all the courtiers turned around at the same time, to face the audience, and it was revealed that they were all wearing dog masks.

The audience applauded again, and, delighted with the reaction and flooded with sheer relief that nothing had gone wrong, I stepped downstage ready to speak the Epilogue, high-fiving everyone in the wings as they came offstage. Behind the scenes I saw Nel laughing up into Abbot Ridley's face as he put a congratulatory hand on her shoulder. She then leaned up, and, euphoric, kissed him quickly on the lips. It was just a peck, but it was still a kiss. I groaned inwardly. I thought then I might have some pieces to pick up at Christmas. But I couldn't think about that now. In the middle of the stage a noose dangled, lowered from above by the art types. I walked centre stage, and, as I'd done in our many rehearsals, put my head into the noose. It was, of course, deliberately loose, and was just meant to symbolise the danger the poet had placed himself in by telling this story. I began the traditional appeal to the audience for leniency, which brought the play to a close:

If I have offended,
Put rope about my throat
And place me in the ground
In just a hard-wood coat.
Tell the revel masters
That I am in the earth
And tell the playhouse owners
To put an end to mirth,
But then ask yourself this
Before you let me go:
Was it really I
Who offended so?
What about these Dogs
Who live upon this Isle,
Who run affairs of state
And hide behind a smile?
And ask yourself yet more
Once I am gone away,
If they have lost their target
Who is now the prey?

Throughout this final speech something odd began to happen. The noose was getting tighter and tighter around my neck, and by the end I could hardly choke out the final lines. I stumbled over the final words, and *prey* was more of a whisper than the near-shout it was meant to be. I looked up. What the hell were the art dudes *doing*? Had they put the noose on one of the candelabra winches? Were they pulling me up instead of the candles? They were going to strangle me. But beyond the darkness I couldn't see anyone on the platform where the winches were. Just blackness. I felt myself begin to lift and went onto my tiptoes to ease the pressure. I looked out into the applauding audience, desperately trying to communicate what was wrong, but just saw rapt, appreciative faces who'd enjoyed their deliciously dark night and thought this was all part of the staging. I searched for Shafeen and found him. He alone looked concerned, and sat forward. I could see his mouth form the word *Greer*. The blood was trapped in my head and started whooshing in my ears. My lungs burned as I gasped for air. I tried to say *Shafeen*, but it was only a croak. I felt as if my head was going to explode. Shafeen now leaped to his feet. But it was too late.

Before he got to me, I'd be gone.

Scene viii

What happened next I will never forget as long as I live, and whatever they say in the hospital, I know it was real.

I could feel myself being lowered to the ground until first my toes, then the balls of my feet, then my heels were on the stage. The pressure of the noose loosened marginally, but it was enough. The rope was still there, but I could breathe. It felt as tight, or as loose, as (I imagine) a dog collar. The blood subsided a little from my head. I still had the noose around my neck, but my feet were flat on the ground. I opened my eyes.

About six feet in front of me, at the very lip of the stage, was Abbot Ridley, dressed as the Grand Stag, facing me. He loomed enormously tall, with the antlers growing out of his head like branches and his face a pool of blackness under the red cowl. But that wasn't the weird thing. The weird thing was that there was another Grand Stag next to him, someone smaller and slighter. And next to him, another one, a bit taller again. In fact, there was a circle of Grand Stags surrounding me, all in red cowled cloaks, all wearing antlers on their foreheads, all looking inwards. All the candelabras were now burning in a charmed circle around them, and their antlers flickered in the flames. Each of them had crossed their black gloved hands on their chest, and on each of their left hands flickered a ruby ring, kindled by the candlelight. I looked beyond the forest of antlers into the dark auditorium. The audience was gone, all gone. When I realised that, I was more afraid than I'd ever been in my life. I suddenly wanted Shafeen very badly.

The tallest figure raised his ruby-ringed hand to his hood to sweep it back from his face. I knew, with terrible foreboding, that I was about to see the face of Abbot Ridley, the newest Grand Stag. But I was wrong.

As the hood was drawn back the face that was revealed belonged to the Old Abbot.

I tried to protest – *But you're dead!* – but my poor strangulated throat could make no more than a raven's croak.

The Old Abbot fixed me with his eyes. The last time he'd spoken to me, I'd still thought him a lovely, twinkly Santa Claus-type guy; now his gaze was cold and judgemental. He lowered his ruby-ringed hand once more and pointed it right at my face.

'Greer MacDonald,' his voice rang out in the empty theatre. 'By the power vested in me by the Dark Order of the Grand Stag, I convict you of the murder of one of our number, Henry Charles Philip Arthur George de Warlencourt. You will be hanged by the neck until you are dead, unless you enter a plea in mitigation.'

I couldn't actually believe what he was saying. This was a nightmare. The noose tightened around my throat once more.

'Have you anything to say?'

I had a million things to say. That I hadn't murdered

Henry – he had fallen. That I would never have wanted him dead. That I wanted him back, but the rope squeezed my throat to a choking silence.

It also again raised me slightly to the balls of my feet. I strained to ease the pressure.

'For the second time, I ask you: have you anything to say?'

Red spots danced before my eyes. I tried and failed to push my fingers under the noose to loosen the grip of the rope. I was now on the point of my tiptoes, like some crazy ballerina, desperately scrabbling to keep some purchase on the ground.

'For the third and final time, I ask you: have you anything to say?'

I was now in the air – my feet had left the stage. I knew if I blacked out now it was all over, but the darkness was falling over my eyes and it seemed that nothing could keep it at bay.

Then I had one of those moments that happen in movies, one of those montages that filmmakers think you have in the last moments of your life, like at the end of *Requiem for a Dream*.

But this wasn't my life flashing before my eyes.

This was definitely edited highlights.

First, I was in the STAGS chapel at the Requiem Mass, the memorial for the very Abbot who was trying me now. I was listening to the chapel choir singing the *Miserere*, the cold clarity of the notes chilling my very blood. Then I heard Abbot Ridley's voice saying: *Greer, history's not carved in stone.* I was in the crypt of Longcross church among the graves, my fingers feeling the carved grooves in the marble of the family tomb, the deeply scored black letters resolving before my eyes. *Carved in stone.* Then I could no longer see, but I could hear Shafeen's voice. 'Greer!' he cried out of the darkness. 'You know what to say, Greer! *You know what to say!*'

He was right.

I knew what to say.

I opened my dry mouth and with the last of my breath I said it.

The neck verse.

'Miserere mei, Deus, secundum magnam misericordiam tuam.'

Instantly the rope holding me up snapped, and, no longer supported, I fell to the stage. There was an unbearable, burning pain – in, of all places, my *thumb*.

And then everything went black.

Scene ix

When I woke up to white sheets and bright lights, I said the least original thing you could possibly say.

'Where am I?'

'You're in Alnwick Cottage Hospital.'

It wasn't so much the answer that surprised me as the speaker.

For sitting by my bed, living and breathing, was Henry de Warlencourt.

He looked exactly the same. Hair so blond, eyes so blue. He wore a white shirt, open at the throat, a tweed jacket, blue jeans and dark-brown boots. He wasn't maimed or scarred. He was perfect. I'd been wrong about Louis. He'd never looked like this.

'You're alive.'

'And so are you.'

'It worked then. The play – it brought you back.'

'Is that what you were trying to do?'

I couldn't take credit for that. 'Not so much me as Cass. She knew all along.'

'God love her.' He smiled, and my heart just about stopped.

318

'My sweet little cuz.' Then his face got all serious. 'What about you? Were *you* trying to bring me back?'

'I'll answer you that one if you answer me another. Did you die?'

He took hold of my hand, avoiding the dressing on my thumb. The gold signet ring, with the little antler design, was back on his finger. His grip was warm and strong and real.

'What do you think?'

He felt very much alive to me. 'OK then. Where did you go after you . . . fell off the waterfall?'

'Maybe nowhere,' he said. 'If the play brought me back, maybe I was just . . . waiting, in the ether.'

'But that's *impossible*.'

'Is it?'

He smiled again, then relented. 'Where did Sherlock Holmes go after he fell off the Reichenbach Falls?'

I thought about this. 'He went home.'

'Exactly. He went home. To 221b Baker Street.'

'Are you saying you went home? To Longcross?'

'If you're discounting the ether theory, that's the only logical explanation, isn't it?'

'Well, it would explain why your room looked lived in. If it was. And that's why Perfect wouldn't treat Louis as the master.'

'He'll be master soon enough.'

'How can he be? Either we brought you back or you never went away, but either way you're here, so how can he be master?'

'He has a piece of paper saying that I'm dead.'

'Did that come from you?'

319

'I don't know what you mean.'

I narrowed my eyes. 'Yes, you do.'

He smiled at that. 'Let's not fight. I'll have to get you more flowers.' He nodded at my bedside table. There was a bunch of beautiful red roses, the colour of blood.

'From the stable-yard?' I remembered them crowding over the stone arch, even in the snow.

'Yes. They're dog roses. I thought you'd enjoy the irony.'

I smiled. 'Won't Louis mind you taking them?'

'It isn't his eighteenth birthday until tomorrow. I'm still the heir to Longcross for another day, so those roses –', he pointed – 'are still my birthright.'

'How can he inherit if you're still around?'

'I've been missing for more than a year and a day. Under the terms of the entail, he can legally inherit.'

'That doesn't seem very long.'

Henry stretched his long, be-jeaned legs. 'That's because it was written in an era when you were unlikely to live to see forty, and a nobleman was required to go off and fight crusades, foreign kings, the Scots, you name it. Louis will inherit on his birthday tomorrow. Unless –' his eyes twinkled – 'I make a guest appearance at the party.'

'Why would you let him inherit like that?'

'Let's just say I might need to stay dead for a little while longer.'

'Why?'

'Greer,' he said, spreading his hands, 'I have to retain some mystery, don't I?'

'Tell me this then. *Were* you going to kill me? You said you were, at the top of the falls.'

That stopped him in his tracks.

I looked at him sharply. 'Were you? You were going to kill Nel, and Shafeen. And Gemma Delaney the year before, and God knows how many others. What about the hunting books?'

'Not in my time, Greer. Whatever the Order did before or since, I never killed anyone. It was just a bit of fun.'

'Who for? Is this one of those "the fox enjoys hunting" conversations?'

He leaned forward and took my hand again, this time in both of his. 'Didn't you enjoy that weekend? If you are really honest with yourself? You came back to Longcross a second time, didn't you? The thrill of the chase doesn't just belong to the hunter, you know.'

I wasn't going to let him get away with this. 'That's so *twisted*. You did some pretty bad stuff, Henry.'

Then he did something I'd never seen him do before. He put his palms over his eyes and spoke without taking them away. For the first time in this, the weirdest of conversations, he didn't sound confident. He sounded broken. 'You don't know. You can't know. You can't understand what shapes a child.'

'You're surely not asking me to feel sorry for you. With all you've got?'

'I'm just saying. You are bought up thinking things are normal, and you don't find out they aren't until you're too old to change.'

Suddenly I thought of the baby elephants so used to being tied up with a piece of twine, so accepting, that it never occurred to them to break free as they grew. But I couldn't *pity* Henry, could I? 'You were going to kill me, and make it look like an accident. You said so to my face.'

He took the hands away. His face was deadly serious. 'No, Greer. Not you. Never you.'

I looked him right in his eyes, the blue eyes I'd never forgotten. 'You could do it now,' I whispered. 'I can't really move.' It was true. I was anchored by a monitor and a drip. 'You could put a pillow over my face.'

He looked at me and I looked at him. It was a really strange moment, oddly intimate, the invitation to kill. But it was an invitation I only felt safe enough to offer because I knew he'd never do it.

'No. I'm not a murderer.'

The moment had come and gone, and a strange lightness replaced it. 'And if you are alive,' I said, teasing now, 'neither am I. Not even a manslaughterer,' I said, remembering the word I'd once invented.

'Better say *manslayer*. That's what they branded Ben Jonson.'

'So you're saying I *am* a manslayer? Am I or not?'

'Well, have you killed anyone?'

'Besides you, you mean?' It was such an odd thing to joke about, but here we were, bantering about bloodshed.

'Only you have the answer,' he said meaningfully.

'God, you're just as annoying as ever!' I exclaimed. 'Being dead hasn't improved you.'

At that he threw back his head and laughed. 'Speaking of coming back from the dead,' he said, 'I'd better go and tell them you're awake.'

I panicked a bit, and grabbed for the hand I'd once let go of at the top of a waterfall. 'You will come back, won't you?'

'Don't worry,' he said, 'you'll see me again.' And before I could stop him, he leaned in and kissed me full on the lips.

Then, as he'd done a year before, he pulled his hand from mine and was gone.

Scene x

When I woke up to white sheets and bright lights, I said the least original thing you could possibly say.

'Where am I?'

'You're in Alnwick Cottage Hospital.'

I got the biggest sense of déjà vu ever. You know when you are having a dream and you think you've woken up, but you're actually still in the dream and then later you wake up *again*. I totally had that. This had happened to me before, except this time it wasn't Henry who answered me. It was Shafeen.

'Hello, you.' He looked like he hadn't slept – he was all stubbly and his hair was ruffled, but he looked absolutely lovely. He leaned in and kissed me on the lips still imprinted with Henry's kiss. I blinked guiltily.

'Did you see Henry?' My voice was a crow's croak, and my throat absolutely killed. So weird – it hadn't hurt at all when I'd been talking to Henry.

'Henry?' He frowned.

'He was here.'

Shafeen didn't look shocked, jump up or run out into the

corridor. He just smiled gently and held my hand, in the same way Henry had. 'They said this might happen.'

'That what might happen?'

'They had you on some pretty serious drugs, Greer. An induced sleep, while the swelling in your windpipe went down. The nurse said there might be some confusion when you woke.'

'How long was I out?'

'Two days.'

'So it's . . . 16th December.' The play had been on the 14th, the day we'd broken up. (Posh schools have really long holidays.) 'Henry had said Louis's birthday was on the 17th. Tomorrow. He was here today.' I tried to raise myself on the pillows.

'Hey, hey. They said you weren't to get excited and you weren't to talk too much. You're doing both.'

'What about the flowers?'

'Those'll be from the STAGS hothouses. Abbot Ridley said he was sending some from the students and staff. He's a class act.'

'You've changed your tune.'

Shafeen shrugged. 'He was great when you were choking. I knew something was wrong and ran down to the stage. I lifted you up, but it was him who cut you down.'

'How?'

'He drew his Earl of Greenwich sword and sliced through the rope. I thought Nel was going to burst.'

I smiled, and even that was a bit painful. 'Where is Nel?'

'She's been here the whole time too. But they only want you to have one visitor at a time at the moment. I got first dibs.'

'Awww.' I tried to sit up, and as soon as I put my left hand down to lift myself it hurt. 'And did I burn my hand?'

'I guess. Perhaps when you fell to the stage. There were lots of candles around.'

'Yes. At the trial the Grand Stags were all standing inside them. Like a circle of fire.'

'What trial?'

I goggled up at him. '*My* trial. By the Dark Order of the Grand Stag. And there are far more of them than we thought, by the way. The Grand Master must be a fixed-term office, like we guessed.'

'Back up,' said Shafeen. 'Trial for *what*?'

'For murder.'

'*Murder?*'

'Henry's murder. But it's OK. He's alive. And so'm I, because I said the neck verse. You told me to.'

'*I* did?'

He was starting to sound like an echo. 'Yes. You shouted out.'

'Greer,' he said, looking concerned, 'are you awake? You're making no sense. What are you talking about?' We stared at each other, both equally confused.

'Look,' I said eventually, 'tell me properly what happened. What you saw, from the audience.'

Shafeen took a deep breath. 'All right. So, you spoke the Epilogue – which was great, by the way – but by the last line you started to sound a bit strangled. But I'd never seen it in rehearsal, and I didn't know about the noose thing and, sorry to sound like I'm your dad or something, but I *never* would have agreed to you doing that. Anyway, I saw your toes actually lifting off the ground, and your face started to go this strange purple colour. So that's when I ran down to the stage and they drew

326

the curtain over you. By this time most of the cast were onstage. Some of them were screaming – mostly Nel, if I'm honest – but you couldn't hear a thing in the auditorium apparently because they were all cheering. The audience clapped through the whole thing, and you might want to know you got a standing ovation.'

'Cool,' I said wryly. 'Glad everyone enjoyed my near-death experience so much.'

'So I lifted you up, like I said, to ease the pressure on your throat, and Abbot Ridley cut you down, like some superhero, and somebody called an ambulance. You gave us quite a fright, you know?' I could see he was understating it, and suddenly felt very sorry for what he'd been through.

'How long was I out for?'

'About two minutes, no more.'

'Two *minutes*?'

'Yes. Why?'

I told him about the trial, and the circle of Grand Stags dressed in red; the sentence and the neck verse.

'No.' He shook his head. 'No judgements by age-old cults, sorry. I think I would remember. You came round almost at once. Then we kept you quiet onstage until the paramedics got there, and they gave you a shot straight away. And told us all to clear off. So we left you with them and they brought you here – they wouldn't let anyone travel in the ambulance, but we followed in Nel's car. You've been out since.'

'And how did . . . the hanging . . . happen?'

'The noose had been put on one of the candelabra winches by mistake and just raised you up when they were lifting the lights ready for the final curtain.'

'That's what I thought.'

'Then they put you out because you'd suffered trauma to the throat and, like I told you, they wanted to reduce the swelling and bruising before they let you wake. Otherwise you might have found it hard to swallow. Oh yes, and breathe.'

He was trying to make a joke, and I could see what an effort it was. What a strain he'd been under. 'Yeah. Pretty essential, that whole breathing thing,' I joked back weakly.

Then I eased back on my pillows. 'It was all a dream,' I said, as though I was in some lame movie like *Vanilla Sky*. Obviously I was massively relieved that the *trial* had been a dream – well, a nightmare – but the thought that Henry must have been a dream too made me, stupidly, feel like crying. He did *feel* less real now; he was fading from sight, just as dreams do the longer you've been awake, as the real world takes over.

It all made sense. How *could* any of it be real? That would be nuts. I always knew logically Henry couldn't have survived that fall from Conrad's Force. My fevered brain had conjured him, just as it had invented that Gothic onstage trial by the Dark Order of the Grand Stag. Then I groaned. 'Jeesus. What must everyone have thought?'

'Nobody thought anything,' said Shafeen. 'You know STAGS. They are great at hushing stuff up. Centuries of practice. While we were all with the paramedics, old Ridley got some of the Friars to ply Professor Nashe with sherry. Once he knew you were going to be all right, he took her off to dinner. By the way, she sent a message through him that she would have loved to have met you but she understood you were tired after the play. That was the story Ridley fed her. She hoped you were "sensible of what a great achievement the play was", and that she was looking forward to meeting you "when you went up to Oxford". Not *if*, Greer, *when*. It looks like it might be a slam-dunk.' He took both my hands now and his eyes were shining. The future seemed assured. 'She's gone now and taken *The Isle of Dogs* to submit it to the British Library. They're going to call it the Longcross Manuscript.'

Just as well. After all the trauma, I didn't really want anything else to do with the play. If it got me into Oxford that was enough. And I supposed that the British Library was the right place for it. I had thought that they should nail *The Isle of Dogs* into a wooden crate and lock it in some vast warehouse like the Ark of the Covenant, but I supposed now that Henry's resurrection was all part of my dream, they could do what they wanted with it. It had no power to raise the dead. It was just a dusty old play.

'The Abbot's been in once or twice, you know? And he sent the flowers, like I said.'

I looked at the blood-red blooms by my bed. I couldn't for the life of me place where red dog roses grew at STAGS, but I could see them plain as day growing over the stable arch at Longcross. Henry had said they were from him. My eyes started to prickle.

Shafeen looked at me closely – he could always read my emotions, but luckily not always the reasons for them. 'Listen,' he said gently, 'it's a lot to take in. Let me fetch the nurse. I don't want you getting all spun out. This confusion is probably totally normal when you've been in a medically induced sleep. There's a lot of time for freaky dreams in two days.' He got up. 'I should probably tell someone you're awake anyway . . .'

And I got that sense of déjà vu all over again.

Scene xi

A cheerful nurse came bustling in wearing teal scrubs.

She was probably in her twenties, had a north-eastern accent and called me 'hinny'. I liked her at once.

She picked up my chart. 'What've we got here? Room K9, otherwise known as Greer MacDonald.'

'Hi,' I said.

'*Partial asphyxiation during school play*,' she read. 'That's a new one on me.'

'Me too.'

'I'm Annie,' she said, taking hold of my wrist to read my pulse. 'You're looking very chipper.' She beamed at me. 'Although if I had a nice young man sitting by my bedside day and night, waiting for me to flutter me eyelashes, I'd be chipper too.'

Did she mean Henry? Had she seen him? 'Which young man?'

'The tall, dark and handsome one. Keep hold of him, hinny.'

'I intend to,' I said. But I couldn't shake the crazy feeling of – was it *hope*? – when she'd mentioned a young man at my bedside. 'Was there . . . was there another young man?'

She was doing that thing when they hold up your eyelids

and shine a light in your eyes. 'I never saw one, but that doesn't mean there wasn't. I've only just come on shift and you have been here for a while. You lining them up, hinny?'

I smiled weakly. She wrapped a blood-pressure cuff around my arm and pumped it up until it squeezed. While she took the reading she said, 'We called your dad. He's coming back from Mad . . . Mad . . .'

'Madagascar.'

'That's the one.' She released the cuff and it deflated itself with a hiss. As she pulled it off my arm it grazed the dressing on my hand and I winced. My thumb looked like Mr Bump, it was so round and fat and wrapped in bandages.

'What's wrong with my thumb?'

'I'm not sure, pet.' She unhooked the chart again from the end of my bed. 'The paramedics wrapped it up at your school. It says *minor burn* here.'

'Probably one of the candles,' I said, more to myself than to her.

'We'll know soon enough, hinny. I'll be back to change the dressing after the doctor's done his rounds. Don't worry, though. Your thumb's still there – you'll still be able to play PlayStation.' I was starting to like her very much.

She looked through the little square window in my door. 'Meantime, you've got another visitor. A young lady this time – sorry.' And she winked.

Chanel held the door for Nurse Annie, and then came right over to the bed and gave me a massive hug. I loved that girl.

'Don't *ever* do that again,' she said into my hair.

I did a kind of laughing sob thing. 'I'm not planning to.'

'I got the fright of my life.'

'Me too,' I said. 'Me too.'

'God,' she said, 'your poor neck. You've got a rope-shaped bruise.'

I hadn't seen it, and was not sure I wanted to. 'Guess I'll be rocking the chokers at Christmas.'

'Are you OK?'

'Yes, I'm fine now. Just fine. A bit croaky. Maybe I'll set up a chatline.'

She ignored the gag, sat down in the visitors' chair and looked around the room, anywhere but at me. She seemed twitchy and squirrelly. She fiddled with the petals of the dog roses. 'These are nice.'

I thought it best not to say they were from Abbot Ridley. 'Nel,' I said, 'are *you* OK?'

'Yes,' she said. 'Fine and dandy. Fine-a-doodle-do.'

I looked at her directly. 'Nel? Have you got something to tell me?'

She looked like she was going to burst. 'Yes,' she said. 'But I promised I'd wait for Shafeen.'

'Promised why?' Then I had a lightbulb moment. 'Is it about the Abbot?'

Now she met my gaze, eyes round. 'That's *spooky*. Yes.'

'I saw you kissing.'

'Oh, *that* one,' she said inexplicably, reddening. 'Yeah, he kissed me after the play.'

'It looked like *you* kissed *him*.'

She shrugged, not quite meeting my eyes. 'Maybe.'

'Chanel,' I said, deliberately using her full name, 'what are you *doing*?'

Before she could answer, Shafeen opened the door a fraction and squeezed in. He actually addressed Nel first.

'Did you find out?'

'Yes,' she said.

He kissed me and sat down on the end of the bed.

I looked from one to the other. 'Guys, what's going on? What *is* all this?'

Nel took a breath. 'I've been nosing about this place. It's been pretty boring waiting for you to wake up.'

'Sor-reee.'

She flapped her hand at me as if to say, *It's OK.* 'So I found a white coat and put it on, and started asking questions.'

I decided to ignore for the moment the nonchalant way Nel had impersonated a medical professional. 'About *me?*'

'No, another patient. The Old Abbot.' She looked at Shafeen and then back at me. 'Thing is, there's no record of him. Nothing at all. He didn't even come here, let alone die here.'

'You're sure?'

'I checked the admissions manifest, and talked to the House Officer.'

A chill goosebumped my skin. 'So he *is* alive,' I whispered.

'So it seems.'

'And if he is, that *was* him putting me on trial.'

Then of course I had to tell Nel about my trial by the Dark Order of the Grand Stag.

'But even if we accept that the Abbot is alive, that trial *can't* have happened,' she said. 'We were all there on the stage of the theatre. You were in our sight the whole time.'

'Except,' said Shafeen slowly, 'when the paramedics threw us out.'

'But those are *paramedics*.'

'The same paramedics who brought the Abbot to this hospital, where he never arrived?' asked Shafeen pointedly. 'The same paramedics who took Henry's "body" away from Longcross?'

'Shit.'

'Yes.'

'Are you saying that . . . the trial happened on the stage once they'd thrown you all out?' I asked.

'No. Yes. I don't know. I know it sounds a bit far-fetched . . .'

'A *bit* . . .'

'I'm just saying that *something's* going on,' he insisted. 'Something really grim. Something happened to upset the Dark Order of the Grand Stag and now they're really pissed off.'

'It must be the death of Henry. That's what they told me. They called him *one of their number*.'

'Then he must have been a Grand Stag. If the DOGS were avenging him, I mean,' said Shafeen.

'I suppose. But this is all guesswork.'

Nel said suddenly, 'When's the last time you checked in with **mrs_de_warlencourt**?'

'Well,' I said, indicating my monitor and my drip, 'I've been pretty tied up.'

'Let's look now.' She flipped out her Saros 8S and swiped it open. She passed it to me. 'Sign in,' she said.

Slightly hampered as I had only one thumb, I signed into my Instagram. Sure enough, a message from **mrs_de_warlencourt** popped up. It was a single line.

There is another Place.

'Another fricking riddle,' sighed Nel. 'If there's another place, what was the first place? STAGS? Longcross?'

I was silent for a moment, looking at the message, letter by letter. Then I said, 'Remember Friar Skelton?'

'The old history friar? What made you think of him?'

'He might have been a kid killer, but he was a helluva teacher. I've never forgotten what he said about Hannibal and the elephants. Remember? That *Hannibal waged war with elephants* and *Hannibal waged war, with elephants* are two very different things? The comma makes all the difference.'

'But there's no comma in this.'

'No, I meant, he's the one who taught us to watch out for punctuation.'

'So?'

'**mrs_de_warlencourt** never uses capitals by accident. When she wrote *I think you'll find this Quite Interesting,* and used upper-case letters, she was pointing us to the Q and the I, because that's what the show was called that told us about the neck verse – *QI.* And the commemorative plaque on the theatre had the name "Gabriel Spenser" in inverted commas, to denote the fact that it was an alias . . .'

'I spotted that!' crowed Nel.

'And I shut you up. I'm sorry,' said Shafeen.

'So if she's using a capital P for Place, I think she means something by it. I think it's a proper name.'

At that moment Nurse Annie came in with a huge bunch of cellophane-wrapped florist's flowers. Much fancier than my bunch of roses from Abbot Ridley. 'Who's a popular lass, then?' She laid them on my lap as if I'd just won an Oscar.

'Whoa. Who are *they* from?' asked Nel.

I read the card. 'What the actual *hell*?'

'What?'

Unable to speak, I showed the little card to Nel and Shafeen. And this is what they read:

To Greer,
Get well soon!
With love and best wishes from
Abbot Ridley, the friars and all the students at STAGS.

'If *these* flowers are from the school, who are the other ones from?' I said.

'Never mind that now,' said Nurse Annie, putting her hands on her hips. 'I'm sure I said one visitor at a time. Greer needs to rest, and you two do too. You look like a couple of zombies. Now go back to your school and I don't want to see either of you before proper visiting hours tomorrow.'

There was nothing more we could say. She bustled them out of the room before we could exchange another word.

Scene xii

I thought I would never sleep, but I did, and dogs chased me through my dreams, carrying scarlet roses in their jaws.

On 17th December, the day of Louis de Warlencourt's eighteenth birthday, I woke feeling tired and confused, but stronger. The new flashy flowers were in a vase at my bedside, literally overshadowing the blood-red blooms. I sat up and reached behind the fancy-pants bouquet to touch the mouse-soft scarlet petals of the roses. 'Who brought you?' I said.

I'd slept through the morning visiting hours, but Nurse Annie told me that Shafeen and Nel had been there, faithful as ever, only to be turned away as I needed my rest. I had plenty of thinking time stretching ahead until the evening, but lying there in that bed, my own thoughts and theories crowded in on me, driving me crazy. The mystery of the flowers, the mystery of *another Place*. Was the Old Abbot really alive? Was Henry really dead? Had I been on trial? Was I a manslayer? Henry – or the dream Henry – had told me that only I had the answer. How could I?

I sat up. I needed to get out of room K9.

Much to my surprise, when I asked to get up Nurse Annie

said, 'Yes, once the doctor has seen you.' I waited impatiently for the doctor, who seemed pretty late, but when he arrived, he seemed about a decade too early. He seriously looked about twelve years old, like Michael J. Fox in *Doc Hollywood*. Hilariously, according to his nametag, he was called Doctor Kyd.

He looked at my chart first and me second. 'How's the throat?'

'Croaky but fine.'

'Good.' He took out one of those wooden lolly sticks and lifted my chin to peer at my neck. Then he said *open wide* and used the same stick to flatten my tongue and look down my throat. 'The bruising's going down nicely and your windpipe has opened back up.' He chucked the stick in the bin and made a note on my chart. He seemed pretty professional. Maybe he wasn't such a newb after all.

'Thumb?'

I held it up in a comedy thumbs-up.

'Any pain?'

'Not unless I touch it.'

'Then don't,' he said, and I started to like him too.

He sat down in the chair. 'Anything else to report?'

I hesitated, not sure whether to bring it up. 'I've had some pretty crazy dreams.'

He put his head to one side. 'How crazy?'

'Well, there was this guy – a friend. I knew him from school and he was . . . in an accident a year ago. Died. And last night, well, yesterday really, I dreamed that he was here.'

'Here in the hospital?'

'Sitting in the same chair you are.'

Doctor Kyd studied me for a minute. 'He died a year ago, you say?'

'Yeah. Why?'

He clasped his hands together. 'There's this thing called the "Anniversary Effect". It's when you start getting visions or flashbacks a year after a traumatic event. In your case, your friend's accident. The anniversary opens up the neurological floodgates, so to speak.'

I wished it were that simple.

'Would you like to talk to someone?'

'You mean, get my head shrunk?'

He smiled. 'If you like. We prefer to call it a post-traumatic psychological assessment.'

I pulled a face. 'Let's cross that bridge when I jump off it.'

He laughed. 'Fair enough. But the option's there.'

'Thanks. So can I get up or not?'

He looked at me closely again, in an assessing kind of way. 'All right,' he said. 'But take it easy.'

I did. I had a gentle look around, rolling my drip about with me like a skinny metal friend. The cottage hospital was really cute. There was a Christmas tree in the reception area with brightly wrapped presents underneath it for sick kids. The automatic doors swished open and closed as people came and went, and fluorescent ambulances stopped outside. I looked closely at the green-clad paramedics, competently going about their work. I couldn't believe these breezy professionals would get mixed up in anything to do with the DOGS. I moved quickly past the draughty doors and carried on with my tour.

I found a little chapel where you could pray for the sick.

I lit a candle for whoever it was I might have killed – no easy feat with my Mr Bump thumb, I can tell you. I looked at the modern stained-glass window. Without St Aidan and the white stag, it looked sort of wrong. I took a ride in the lift and discovered a little library upstairs. Me and my drip buddy shuffled between the shelves. There was a window with little cushions on the sill and a view that looked onto Alnwick Castle, a grey, grim-looking place with snow on the turrets. I remembered what Friar Waterlow had said about the only surviving reference to *The Isle of Dogs*, written in Ben Jonson's hand, being held in the castle collection. I turned away from the view. I couldn't think about Ben Jonson any more.

Instead I looked along the shelves for Arthur Conan Doyle, and found a whole Sherlock Holmes collection. Henry's voice rang in my head. *He went home to 221b Baker Street*. I selected *The Adventure of the Empty House*, the one where Holmes comes back to life following his grand battle with Professor Moriarty at the Reichenbach Falls. I took it to the window seat and quickly became engrossed. It was just what I needed to take me away from my own thoughts. In the story it was Holmes's brother Mycroft who kept Sherlock's rooms ready for his return. Had someone in Henry's family done the same for him? Just as I got to that bit when Holmes reveals himself to a gobsmacked Watson, an orderly came to get me – my dad was on the phone.

He was on a very crackly line from Madagascar airport. Apparently he'd phoned about a million times, but I'd been asleep. Obviously he was properly freaked out and ready to get the next plane home, but I talked him off the ledge, telling him that I was fine, that I'd see him in a week, that we'd have a lovely Christmas together. After that it was time for a pretty disgusting dinner, then when the evening visiting hours finally rolled around I was back in my bed, desperate to talk to my friends.

When the knock came at my door I was all ready to get into it again with Nel and Shafeen.

But I didn't get the visitor I expected.

'Not sure if this one's a boy or a girl,' said Nurse Annie, well-intentioned but not exactly PC. 'But it's very handsome.'

It was Cass.

Scene xiii

Handsome was the word for Cass that night.

She was in a wine-coloured velvet smoking jacket, a snow-white dress shirt and a black bow tie untied at the throat. Her hair was slicked back from her face, and she was wearing a slick of dark plum lipstick. She looked wonderful.

She bent and kissed me on both cheeks in that upper-class way. She asked all the usual questions and then put something small and solid in my hands. 'I brought you this,' she said.

It was wrapped in a scarlet (what else?) cloth napkin – no paper serviettes at Longcross. I folded back the cloth, and found a slice of cake. It was one of those heavy, old-fashioned fruit cakes, densely packed with dried fruit and with a layer of marzipan and white icing. I balanced it upright on my lap – there was an L piped on the top. 'Louis wanted you to have some,' she said. 'It's his birthday cake.'

Of course. 'It's his birthday today, right? Is he having a party?'

'Yes. It's going on right now.'

'God, you shouldn't have come all this way in the middle of his do, just for me.' Then a thought struck. 'Cass,' I said gently, 'isn't it *your* birthday too? You know, you being a twin and all?' I tried to make light of it.

She clasped her hands together. 'Yes. Yes, it is.' She didn't quite meet my eyes. It struck me then, with a pang of sympathy, just how coconuts this whole entail thing was. Just like that, she had ceased to matter, to the extent that she could leave her own party and no one would care. I wondered if she'd even got a cake.

As if she'd read my mind she said, 'It's only an hour in the car. And I needed a break. I think –' she forced a smile – 'it will go on all night. Louis is pretty happy.'

My stomach shrivelled with hope and foreboding. 'I bet he is. Master of all he surveys now, I guess.'

'I guess,' she repeated. She bit her lip a little.

'Any . . .' I didn't know how to ask if her spectral cousin had done a *Sixth Sense* and turned up at the party, 'special guests?'

'Oh,' she said, looking a bit awkward. 'That is, of course you would all have been invited – Louis especially wanted me to say that – but you were . . . here, and Shafeen and Nel wanted to stay with you.'

'I wasn't fishing for an invite. I just meant, who was there?'

'Just family really.'

That's what I was afraid of. 'Surprise appearances?'

'Well, the London lot are there. And Mummy and Daddy made it down from Scotland, despite the snow.'

I breathed again. So Henry had been a dream after all. 'Nice,' I said.

'Yes. Usually when there's even a flake of snow they can't

get –' She stopped and her face drained of colour. She was staring fixedly at something on my bedside table. It was quite unsettling.

'The flowers,' she croaked, sounding a bit like me.

'I know,' I said. 'They're from the school. Pretty flash, hey?'

'Not those. The dog roses.' She put her hands to her heart in a curiously theatrical way. 'They're from Longcross.'

My own heart started to beat faster.

She turned her gaze on me. 'You've seen him, haven't you?' Her eyes seemed huge and were shining unnaturally brightly. 'Haven't you?'

I didn't toy with her by asking who she meant. But I didn't want to fuel whatever fire was burning in those eyes. 'I *thought* I did,' I said gently and evenly. 'But I've been on some pretty hardcore drugs.'

'Then how do you explain the flowers?'

'I don't. I can't.'

'Did he say he'd brought them?'

'Yes.'

'Then he's there.' She laughed with pure joy and clapped her hands together. 'He went home. That's right, isn't it?'

I shifted uncomfortably. 'He said something about 221b Baker Street.'

'He's in London?'

'No. It's a . . . thing we have, about Sherlock Holmes. Holmes fell off a waterfall, and then he went home.'

She stood. 'I've got to go.'

'Where?'

'Back to Longcross, of course.'

I had a horrible feeling that she wasn't rushing back to Louis, but to Henry.

She leaned in and kissed my cheek, not poshly this time but properly, firmly, affectionately, as if she was thanking me for something.

'Oh, and Ty's waiting to see you,' she said as she straightened up. 'Can you tell her to be quick?'

'*Ty's* here?'

'She was at the party too, and when I said I was coming to see you, she wanted to come with me. But they have this one-at-a-time rule . . .'

'I know, I know . . .'

'So she said she'd wait.'

'OK. Thanks, Cass. And thanks for the cake. Thank Louis too.'

She ducked her head and left me alone with the little iced slice on my lap. I put it on the bedside table, next to the Longcross roses. It was very nice of her, and Louis, and I'm sure it was delicious, but there was absolutely no way in the world I was going to eat it.

Scene xiv

I wasn't really sure why Ty had come to visit, unless it was just to keep Cass company in the car.

I mean, it was nice of her and all, but we'd never been super-close, apart from that night of the deciphering, and that was evidenced by the fact that she didn't even sit down, but just sort of hovered, fiddling with her hair.

Like everyone else she noticed my neck first and the flowers second. 'I can't stay very long,' she said. 'That creepy gamekeeper brought us in the estate car, and I don't think he's a patient man.'

I smiled. 'Ty,' I said, 'you look amazing.'

She was in a red dress with a sequinned bodice and a sticky-out skirt of red net. She had very dramatic, glittery red eye make-up on her eyelids. At the edge of her eyes she'd stuck little ruby crystals. They looked like tears of blood.

'Thanks.'

'How's the party?'

'Banging,' she said. 'I never seen anything like it. They got an orchestra, Greer. And these waiters walking around like penguins with trays of food and drink. And later, they reckon, fireworks.'

346

'Cool,' I said. 'Enjoy.'

'Thanks,' she said again. There was a long, awkward pause.

'OK,' she said. 'Glad you're still alive. Gotta go.'

Gotta go. Where had I heard that phrase before? It was a common enough phrase, but I hadn't just heard it, I'd seen it *written down.* As she was disappearing through the door I remembered just in time. I sat up straight and called: '`mrs_de_warlencourt`!'

She turned around.

Her eyes were wide and guilty, and in that moment I knew.

There was a long silence. 'Talk to me,' I commanded, channelling a bit of Cass. She gave a small sigh and closed the door behind her. This time she did take the chair and pulled it close by my bedside.

'His name was Leon Morgan. He came over on the *Empire Windrush* from Jamaica in 1948. It was the first time he'd been on a ship that big. He was so excited, Greer. Excited to be coming to England with his mum and dad and his little sister. When they landed, someone in the Foreign Office was kind to the family. They told them about this school in the north of England that would give a scholarship to a clever little boy. An old school, a church school, a good place. They were godly people, and Leon's parents knew they couldn't give him a chance like that in a million years, however hard they worked. So, although they missed him every day, they let him go. And he never came back.'

I didn't breathe.

'They knew he'd gone with some friends to a country house

for the weekend and there'd been an accident. They knew what had happened, however unbelievable, because Leon had sent them a letter, which arrived after he died, but they couldn't prove a thing. They had no power, no friends in this country. So they could do nothing. His mum and dad never got over it. Neither did his little sister. My grandma.'

I was horrified. Horrified for Leon. Horrified for his poor parents reading a letter from a dead boy. And horrified at myself. How could I have been so stupid? How could I have fantasised over Henry's return? How could I have flirted with death like that? I knew what he was, what his heritage was, but he'd charmed me even from beyond the grave. He'd even been a rival for Shafeen, beautiful lovely Shafeen. Suddenly I wanted Shafeen very much – I wanted to see him right now, that instant, and reassure him that Henry was my past but he was my future. I was ready, at last, to take us to the next level – to finish what we'd started at Longcross in the Queen's Chamber. I couldn't believe I'd ever thought more of Henry than of him. And worse than that, worst of all, I'd thought far more of Henry than of this kid, this footnote who wasn't a footnote. Leon Morgan was a real person. I remembered we'd talked about him, Henry and I, in that last fateful conversation at the top of Conrad's Force. That anonymous 'African son' listed casually as one of the Order's kills. Then I'd been more focused on saving my own skin. I'd never considered that other poor child – the one who never went home.

When I could speak I said, 'I thought he was from Africa.'

'Who said that?'

Henry. 'I dunno – rumours.'

'Rumours put about by people who don't know the difference between Africa and the West Indies? Black is black, right?'

I was very much afraid she might be right.

'I tried to tell you I wasn't just a token character, didn't I?' said Ty. 'I'm much deeper into this thing than any of you. You've only had a year of it. For me . . . it's been my whole life.' She breathed in a long, deep breath. 'And now I'm coming for them, Greer. I'm gonna let slip the dogs of war. That's why I worked so damn hard to get the best grades in my school on the Isle of Dogs. That's why I applied to STAGS. That's why I read every webpage on the Internet about Henry de Warlencourt. And that's why I got in touch with you.'

'How did you know so much? About me? About everything?'

'I made it my business to know. This is my mission, Greer, you get me? I'm going to get them bastards who did my Great-Uncle Leon, if it's the last thing I do.'

I believed her. She looked supremely confident and a little dangerous – Queen Cynthia all over again.

'So you're not in love with Louis then.'

She flashed a brilliant smile. 'Told you I could act, didn't I? No, I'm not in love with him. Besides, I think, despite her "poor little me" act, Cass and Louis are still pretty tight.'

'Still?'

'Oh yes,' she said. 'There's no room for anyone else in *that* twisted little relationship. But there's no way in this world *I* would get together with any of that family. The only place I'll ever be **mrs_de_warlencourt** is on Instagram.'

Visitors, alive and dead, had been taking my hand for the past two days. Now, I took hers. 'Ty,' I said, 'you've been a greater friend to me than I've been to you. I should have done much better. But I'd like to try.'

She didn't reply but looked at our hands on the coverlet – one black, one white. 'I should go,' she said, withdrawing hers.

I grabbed at it, just as I'd tried to hold onto Henry. That seemed unbelievable now. 'Stay,' I said urgently. 'Don't go back. Just tell Cass – tell her you're unwell, or tired. Tell her anything. Just don't go back.'

'I'm not finished yet.'

'At least let us help you.'

She shook her head. 'You've got to get well. This is my thing.'

'It's *our* thing,' I said.

And then I did what I should have done in the first place. I told her. I clued her in. And I held nothing back. She should be, would be, part of our gang. I told her everything about last year, the huntin' shootin' fishin'. I told her about Shafeen's dad, and what had happened to him at Longcross in 1969. I told her about Henry's death, and even Henry's comeback. Some of it I felt like she already knew. Some of it I felt was new to her. But she listened to it all and then put her hand back in mine. 'Everything you've told me just demonstrates how much they need to be stopped. They're planning something, Greer, something big. And I have to be in the right place at the right time.'

That reminded me. 'Where is *another Place*?'

'Cumberland Place,' she said quietly. 'The London home of the de Warlecourt family. The twins were brought up there. I'm pretty sure it's the HQ of the Dark Order of the Grand Stag. That's where the power lies.'

'What sort of power?'

'I don't know yet. And that's why I have to go back.'

Gently, she took her hand away. She got up, and the red skirts fell around her. She hesitated. 'The friend thing – I'd really like that. There's always next term.'

'Yes,' I said, heart sinking. 'Next term.'

'And now,' she said, this time with a smile, 'I really gotta go.'

As she went for the door once more, I got an overpowering, terrible feeling that I wasn't going to see her again.

'Ty!' I called.

She turned back.

'Be careful.'

Scene xv

And then, at last, I got the visitors I'd expected all along.

I was pretty exhausted, but I was dying to tell Shafeen and Nel what I'd learned from Ty. But, in a massively frustrating piece of timing, we'd had no time to say more than hello when Nurse Annie bustled in.

She wagged her finger at us. 'You two are terrible at this one-at-a-time thing. One of you'll have to hop it.'

Now, I liked Nurse Annie just fine, but at that point I could cheerfully have killed her.

Shafeen took a more considered approach. 'Oh come on, Annie,' he said. 'We'll be good, I promise. And then we'll all get a proper night's sleep. Just like the nurse ordered.'

It worked. 'All right, hinny,' she said. She was obviously Shafeen's slave already. 'So long as you don't mind me changing this dressing. You two jump on the bed, cos I'll be needing this chair. And I haven't seen this wound yet so if there's a bit o' blood, don't go fainting on me – I don't have the beds.'

I was actually pleased they were there, because the snipping of the scissors and the pulling of the bandage was just painful enough to make me glad of the distraction. Obviously I couldn't tell them about Leon Morgan yet, but we chit-chatted in a totally bogus way about Louis's eighteenth and other irrelevant stuff, until the nurse stopped us with an exclamation.

'Well, God save us,' she said, sitting back in her chair. 'I've never seen the like of *that* before.'

I looked at my thumb and my blood turned to ice.

Only you have the answer, said Henry's voice in my head.

There was no blood on the pad of my thumb, but there was a burn.

More specifically, a brand.

And it said, simply:

M

HISTORY OF S.T.A.G.S.

S.T.A.G.S. was founded in the seventh century by St Aidan the Great. The name Aidan means 'fire' in Gaelic, and he is considered to be a protector against fire. He was dubbed 'the Great' in order to distinguish him from the lesser saint St Aidan of Ferns. Our St Aidan was born in Ireland, and became a monk on the Scottish island of Iona. He travelled to Northumbria, where he was made Bishop of Lindisfarne. Realising the value of education, he founded a school in the hope that he would train the next generation of Christian leaders. The school began with just twelve boys as pupils, but it grew into a centre of education and a jewelhouse of scholarly knowledge.

Aidan was canonised upon the performance of a miracle; he saved a stag from the hunt by turning him invisible. That stag gave the school an emblem, and a name. Today, after a thousand years of exceptional scholarship, S.T.A.G.S. has educated a dozen British prime ministers and countless members of both houses of parliament. St Aidan's dream that he would train the future leaders of men has become a reality.

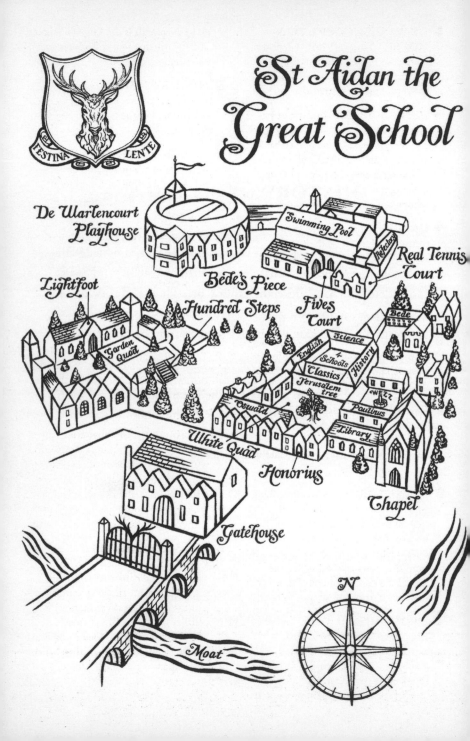

DE WARLENCOURT PLAY-HOUSE – built in 1969, the theatre is an exact replica of the sixteenth-century Swan Theatre which used to stand on London's bankside.

BEDE LIBRARY (incorporating the Scriptorium) – named after the Venerable Bede, the library has several notable architectural features, including the medieval Scriptorium, a remnant of the original monastery school, and the Tudor Reading Room.

GATEHOUSE – the gatehouse forms the entrance to the school, reached by crossing the medieval moat. In the days of the monastery school, the drawbridge was raised at night to keep marauding Scots away from the treasures of the chapel.

BEDE'S PIECE STAGS boasts extensive playing fields, named for a piece of common land enclosed by the school during the eighteenth century.

CHAPEL – Founded in 683, the chapel is the oldest surviving building of the first monastery school. The stained-glass window of Aidan and the stag is original.

REFECTORY – This long building with vaulted ceilings was rebuilt at the time of the Civil War after a fire. The wooden benches and tables on which the students dine are the original ones from the monastery, on which the monks ate their breakfast of bread and beer.

ENGLISH SCHOOLS – In the reign of Edward VI, New Quad – a quadrangle of exquisite Tudor buildings – was built at STAGS to represent the four pillars of learning. The first of the schools (always referred to in the plural) is the English Schools, and the original sign still remains carved above the door.

HISTORY SCHOOLS – The second side of the quad, the History Schools houses the original copy of Bede's work.

CLASSICS SCHOOLS – The third side of the quad, the Classics Schools still fulfills its function of teaching Latin, the language of law and learning.

SCIENCE LABS – Originally the Theology Schools, the fourth side of the quad, despite its Tudor appearance and theological sign carved in stone, now houses STAGS' extensive science laboratories.

THE HUNDRED STEPS – this ancient stone stairway connects the upper and lower schools. Legend has it that in 1348 Edmund de Warlencourt rode up the hundred steps on his horse for a wager.

POOL – The STAGS swimming pool is Olympic-sized and fully compliant with the regulations of the Fédération Internationale de Natation. It is 164 feet long, 82 feet wide and 6 feet deep, with eight swimming lanes marked with rope and buoys.

FIVES AND REAL TENNIS COURTS – Both courts are fully enclosed, and constructed of their original timbers. The Real Tennis court is fashioned after Charles II's court at Hampton Court Palace. The Fives court is designed to replicate one of the exterior bays of the chapel, where the game was first played after Mass.

HOUSES AT S.T.A.G.S.

HONORIUS

Honorius was Archbishop of Canterbury in the seventh century. His is the oldest and grandest house at STAGS. The White Quad, dating from the tweltfh century, features at its centre the Jerusalem Tree, a cedar tree grown from a seed brought home from the Crusades by Conrad de Warlencourt.

Honorius house colours: a white stag's head on a ground of red and gold with a cedar tree as a charge.

BEDE

The Venerable Bede was an English Benedictine monk who wrote *The Ecclesiastical History of the English People*, a draft of which survives in the Scriptorium at STAGS. Bede house incorporates the extensive playing fields known as Bede's Piece.

Bede house colours: a white stag's head on a ground of red and blue, with a book as a charge.

OSWALD

Oswald was king of Northumbria from 634, uniting the kingdoms of Bernicia and Deira to become the most powerful ruler in Britain. Oswald did much to promote the spread of Christianity in the north, and fittingly the school chapel can be found in his house.

Oswald house colours: a white stag's head on a ground of red and green with a crown as a charge.

PAULINUS

Paulinus was a Roman missionary and the first Bishop of York. The Paulinus Well, built during the bishop's mission to Northumbria in the seventh century, stands in the middle of Paulinus quad. The waters at its depths were said, upon drinking, to turn a sinful man to God.

Paulinus house colours: a white stag's head on a ground of red and purple with a well as a charge.

LIGHTFOOT

Lightfoot is the girls' house at STAGS, and is the newest of all the houses, built originally as a dwelling for masters in 1550. It is a handsome Tudor building with its own Garden Quad, and it was first named Aidan's House. The name was changed when Bishop Joseph Lightfoot of Durham successfully lobbied for the admission of girls in 1880. Since then, Lightfoot House has borne his name.

Lightfoot house colours: a white stag's head on a ground of red and silver, with a bishop's mitre as a charge.

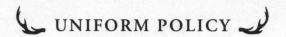 UNIFORM POLICY

By the first day of Michaelmas Term, all students must be equipped with the following uniform:

- Black Tudor coat
- Scarlet stockings (unless you are a Medieval, in which case you may wear knee-high stockings of a design of your choosing)
- Narrow brown deer-leather belt
- Plain white wing-collar shirt
- White clerical tie
- Black knee breeches
- Black deer-leather lace-up shoes
- Regulation black PE kit with STAGS crest

Uniform may be purchased from our suppliers: Keytes of Berwick-upon-Tweed.

The STAGS uniform must be strictly observed year round. A scarf in the colours of one's house may be worn during Michaelmas and Hilary Terms.

GLOSSARY

JUSTITIUM – a short holiday that falls roughly in the middle of each term, when students are permitted to return home if they wish

MEDIEVALS – the prefects, usually between three and six in number, chosen from among the final-year students at STAGS

PROBITIONES – final examinations at STAGS, set in the final year

FESTINA LENTE – the STAGS school motto: 'Make Haste Slowly'

MEDIEVAL anything traditional or historical, in line with the highly prized values of the school

SAVAGE – anything modern or technological, considered not in keeping with the ethos of STAGS

The Real Isle of Dogs

The Isle of Dogs was a real play.

Ben Jonson was said to have written it in collaboration with fellow playwright Thomas Nashe, but as Nashe denied any involvement when things got sticky I haven't given him any of the credit. His name does appear in this book, however, if you look carefully.

The Isle of Dogs was performed by Pembroke's Men in July 1597, at one of the playhouses on London's Bankside, probably The Swan. A report was immediately made by one of Elizabeth I's informers and her response was swift and severe. The theatres were closed at once and the order went out for a number of playhouses to be destroyed. Nashe fled the city while Jonson and his players burned every copy of the play. But Jonson, along with Gabriel Spenser and Robert Shaw, were caught and imprisoned in the Marshalsea. In August they were tried by Elizabeth's foremost advisors, William and Robert Cecil. They were father and son.

The three actors protested their satire was innocent, even in the face of torture, and in October of the same year walked free. Their defiance meant that many other Crown cases against London theatres and playwrights collapsed. Had the case against them prevailed, English theatre would have lost, not just Jonson's work, but such plays as *Macbeth*, *King Lear* and *Hamlet*.

Jonson and Spenser might have formed a close comradeship in prison, but they were literally at daggers drawn by September 1598. Jonson killed Spenser in a duel in Hogsden Fields (modern day Hoxton) despite the fact that, according to Jonson, Spenser's sword was ten inches longer than his. Jonson found himself in prison once more, but this time for murder. He was sentenced to death, but pleaded Benefit of the Clergy, speaking the 'neck verse' to avoid the noose. His possessions were confiscated, and his thumb branded, but he was freed and went on to write his greatest works, including *The Alchemist* and *Volpone*.

No one knows what the real *Isle of Dogs* was about. The imagery of dogs in Elizabethan times, with their fawning and licking ways, could easily be repurposed as a swipe at flattering courtiers like the Cecils. In the atmosphere of a mounting rivalry between the father and son team and Elizabeth's great favourite, Robert Devereux, Earl of Essex, Ben Jonson may have used his play to support the young earl. But the closeness of the geographical Isle of Dogs to the queen's palace at Greenwich, and the fact that the Crown reacted so harshly to the play, is highly suggestive of the theory that Jonson took aim at Elizabeth I herself.

Wherever the truth lies, I owe Ben Jonson an apology for my version of *The Isle of Dogs*. I did my best considering that the real play is lost forever.

Or is it?

Author's Note

Miserere by Gregorio Allegri was, and is, an important piece of music in my life.

When we'd just got just married my husband and I used to sit in our little kitchen in the after-dinner twilight listening to it, and it was like cold water going down your back. I don't know how we discovered it – probably in some film or other – but it just spoke to us.

Now you've been Medieval enough to finish this book please allow yourself a Savage moment to go on YouTube and listen to *Miserere*. In true S.T.A.G.S. tradition it's probably best to go for the choir of Kings College, Cambridge, one of the oldest choirs in England (plus they have a kick-ass chapel).

I never knew, all those years ago, that the words to *Miserere* were the 'neck verse', never realised that it would have such significance to me years later when I wrote this book. But if it has significance to me, that's nothing to the significance it had to Ben Jonson when, hundreds of years ago, that short string of Latin words saved his life. He was *literally* saved by the book, and if that's not an argument for reading, I don't know what is. You know those bumper stickers that say: *If you can read this you're driving too close?* Well, if you are reading *this*, then that means you got to the end of a book, and that means you're a *reader*, and that means that, like Ben Jonson, you'll be just fine.

M. A. Bennett

Acknowledgements

Firstly, I have to thank Jane Harris and Emma Matthewson at Hot Key Books for allowing me to carry on the *S.T.A.G.S.* story. Thank you to Emma also for her fantastic editing skills, to Holly Kyte for her thorough copy-edit and to Talya Baker for her meticulous editing and proofreading.

Thank you to my agent and friend Teresa Chris, who leads me through this wonderful world of books.

In that world I am grateful to a team of Medievals and a team of Savages in equal measure. The Medievals are the librarians who support my work so enthusiastically, especially in schools. And the Savages are the bloggers who champion my books on social media. Thank you all.

Family next. Thanks to Sacha for his knowledge of films, for room K9, and for the invaluable support he gives to me and my work. Thanks to Conrad who, although he is a full-on Savage, still helps me with references from his digital world. And even more thanks to Ruby, who is a bit more Medieval, and not only reads every word I write, but gives me advice along the way.

Two biographies of Ben Jonson helped me to understand his world. *Ben Jonson, A Life* by Ian Donaldson, and *Ben Jonson, A Literary Life* by W. David Kay.

I was also inspired by the Kingscote books by Antonia Forest, far and away my favourite school series. The twins, the theatre, the boarding school – she was there before me. If you haven't read them, you must.

On the Savage front, two TV shows in particular influenced this book. Firstly, *QI* (BBC2) brought *The Isle of Dogs* back into my consciousness after many years of having forgotten about it. The exact clip which set me off on this journey is referenced in the book. I also gleaned a lot of information from the Channel 5 documentary *Elizabeth I*, which helped me to understand the later years of the queen's life.

I'm lucky enough to visit lots of schools. Thank you to all the kids who couldn't wait to find out what happened after *S.T.A.G.S.* – this book is for you.

Thanks to my sister, archaeologist Veronica Fiorato, for her knowledge of ancient manuscripts and their preservation.

Thanks to Morgan Headley for letting me borrow her name for Ty's surname.

Lastly my thanks to actor Sebastian Armesto, who played Ben Jonson in the film *Anonymous* (2011), for his insights into the playwright's character, and being the nearest thing I can imagine to meeting Ben Jonson in real life.

Hello!

Thank you for picking up **DOGS**.

DOGS is the second book in my STAGS series, about St Aidan the Great School, an exclusive private school with a dark secret. *STAGS* was the story of Greer McDonald, an ordinary girl who wins a scholarship to an exclusive English boarding school, St Aidan the Great, and is then invited, by the richest clique in the school, on a country house weekend to Longcross Hall, where the promised traditional bloodsports – Huntin' Shootin' Fishin' – take a dark turn.

The book was born out of the fact that I've had an interesting relationship with the upper classes myself. My grandmother, Ina Hoggarth, worked at Langcliffe Hall, a big stately home in the north of England. When I was born, my mother worked full-time, so I was raised by my grandmother in the housekeeper's cottage. Living in the grounds of a great house I saw at first hand the upper classes at play. The Hall had a grouse moor and the family often hosted shooting parties during the season. My grandmother would work all weekend and come home on Sunday, dog-tired, with stories of the weekend's sport. The gamekeeper, improbably named Perfect, would bring us a brace of pheasants for our Sunday dinner, still warm, floppy-necked and riddled with shot. Of course, while I was growing up in the housekeeper's cottage, and attending the local comprehensive school, the sons of the big house were living a very different life. As a teenager, I would see them in the village pub during the holidays, but during term time they were at Ampleforth College, an exclusive boarding school in North Yorkshire run by Benedictine monks. Years later, I would write about another exclusive school run by Friars and an Abbot, but I would weave into that dark foundation everything I'd learned at my grandmother's knee about huntin' shootin' and fishin'. It is at this school, St Aidan the Great, that the events of **DOGS** unfold, picking up exactly where the story of **STAGS** left off . . .

If you would like to find out more about my books, you can visit **www.bit.ly/MABennett** (case-sensitive) and become part of the **M. A. Bennett Readers' Club**. It only takes a few moments to sign up, and there are no catches or costs.

Hot Key Books will keep your data private and confidential, and it will never be passed on to a third party. We won't spam you with loads of emails, just get in touch now and again with news about my books, and you can unsubscribe any time you want.

And if you would like to get involved in a wider conversation about my books, please do review *DOGS* on Amazon, on Goodreads, on any other e-store, on your own blog and social media accounts, or talk about it with friends, family or reader groups! Sharing your thoughts helps other readers, and I always enjoy hearing about what people experience from my writing.

Thank you again for reading *DOGS*.

All the best,

M. A. Bennett

M. A. Bennett

M. A. Bennett is half Venetian and was born in Manchester, England, and raised in the Yorkshire Dales. She is a history graduate of Oxford University and the University of Venice, where she specialised in the study of Shakespeare's plays as a historical source. After university she studied art and has since worked as an illustrator, an actress and a film reviewer. She also designed tour visuals for rock bands, including U2 and the Rolling Stones. She was married on the Grand Canal in Venice and lives in north London with her husband, son and daughter. Her first YA novel, *S.T.A.G.S.*, was published in 2017 and was shortlisted for the YA BOOK PRIZE 2018, won the Warwickshire Secondary Book Award 2019 and Gold in the Sussex Coast Schools Amazing Book Award 2019, both voted by students, and won the Great Reads 'Most Read' 2018 Senior Award. *D.O.G.S.*, the second in the world of STAGS, followed in 2019.

Follow her at @MABennettAuthor on Twitter and at @mabennettauthor on Instagram.

Want to read
NEW BOOKS
before anyone else?

Like getting
FREE BOOKS?

Enjoy sharing your
OPINIONS?

Discover
READERS FIRST

Read. Love. Share.

Get your first free book just by signing up at
readersfirst.co.uk

HOT KEY BOOKS

Thank you for choosing a Hot Key book.

If you want to know more about our authors and what we publish, you can find us online.

You can start at our website

www.hotkeybooks.com

And you can also find us on:

We hope to see you soon!